MW01487418

DARK ALLIANCE

TURBULENT WATERS

THE CHILDREN OF THE GODS
BOOK SIXTY-NINE

I. T. LUCAS

Published by Evening Star Press

EveningStarPress.com

ISBN-13: 978-1-957139-55-5

JADE

*D*awn had broken over the sky hours ago, but Jade was still in bed, reluctant to leave the warmth of Phinas's arms.

It wasn't like her to linger between the sheets when the sun was up, and it wasn't like her to spend a night with a male either, but it had been surprisingly pleasant.

Despite lacking even a shadow of aggression or dominance, their bed play had been unexpectedly satisfying. It had been a very different experience for her, and she suspected it had been just as different for Phinas.

To make it work, both had throttled down their dominant tendencies, but not for the same reasons.

Jade had stifled her aggressive urges to avoid challenging Phinas, who wouldn't have been able to respond with enough physical strength and would have felt humiliated. On his part, Phinas had probably been gentler with her than he would have been with his immortal or human partners to avoid spurring her aggression, which was ironic given that he didn't need to worry about hurting her.

Nevertheless, their joining had been incredible.

Phinas's potent venom had no doubt contributed to the languid sense of satisfaction and well-being she was experiencing, but it would have been just as good even without the venom-induced euphoric trip and string of climaxes.

Unexpectedly, Jade had found emotional respite in Phinas's arms.

Within his embrace, the pain of loss felt less acute, the need for revenge burned less fiercely, and the weight of duty was lighter.

Still, as wonderful as those stolen moments were, it was time to get up and face the world. She needed to check whether Merlin had already extracted some of the trackers from her people, and they had to figure out a way to speed up the removal operation.

The sooner they got rid of those trackers, the sooner they would leave Igor blind in the water.

"I need to get going." She pushed out of Phinas's arms.

"Don't go." He pulled her back. "Stay a little longer."

She let him hold her, enjoying the feel of his large hands as they roved over her back, caressing gently, leisurely.

"I wish I could." She kissed his lips. "But we both have duties to attend to. Besides, I'm hungry, and you are as well. I can hear your stomach rumbling."

He licked his lips. "By now, Isla and her helpers have probably prepared breakfast, and if it's even half as good as dinner was last night, it's going to be a treat." He squeezed her bottom before releasing her.

Jade frowned as it occurred to her that Phinas shouldn't have even known who Isla was, let alone that she was in charge of the kitchen. Isla must have been the one who had approached him to complain about the way humans had been treated in Igor's compound, specifically the breeding with Kra-ell males, and that was what had made him confront her about it last night and sparked their argument.

The thing was, Igor hadn't been terrible to the humans, and he hadn't mistreated them any worse than Jade had done when she'd been in charge of her own compound, so any accusations Isla had voiced were directed at her as well.

Why had she approached Phinas, though?

If Isla wanted help from the liberators, Tom or Yamanu were the more obvious choices.

Perhaps Phinas seemed more approachable?

Jade had to concede that he had a certain charm about him, while Tom seemed standoffish, which was second nature to any god, even one as decent as he was. Yamanu was easygoing and friendly, but his physical size was intimidating.

She needed to have a talk with the woman and see what her problem was. The human hadn't produced any hybrid children, and as far as Jade knew, Isla hadn't accommodated any Kra-ell males either. She wasn't the type they usually preferred. But before she accused the female, she needed to ensure it had been her.

"I didn't know that you were on a first-name basis with my humans. When did you get acquainted with Isla?"

Realizing his mistake, Phinas's eyes widened briefly, but even though it didn't last more than a split second, Jade caught it.

"I met her in the kitchen when I went to thank the cooks for the fabulous meal and to offer my men's help to clean up after dinner."

"That was nice of you. Did Isla accept the offer?"

"Nope. She said that the humans were happy to prepare our meals and clean up after them in gratitude for us freeing them from Igor and protecting them on the voyage."

3

Jade had her confirmation. It had been Isla who had complained.

"Let's get going. I'll accompany you to the dining hall, but since I don't eat the same food you do, I will not stay."

"Right." He rubbed a hand over his stubble. "When was the last time you fed?" He grimaced. "Don't tell me you haven't had any blood since draining Valstar?"

At the reminder, bile rose in Jade's throat.

She'd never taken such a copious quantity of blood before, but she hadn't had a choice. It had been the only way for her to keep Igor's second-in-command incapacitated while Tom and his Guardians had stormed the compound. Bashing Valstar over the head with a chair might have also done the trick, but not for long. He wouldn't have stayed down, and Jade couldn't risk him activating the explosives that Igor had put under the compound.

When Pavel had arrived with the chains to bind Valstar, she'd left the kid to guard the prisoner and went on a killing spree, eliminating four of her people's murderers. Regrettably, her number one target was still at large, and she wouldn't rest until she'd eliminated him as well.

"I haven't fed since then," she admitted. "I was nauseous for a long time after that, and when I finally felt thirsty again, we were on the move, and I didn't have time."

Phinas cocked his head. "So you don't feel hungry? Only thirsty?"

"It's a combination of both. I can drink water and some other liquids, and that satisfies most of the thirst, but only blood can eliminate it altogether."

A smile lifting one corner of his lips, he tapped his neck. "How about you feed from me? Once you've quenched your thirst, you can join me for coffee while I eat."

4

As her eyes followed his fingers to the carotid artery he was tapping, her tongue darted over her lips, and she swallowed.

The Kra-ell didn't feed from their partners to satisfy the thirst, but it was a most enjoyable part of the sexual experience that she hadn't dared broach with Phinas yet.

Their relationship was bridging species and cultures, and she was hesitant about introducing blood-sucking into their play. It could easily turn him off, and she couldn't afford to lose him.

She needed Phinas for more than just the pleasures of the flesh or companionship. He was a valuable source of information about the clan and its internal politics.

"We don't use our bed partners as a food source."

"Why not? I'm bigger than the goats and sheep you have in the cargo bay, and I certainly smell better. If they are fine after you get your fill, I will be fine as well."

He might be, but he also might get lightheaded, and that wasn't an option when Igor could strike at the ship at any moment.

It had been fifty-three hours since the clan had taken over the compound, and despite their best efforts to avoid detection, Jade had no doubt that Igor's counterattack was imminent.

He wouldn't let the clan abscond with his people without utilizing every possible weapon in his arsenal, to which there was no limit. He could probably get his hands on a nuclear warhead if he wanted one.

"I'm not going to feed from you." She slid out of bed.

Phinas narrowed his eyes at her. "You said goats and sheep were passable, so your refusal can't be because you prefer their taste to mine."

"I don't prefer it, and I know that your blood will taste exquisite. But the Kra-ell only take a little from their partners to enhance pleasure during intimate moments. We don't feed from them." She padded to the bathroom.

"You didn't take from me even once." He followed her inside. "And you had at least three opportunities."

"I didn't think you'd enjoy it."

"I'm sure I will." His big nude body filling the doorway, Phinas leaned against the doorjamb and gripped his straining erection. "I'm looking forward to it."

His very obvious physical reaction indicated that he was turned on by the prospect of her bite.

Jade smiled. "Tonight, then." She pushed on his chest to clear the doorway and closed the door in his face.

"Is that a promise?" he asked from the other side.

"It is."

2

PHINAS

*T*he promise of Jade's bite put a smile on Phinas's face and pumped even more blood into his erection, but instead of being invited to join her in the shower, he got the door slammed in his face.

It was very disappointing.

The female was comfortable with her nudity, so a desire for privacy couldn't be the reason for her behavior. Perhaps the physical manifestation of his excitement was or Jade was just in a rush to get to her duties. Whatever her reason, it was evident that she didn't want to go another round with him.

Reluctantly, Phinas walked to the cabin's other bedroom and got into the shower.

He shouldn't be surprised. With Jade, everything was about duty and responsibility, and her personal enjoyment was not a priority.

Phinas could respect that, and the truth was that he wasn't all that different. Duty came first for him as well, but since he was supposed to befriend the Kra-ell leader, he was actually doing his job.

Not that it was a hardship, and not that he would have

stayed away from Jade if he hadn't been directed to get close to her. She was the hottest female he'd ever been with, and he enjoyed her company more than anyone else's.

It was so strange and unexpected that Phinas was starting to think that the Fates had something to do with it. Except, he didn't believe in the Fates.

He was a loner by nature, and he'd never been particularly close to anyone, but for some inexplicable reason he felt at home with Jade, who wasn't even from the same species and whose culture and belief system were alien to him.

Perhaps it was the luxurious cruise ship?

It created an illusion of a vacation and contributed to a romantic atmosphere.

Or was it the looming danger?

Those intimate moments with Jade were even more precious, given that they didn't know what Igor's next move would be, nor when the attack would come.

Jade was under even more pressure. She'd assumed leadership of the compound's population and was tasked with reorganizing its social structure in a way that would satisfy the three different groups.

Phinas didn't envy her the task. He was okay with leading men into battle, but that was the extent of his leadership skills. Unless it concerned security, he didn't want to tell people how to live their lives and what they were allowed or forbidden to do. That was Kalugal's job, and he was very flexible with his guidelines.

His men were supposed to adhere to common standards of decency, and since joining the clan they were also supposed to follow clan law, but no one policed them to enforce the rules.

Done with the shower, Phinas wrapped a towel around his hips and walked into the cabin's living room.

The sight that greeted him had his erection inflate in an instant.

Jade looked good enough to eat in a pair of his undershorts, a pair of his socks, and nothing else. Bent over, with her magnificent ass in his face, she was picking up clothes off the floor.

Regrettably, he'd already surmised that she wasn't interested in another round of bed play before heading out.

Straightening up, she gave him a sly smile. "I hope you don't mind." She patted her bottom. "I took the liberty of borrowing a pair of your briefs and a pair of socks."

She'd taken them from his duffle bag, but he had no problem with that, except that she hadn't asked in advance. He had no secret items in there, only a stack of clean clothes and a bag of those that needed to be laundered.

"They look better on you than they do on me." He walked into the bedroom and pulled out another pair of shorts for himself.

Using his immortal speed, Phinas put on a pair of jeans and a long-sleeved Henley before returning to the living room. "Do you want to stop by your cabin for a change of clothes?"

Jade waved a hand at his shirt. "If you have another one I can borrow, I can skip stopping by my cabin and go straight down to the cargo bay."

She must be starving if she was so anxious to get there. Or perhaps she wished to avoid explaining to her second-in-command where she'd spent the night.

"It's going to be huge on you." He turned around and pulled a shirt out of his duffle bag.

Shrugging, she took it from him. "We are the same height."

"We are, but I weigh three times as much as you."

Jade cast him an amused smile. "I'm slim, but I'm not light."

He'd noticed that when he'd lifted her last night and carried

9

her to the bedroom. Given her build, he'd expected her weight to be slight and was surprised to find that it was substantial.

Although, given how strong she was, it made sense that she was solidly built.

Evidently, the Kra-ell's body mass was denser than that of humans and immortals.

"Nevertheless, I'm broader."

She pulled the shirt over her head, shimmied into her cargo pants, and tucked it inside them.

"That you are." Her eyes roved over his body.

Jade rolled up the sleeves that were too long, not because her arms were shorter but because her shoulders were narrower. When she was done lacing her boots, Phinas opened the cabin door.

"I'll come with you to the cargo bay, and after you are done feeding, you can join me for coffee in the dining room."

She shook her head. "You have better things to do than watch me eat, but I'll join you for coffee later."

For some reason, Jade didn't want him to see her feed, taking the vein of an animal and sucking its blood.

Did she think it would be a turn-off for him?

Perhaps she'd heard the stupid rumor about his and Aliya's falling out after he'd accompanied the girl on a hunt?

Phinas had told Jade about his short involvement with the young hybrid and had explained why it hadn't worked out between them, but he hadn't mentioned the rumor that had started right after Aliya had chosen Vrog over him. People had assumed he'd gotten turned off after seeing her hunt, but that wasn't the reason.

Should he ask Jade about it or just let it go?

It might be better to wait.

They were still finding their way with each other, and it was going surprisingly well given that they weren't even from the same species. But it was better to be patient and let things evolve between them naturally without pushing for more.

He wrapped his arm around her tiny middle. "What are your plans for the rest of the day?"

She looked at his arm and then lifted her eyes to his. "I have my duties, and you have yours." She looked at his arm again. "I'd rather we didn't display such familiarity in public."

He dropped his arm. "Is it one more of those cultural differences? Or are you embarrassed about being seen with me?"

"It's cultural." Jade started toward the elevators. "The Kra-ell don't hold hands or embrace in public. We don't even shake hands." She pressed the button for the elevator. "Before I was captured, I traveled extensively and spent much time among humans, so I learned to tolerate handshakes, but I'm uncomfortable with casual touching."

Tolerate.

The word was like a knife to Phinas's gut.

Jade had been forced to tolerate so much that he wondered how she'd managed not to fall apart.

Her sons and the other males of her tribe had been slaughtered in front of her eyes, and then she'd been forced to accommodate their murderer sexually and bear him a daughter.

If Toven hadn't promised Jade Igor's kill, Phinas would have taken care of it.

Even though he would be no match for Igor in a hand-to-hand fight, the rage inside him over the evil perpetrated against this amazing female would have given Phinas the strength needed to overcome the much more powerful opponent and tear the guy's throat out with his bare fangs.

As the elevator doors opened, he forced the dark thoughts to a corner of his mind and followed Jade inside. "The truth is that I don't have much to do." It was a waiting game until Igor made his next move, and in the meantime, Phinas and his men were enjoying the clan's luxurious cruise ship. "Dandor wanted to fill the pool with water, but since it's freezing cold and we need to conserve fuel, heating it is out of the question."

Leaning against the wall, Jade cast him an amused smile. "That's a shame. You wanted to teach me how to swim."

"Have you seriously never tried it?"

She shrugged. "I guess it's another cultural difference. The Kra-ell are not great swimmers." She gave him a savage smile. "Back home, there are things in the water that are dangerous even to us."

It occurred to him that amphibian predators were not the only reason for the Kra-ell's reluctance to swim. With how compact their bodies were, they probably couldn't float well.

Then again, even tigers and elephants could swim, so the Kra-ell should be able to manage, and given the current situation, their inability to swim could prove deadly.

"We are on a ship, and we expect an attack. What happens if you find yourself overboard? Will you just sink to the bottom?"

"I can keep myself afloat by treading water."

Phinas frowned. "That's not a good tactic in freezing temperatures." Given their strength, the Kra-ell might be able to keep it up for much longer than humans or even immortals, but eventually the cold would sap their energy. "Can you float on your back?"

"I don't know. I've never tried."

"We have to fill that pool and start training you and your people to flip to your backs to conserve energy. After that, you all need to learn to swim."

She nodded. "You are right. Our humans need to learn that as well. I just hope we have enough time before the attack for everyone to become proficient."

3

JADE

*T*he cruise ship's dining hall was bigger than Jade had expected, but it wasn't full. No purebloods were seated around the tables, which wasn't surprising given that they didn't eat human food, but she'd expected to see at least one or two.

Many of them enjoyed a cup of coffee or tea from time to time and a drink of vodka in the evenings. Besides, mealtime was an excellent opportunity to get to know their liberators and start conversations.

Jade wondered why no one had thought to do that, but she was glad they hadn't.

It wouldn't take her people long to realize that Tom and his guardians were not human.

Several of the hybrids were present, though, and in addition to their nods of greeting, they cast curious looks her way.

"Over here!" One of Phinas's men waved him over.

Given the tight press of his lips, Phinas wasn't enthusiastic about the invitation. Leaning over, he said quietly, "I'd rather be alone with you than join Dandor and Chad."

She would have preferred that as well, but they had appearances to keep up. "Since I'm not eating, you might enjoy their company more. Besides, if the two of us sit separately, rumors will start."

"They will start anyway." He put his hand on the small of her back. "The clan is like a hive, and gossip is everyone's favorite pastime."

Her lips curled in distaste. "I experienced the same in the compound. This deplorable trait seems to transcend cultures and species."

He chuckled. "It would appear so."

"Good morning." Dandor got to his feet and pulled out a chair for her.

The human custom of males rising to their feet when a female joined the table was one of the few Jade would have liked to appropriate for her people, but the seat he offered her was strategically disadvantageous.

"Good morning to you too." She remained standing. "I'd rather not sit with my back to the room. Would you mind switching places with me?"

Dandor had the wall at his back, which was a preferable defensive position.

"No problem." He offered her his seat. "How was your first night aboard the *Aurora*?"

"It was fine." Phinas pretended the question had been directed at him as he pulled out a chair for himself. "I didn't notice the rocking, which was surprising given how choppy the Baltic is this time of year."

Jade stifled a smile.

He hadn't felt the ship rocking because they'd been busy rocking the bed, and after they were done, they'd fallen into such a deep sleep that the boat could have been attacked, and they would have slept through it.

She couldn't speak for him, but she'd slept better than ever. Was it because she'd felt safe in Phinas's arms?

Since he couldn't protect her against a Kra-ell, that didn't make much sense, and yet something about him soothed the storm raging inside of her. Maybe it was his easy charm that had given her such a wonderfully relaxed night, or perhaps it was the fact that he wasn't a Kra-ell and he didn't have any expectations of her. She didn't need to play the role of a leader, she didn't need to play dominance games with him, and she could just be herself.

Did she even know who that self was, though?

Jade had thought she knew, but after her world had come crashing down, a lot of the things she'd considered important had lost meaning, and the only motivation to keep waking up in the morning had been the need for revenge.

"Would you like some coffee?" Phinas asked.

"I would love some."

"I'll get it." Dandor rose to his feet.

As he passed by Yamanu's table, she remembered that the Head Guardian wanted her to meet his mate and her sister, but Jade hoped he'd forgotten about that.

It wasn't that she minded meeting them and getting the introductions out of the way, but she didn't want to spend more time with them than she had to. Her people needed her, and she didn't have the time or the patience for social calls.

The little free time Jade had, she preferred to spend with Phinas.

Noticing her looking their way, one of the women lifted her hand and waved, her sister flashing Jade a smile that revealed a pair of gleaming canines that could pass for fangs.

She was still focused on that anomaly when Yamanu turned around and waved hello.

"Good morning." He rose to his feet and walked over to

their table. "It makes me happy to see the two of you becoming so friendly with one another." He clapped Phinas on the back. "I'm a sucker for romance."

Chad shook his head.

Jade didn't know how to respond to Yamanu's insinuation.

Romance was a human term that was foreign to her. What she and Phinas had were sex and companionship. It wasn't romance, and it wasn't love.

"How can I help you, Yamanu?" Phinas ignored the Guardian's comment.

Yamanu flashed him a toothy smile. "Actually, I came over to invite Jade to our cabin this evening, but since you two seem to have become an item, you are both invited."

Jade lifted her hand. "I can come over to your table right now and be done with the introductions."

The Guardian's expression soured. "Are you declining my invitation again?"

Damn. Had she offended him?

"I'm just trying to be efficient. If all you want is to introduce us, we can save time by doing it right here, right now."

"That's not why I want you to meet my mate and her sister. They will explain when you come over this evening."

Phinas draped his arm over the back of her chair. "We would be delighted to attend a get-together in your cabin. Should I bring a couple of bottles of whiskey?"

The grin returned to Yamanu's face. "I've got the refreshments covered. Just make sure to show up at seven o'clock and have Jade with you."

"We will be there."

4

TOVEN

"Will you be okay by yourself in the cabin?" Toven leaned down and kissed Mia's forehead.

"I'm not going to our cabin. I made plans with Mey and Jin to tour the ship. I'm going to Jin's cabin, and we are going to have coffee and chat and then go on a tour from there."

"When did you make those plans?"

"While you were talking with Yamanu. Is he going with you to see Valstar?"

Toven shook his head. "I'm going alone. Valstar promised me information, and I want to question him at my leisure with no interruptions."

"Have fun." Mia gave him a pat on his rear. "When you are done, call me."

"I will." He kissed her again before returning to the elevator.

When he exited on the Kra-ell level, the two Guardians posted in the hallway were like a double beacon, indicating which cabin Valstar was in.

"Good morning, gentlemen. How is the prisoner behaving so far?"

17

"He's not giving us any trouble," the Guardian on the left said.

Toven made a mental note to learn the names of all the warriors on board. His memory wasn't the best, and although he memorized faces with ease, he had difficulty remembering names. Perhaps it was the artist in him. He'd always found peace while sketching. It was effortless and calming, while writing stories required focus and effort.

"Is anyone watching him on the inside?" he asked.

The Guardian on the right shook his head. "He has chains on his legs and he's under your compulsion. He's been watching television and has barely moved from the couch."

It could be a convincing act, and Toven wasn't taking any chances. He had a dart gun tucked in the waistband of his pants, which felt odd.

Toven had never needed weapons to protect himself. His mind control ability and superior speed and strength had been enough. For the first time ever, he was facing an opponent who was faster and stronger and who might be resistant to his mind control.

No wonder the gods had sought to enslave the Kra-ell. It was disconcerting to be at a physical disadvantage and to have little or no ability to control their minds either. The only real advantage the gods had over the Kra-ell was their technological superiority and their genetic manipulation ability.

"Please, open the door for me." Toven pulled out his dart gun.

The Guardian eyed the weapon. "It worries me that you don't put much faith in your ability to control him with compulsion."

"It should worry you. Valstar could be pretending to be under my control and just waiting for the right moment to strike."

"Where would he go?" the other Guardian asked as he opened the door. "Overboard?"

Nevertheless, his more cautious friend took a step back and pointed his machine gun at the door.

"You have a visitor," the Guardian announced.

Valstar was seated on the couch, a foot-long chain attached on each end to one of his ankles, but his hands were free, and his back was straight. He didn't look like someone who had given up hope, and he didn't look like he was about to attack either.

The television was on, and a movie was playing, but the sound was turned down low.

"Good morning." Toven walked into the cabin and tucked his gun back into his waistband.

Valstar nodded but didn't repeat the greeting.

It wasn't the Kra-ell way.

"Do you want us inside with you?" the cautious Guardian asked.

"I don't, but thank you for the offer."

The guy nodded and closed the door.

When Toven sat down on the armchair facing the couch, Valstar lifted the remote and clicked the television off. "Did you come to collect?"

"Collect on what?"

"I promised you information. I assume that you are here to collect on my promise."

"I want to ask you some questions."

"Go ahead."

"Did you know Igor before you were assigned to the same pod?" Toven used strong compulsion in his voice to ensure Valstar answered immediately and didn't try to devise a way to circumvent the question.

"I didn't," Valstar said. "None of us knew each other, and we

19

didn't get acquainted before being placed in the pod either, which I found odd."

"Why was it odd?"

As Valstar shifted on the couch, the chain attached to his legs dragged on the hardwood floor. "A lottery was held among young Kra-ell that fit a certain profile, and it was mandatory. Those who had gotten picked were summoned to a processing center, and none of us knew anyone else. That was fine, but since we were supposed to settle on Earth and form a tribe, I expected at least an introduction. There was none. We weren't even given each other's names. To this day, I don't know Igor's Kra-ell name."

"How is that possible? Igor couldn't have chosen the name before waking up and discovering that he'd arrived thousands of years later than he'd been supposed to."

Valstar nodded. "At first, he called himself Ingvar, which I assumed was his Kra-ell name at the time. It wasn't one I'd ever heard before, but it sounded like many other Kra-ell names, so I had no reason to question it. Only later, when he changed it to Igor, I learned that Ingvar was a Scandinavian name from which Igor had been derived."

"Ingvar means gods' warrior in old Norse, so it could have come from an even older name used by the Germanic tribes, but how could Igor have learned of it? Were you briefed about Earth's inhabitants?"

Valstar shook his head. "We knew it was habitable because the gods told us it was. They visited it before us, and the king sent the rebels here, the ones who'd sided with the Kra-ell." Valstar tilted his head and offered Toven a crooked smile. "Are you one of the original exiles, or were you born on Earth?"

5

ELEANOR

*E*leanor nudged Emmett's shoulder. "Wake up. You need to get out of bed."

Groaning, he pulled the blanket over his head and turned on his side.

"It's four in the afternoon. If you keep napping, you won't be able to sleep at night. "

Emmett's excuse for sleeping all day was that he was depressed. He didn't like being back in the village, and despite reassurances that it was probably temporary until they caught Igor, he was acting as if his world had fallen apart and Safe Haven was lost to him forever.

He was such a drama king, and Eleanor was tired of being his cheer lady. She had never been the cheerleader type, and assuming the role for Emmett's sake was exhausting.

Maybe it was the wrong approach, and she should yell at him to snap out of it?

Yeah, that jived much better with her character.

"If you are not out of this bed in one minute, I'm going to leave you and go visit my family by myself."

He lowered the blanket and lifted his head to look at her. "I can't be alone right now."

"Then get up and come with me. Parker is looking forward to seeing you."

"He is?"

Her nephew hadn't said anything, but she knew that he liked Emmett, so maybe he could take over the cheerleading role for an hour or so. Besides, Emmett needed an audience to get into his performer persona, which was sure to improve his mood, and even a small family gathering would do. It would help him get out of his head.

"Of course, he is. Vivian told me that he and Ella can't wait to see us."

"We are invited for six." Emmett pulled the blanket back up. "I have two hours until then."

"You need to shower and get dressed." She waved a hand in his direction. "Your beard could use a trim and so could your hair. I can do that for you if you want." Eleanor tried to keep a straight face.

After the one time she'd trimmed his beard and hair for him, Emmett would never let her do it again, and it might convince him to get out of the house and drive to the city for a proper haircut.

"No, thank you. I'd rather do it myself."

That hadn't been her intention. "We can go to the city tomorrow." She patted her hair. "I want to try a Brazilian blowout. I'm tired of how messy my hair gets with even a hint of humidity in the air."

"I love your hair." Emmett flipped the blanket off and swung his legs over the side of the bed. "I don't want you to straighten it."

"Well, tough, because I do." Leaving the door open, Eleanor walked out of the bedroom.

Cecilia lifted her ears and stretched on the windowsill, giving her a questioning look.

"If I feed you again, you'll get fat, and Ana won't let you stay over."

Offended, the cat stretched once again, shifted her pose, and offered Eleanor a view of her butt as she tucked herself into a ball.

Ana had agreed to share her while in the village, and although cats were territorial, Cecilia had no problem calling both houses her own. They had to keep track of who was feeding her and when, because that cat was a glutton and would eat until she blew up.

When Eleanor's phone buzzed in her pocket, she pulled it out and sat on the couch. "What's up, Leon? Do you want me to bring Cecilia over?"

"I'm not calling about the cat. I thought you would want to know that we finally caught the hybrids."

"Hallelujah. I thought that they gave us the slip and were on their way to Igor."

"Yeah, we all did, and I'm glad that I decided to leave two Guardians to watch the Airbnb despite that."

The rental car with the tracker they had planted had been parked in front of the house, but the hybrids hadn't been there since Monday.

"Where were they?"

"I don't know. The Guardians tranquilized them as soon as they got back, loaded them in the car, and are driving them all the way to our downtown warehouse to scan them for implanted trackers. Julian will meet them there so he can remove them if they find any. After that, they will be brought to the dungeon in the keep and questioned. Do you want to attend?"

Leon had gotten to know her well during their time together in Safe Haven, and he knew that she would love that.

"Of course, and I'll bring Emmett along to help interrogate them. What's their ETA?"

"Sometime during the night. We will question them tomorrow morning."

"Good. Vivian invited Emmett and me to dinner, and I would hate to disappoint her. Julian and Ella are invited as well, but if the hybrids are only arriving late at night, Julian doesn't need to leave for the warehouse anytime soon."

6

TOVEN

*T*he cat was out of the bag, or perhaps it had never been inside of it, and Valstar had known from the start that Toven was a god, the same way Jade had known from the first moment she'd seen him.

"What gave me away?"

Valstar smiled. "Did you really think you can pass for a human?"

"Why not? I look human."

"You look like the statues humans erected in honor of their gods. Too perfect, the way all gods are. But even if you managed to make yourself look less exquisite, your incredible compulsion ability would give you away."

"Igor's ability equals or surpasses mine. Is he a god?"

Valstar closed his eyes. "I often wondered if he was a hybrid, part Kra-ell, and part god, but if I had even dared to hint at it, he would have ended me. First of all, it's anathema to the Kra-ell to breed with gods, and vice versa. Secondly, Igor despises the gods, which isn't surprising given how they had used and mistreated the Kra-ell for hundreds of thousands of years, but it is surprising for Igor, who doesn't feel much about anything. They must have done something particularly terrible to him."

"Like produce him and then turn their backs on him. That would make anyone resentful, and especially someone like Igor who is power-hungry."

Valstar shrugged. "Another possibility is that the gods played around with his genes. There were rumors about them conducting secret experiments on Kra-ell. Maybe they gave him his compulsion powers and took away his ability to feel. Maybe they tried to produce the perfect soldier."

It wasn't too big of a leap. Humans had been trying to produce perfect soldiers for decades, and not only via training. The drug experiments were well known, the genetic ones less so.

But who did the gods fight that they needed to create a perfect killing machine?

"What would they have done with such a perfect soldier, though? Wouldn't he pose a threat to his creators?"

Valstar pursed his lips. "Maybe that's why he was sent to Earth. He was a defective specimen who didn't obey his masters."

Toven looked into Valstar's dark eyes. "Perhaps Igor was sent to Earth to kill the gods. You said that the rebels were sent here as punishment. Maybe his job was to eliminate them. Communications with the gods' planet had gone down thousands of years earlier, so no one would have found out about it, and the reputation of the gods' king as a benevolent father and ruler would not have been tarnished."

"The thought crossed my mind," Valstar said. "But I dismissed it. After discovering how much time had elapsed, we made a half-hearted effort to find the gods, but when it became clear that they were relegated to the realm of myths and legends, Igor turned his focus on building a life for us on Earth."

That would have been the logical thing to do, and Igor was ruled by logic, not emotions, so Valstar was probably right.

"When did he start looking for the other survivors?" Toven asked.

"Not right away. The ship was gone, and without it, we couldn't communicate with the other pods. We had to wait until humanity formed global communication networks and finding information became easier."

Toven didn't believe for a second that Igor found the other Kra-ell by looking for clues in the news. The settlers must have been implanted with trackers before ever leaving home, and Igor had waited for human technology to catch up.

"You mean advances in tracking technology. He knew that they were all implanted with trackers, and he also knew how to search for the signal."

"I don't remember being implanted with a tracker, but who knows what the gods did to us. Your guards told me that you are checking everyone from the compound for trackers. What did you find so far?"

Somehow, Valstar was managing to lie to him, which meant that he could resist the compulsion. Either that or he was very skilled at working around it.

He'd been there when the males of other tribes had been slaughtered and their trackers removed to be later implanted in others.

He must be feigning ignorance.

Except, there was no proof Igor had dug out trackers from the bodies of the males he'd killed. The theory was based on the assumption that the settlers had been implanted before boarding the ship to Earth, and the only way Igor could obtain more was by removing them from the dead.

It was a solid assumption, though. Igor had found a way to find some of the Kra-ell, and the only thing that made sense was that he could follow a signal they were emitting.

"All the Kra-ell we checked so far had trackers in them. We gave priority to the purebloods and hybrids, so I don't know what the situation is with the humans. But you must know who has them and who doesn't. You've been with Igor every step of the way."

"Igor didn't share everything with me. I knew that he implanted the Kra-ell who were sent out on missions and the young humans who were sent to study in the university, but the devices were bought from human suppliers, and there was nothing special about them. I didn't know that everyone had them."

"Who did the implanting?"

"We had a human doctor do that."

"Under compulsion, I assume."

Valstar nodded. "Of course. We brought him to the compound blindfolded and then returned him to St. Petersburg after Igor tampered with his memories."

That might be the answer to the inconsistencies. If Igor could thrall in addition to compel, he could erase memories and plant new ones and Valstar might be telling the truth as he knew it.

"Did he compel the doctor to forget what he did? Or did he thrall him?"

Valstar frowned. "Aren't they one and the same?"

The Kra-ell mind manipulation power was a hybrid form of thralling and compulsion, but it was only effective on animals and humans. None of them was as powerful as Igor, who could compel Kra-ell and immortals alike, but not thrall them, or so Toven had believed up until now.

"Let me rephrase. Did Igor command the doctor to forget

what he did, or did he reach into his mind and replace his memories of the compound and its occupants with something more mundane?"

Valstar regarded him with a puzzled expression. "Are you suggesting that he hypnotized the doctor to remember a false memory?"

"In so many words, yes."

"I didn't know that Igor could do that. I think that he just commanded the doctor to forget. It worked well enough on humans."

"What about the Kra-ell? Did it work on them as well?"

Toven knew that it had. Igor had commanded the females not to think about the slaughter of the males of their tribes, which was the same as telling them to forget about it. Jade and Kagra were stronger than most, so they had fought off the command.

"It worked on some," Valstar said. "It didn't work on me, in case you were wondering. I wish it had, so I could claim innocence, but regrettably I remember what I did and regret it even though I had no choice."

"There is always a choice." Toven rose to his feet. "You could have plunged that sword into your own heart instead of obeying Igor's command. That would have earned you a place in the hills of the brave or whatever you call it."

"The fields of the brave." Valstar hung his head. "But you are wrong. By taking my own life, I would have condemned myself to forever walk in the valley of the shamed."

"Even if you did it to save others?"

"My action wouldn't have saved them. The others would have obeyed, and those males would have died despite my sacrifice. Besides, I no longer believe in that nonsense. I stopped believing in the Mother a long time ago."

7

KIAN

*K*ian folded his newspaper and put it on the kitchen counter. For once, the news didn't hold his interest despite the turmoil that had erupted world-wide. The economy was bad everywhere and getting worse, war was raging in some places and social unrest in others, and he couldn't help but wonder if Navuh had anything to do with the global mess.

When things didn't make sense and the world was spiraling into turmoil, Navuh was Kian's usual suspect. Not that the Brotherhood was the only evil force lighting a fire under the pot and stirring things up, but Kian didn't know who else it could be.

Once the Kra-ell crisis was over, he could clear some bandwidth to dedicate to the issue.

According to Lokan, Navuh was focused on raising an intelligent army and shoring up his finances, but perhaps Lokan wasn't as well informed as he thought.

Navuh was a master of compartmentalization, and he didn't share his plans with all of his sons—either his one remaining son by blood or those he'd adopted. The one possible exception was Losham, whose strategic brilliance made him Navuh's right-hand man.

Perhaps Lokan should get in touch with his adopted brother and try to pump him for information. Navuh didn't credit Losham with the successful strategies he'd come up with, taking the credit for himself, and most members of the Brotherhood believed that Navuh was the mastermind behind everything.

Losham was no doubt bitter about it and wanted someone to know that he deserved credit for his successes. He might want to boast to his half-brother and let a few things slip.

As the thumping and grinding noises of Syssi's cappuccino machine pulled Kian out of his reveries, he felt his shoulders lose their tension and a smile curve up his lips. The sounds were soothing, representing home and good times with his family.

"I don't know how Allegra can sleep through this racket." Syssi walked over to the counter with a cup in each hand. "I hoped she would wake up from the noise."

It was after six in the morning, and Syssi needed to get ready for her workday in the lab, but they both knew that waking Allegra up before she was ready would make the rest of the day miserable.

Their daughter loved sleeping, which most of the time was a blessing, but some mornings it was a problem.

Kian took a sip from the perfect cappuccino his wife had made for him and sighed with pleasure. "You've become a master barista and ruined any other coffee place for me."

Syssi grinned. "Practice makes perfect, and there is no better place than home."

"I couldn't agree more." He leaned over and kissed her cheek. "I'm blessed."

"We are both blessed," Syssi corrected him and then chuckled. "Although I have a feeling that our lives won't be as idyllic when Allegra gets older. You should have seen your daughter with Karen's twins yesterday. They are already fighting over her, and she's basking in the attention. I can just imagine those three sixteen years from now."

Kian frowned. "I really don't want to think about my daughter with boys, and there will be at least four vying for her attention. Ethan and Darius will give Ryan and Evan a run for their money, and if Darius is anything like his father, he's going to win."

"What you mean is that you hope Darius will win." Syssi hid her smile behind her cappuccino cup.

"Why would you think that?"

"Because he's the best candidate. Darius's daddy is a three-quarters god, brilliant, charming, and good-looking. If Darius grows up to be like Kalugal, Allegra would be lucky to snag him."

Kian's good mood took a nosedive. "He'll also be conniving and manipulative. In addition, there is the issue of insanity that runs in Kalugal's bloodline. If Toven and Mia produce a son, he would be a much better match for Allegra."

Toven and Mortdh had different mothers, and the insanity gene had come from Mortdh's mother. Toven's descendants should be perfectly fine.

That being said, Toven's daughter had serious issues, and Kian wasn't at all sure that all of them had been the result of the catastrophic accident she'd been involved in.

Geraldine was lovely and sweet, and she made Shai happy, but she was a little loony.

Syssi shook her head. "I don't know why you are always so suspicious of Kalugal. I know that you like him and enjoy his company, and you trusted him enough to invite him and his men to live in the village. So far, he's been cooperative, and he even volunteered his men to help with the Kra-ell rescue. I don't understand your problem with him."

"I'm sure Kalugal didn't do that out of the goodness of his heart. He has his own agenda."

"Like what?" Syssi lifted the cup to her lips.

"I don't know. Maybe he wants them to become his allies."

"Since Kalugal is part of the clan, his allies are also ours."

"I'm not sure about that. He and his men are a small group, and he might want to increase the number of people under his control."

Syssi put her cup down. "If you were in his position, wouldn't you do the same thing?"

"Probably," he admitted. "I would shore up the number of my supporters and then push for democratic elections. He could potentially replace me as the leader of the clan."

Syssi laughed. "That's never going to happen, and you know that. We are not a democracy, and this is still Annani's clan. Something about Kalugal just rubs you the wrong way. What is it?"

"The list is long." Kian crossed his arms over his chest. "He seems to know everything that's going on, even things that I made an effort to keep a secret. I don't know how he finds out about them. Kalugal, on the other hand, keeps his business shrouded in mystery. But unlike him, I respect his privacy and don't try to find out what it is."

Syssi arched a brow. "He told you what he's been working on. He developed that Instatock app that has teenagers world-wide enthralled." She lifted her cup and took a sip.

"He only told me about it because Jacki insisted that he needed checks and balances, and I applaud her for it. That much power in the hands of Mortdh's grandson is dangerous. Despite his so-called confession, I'm still wary of what Kalugal plans to do with the app. He's not an honest man."

"In what way? Other than being secretive, that is."

"He used insider information to make his fortune."

"Kalugal had no choice. He escaped Navuh with nothing, and he needed to provide for his men."

Kian shook his head. "I could have forgiven him for doing that if he had used his compulsion ability minimally when he just got here, but he continued the practice long after he was no longer struggling to survive."

For a long moment, Syssi didn't say a thing, but Kian knew she was taking her time to formulate a counterargument.

Putting her cup down, she swiveled her stool, so she was facing him, and put her hand on his knee. "You have a tendency to see things in black and white, my love. Kalugal is a light shade of gray. He has done some unsavory things, but given where and how he grew up, he turned out better than anyone could have expected. Also, he's still a young immortal, and he's still finding his way. You should cut him some slack."

Kian opened his mouth to argue, but then Syssi's words sank in, and he realized that she was right. He couldn't compare the way he grew up with the way Kalugal had grown up in Navuh's camp. While Kian had been taught lessons on morality and decency by his mother and rewarded for practicing them in his life, Kalugal had been taught the exact opposite and rewarded for that.

It was a miracle that his cousin had turned out as good as he had, and given how Kalugal could have used his compulsion power, the transgressions he'd committed were minor.

Lifting Syssi's hand, Kian brought it to his lips and kissed her palm. "You are infinitely wise, my love. In less than a minute, you have managed to change my entire perspective on Kalugal."

"Then I should have spoken up earlier." She smiled. "I just hoped you would realize that on your own."

He chuckled. "I'm too stubborn and dense for that."

As Syssi picked up her cup and took another sip, he knew she had more to say.

"Since you see things in a different light now, you might be open to what I'm going to suggest next. You need to invite him to your war room and make him part of the decision-making. After all, he volunteered his men, and he should be included. The same goes for Phinas. When Yamanu and Toven confer with you and your war room team, Phinas should participate."

"Kalugal is not interested in military operations. Since leaving the Brotherhood, he's been solely interested in business. He didn't mention even once that he would like to be included in the decisions regarding this mission. If he had, I would have invited him."

Syssi arched a brow. "Really?"

"Not willingly or happily, but I would have felt obligated. He volunteered his men, his jet, and even offered to help financially. In fact, I expected him to use that as an in, but he never did."

"Maybe he's waiting to be invited."

Kalugal wasn't shy, and when he wanted something, he had no problem asking for it, but Syssi had a point. The decent thing to do would be to offer. If Kalugal didn't want to join, he could decline the invitation.

Hopefully, it would be precisely what Kalugal would do.

Despite his epiphany, Kian still wasn't comfortable with Kalugal being privy to everything that was going on in the war room. Too much information was freely exchanged, and Kalugal might learn more than Kian was comfortable with him knowing.

8

KALUGAL

"I'll be there in half an hour." Kalugal ended the call just as Jacki walked into his home office with Darius draped over her shoulder.

"Who was it?" She bounced lightly on her feet while patting their son's tiny back.

It took forever to feed Darius and just as long to get him to burp, and when he did, it was almost always accompanied by a geyser of clumpy, stinky spit-up. He was the sweetest and most beautiful boy, but he wasn't an easy child to raise.

"Kian." Kalugal smoothed his thumb and forefinger over his short beard. "He wants me to stop by his office before I leave for the city."

"Is there a problem?" Jacki stopped bouncing their son. "Did something happen to our guys?"

"Nothing happened. Kian said that he wanted to discuss plans for the future, and he sounded a lot nicer than usual, which made me suspicious. He must want something."

Usually, he and his cousin engaged in a semi-taunting banter that kept them both on their toes and was quite enjoyable, but this time Kian had been polite, cordial and, most alarmingly, his tone of voice had been warm.

The only times Kalugal had heard Kian use that tone was when talking to his wife or daughter.

"If Kian wanted something, he would have asked for it." Jacki resumed her rocking and bouncing. "Subtlety is not one of his best traits." She chuckled softly. "He's as subtle as a brick."

"True. But he hates asking for favors. Maybe he needs money to finance the Kra-ell exodus."

"You said that Roni managed to snag the evil dude's money, and that there was a lot of it. Kian can finance the operation using that."

"That's true as well." Kalugal pushed to his feet and reached for his son. "I'll burp him."

Jacki shook her head. "You are already dressed for work, and you know what happens when he burps. It's usually accompanied by a geyser."

"I'll put the cloth over my shoulder, and if he shoots over it, I'll change clothes. I want to hold him for a little while before I have to go."

He couldn't leave the house before getting his fix. Otherwise, he wouldn't last the six hours or so that he forced himself to spend in the office each day of the week.

Jacki's eyes softened. "Alright." She handed him their little bundle of joy along with the burping cloth.

Holding his child against his chest and inhaling the sweet baby smell was like a drug Kalugal was getting more and more addicted to each day, and as euphoria washed over him and his eyes nearly rolled back in his head, he couldn't care less about the stinky burps or the cottage-cheese-like projectile.

The love he felt for this tiny being was mind-boggling in its intensity.

Kalugal couldn't comprehend how his own father had been cold and indifferent to him and his brother.

His mother claimed that Navuh cared about him and Lokan, and that he'd been cold to them because he couldn't risk showing them more attention than the other sons he'd claimed as his own but who weren't his by blood.

Kalugal didn't believe her.

Navuh had never shown him even a smidgen of affection, and no one was that good of an actor. His mother wasn't lying to him, but she was lying to herself. Areana saw Navuh through the prism of their mate-bond, with love blinding her to her mate's true nature.

Then again, maybe Navuh was different with her, showing her a side of himself that he didn't show anyone else.

Some men were like that, caring only for their mates and not for their offspring, but Kalugal couldn't understand that either. Wasn't procreation the primary purpose of mating? And weren't fathers supposed to be fiercely protective of their children to ensure their survival?

But as with most everything else in creation, nothing was ever perfect or functioned entirely as intended. People, whether human or immortal, were faulty creatures, with some more broken than others.

As the burp came, it was accompanied by the usual spit-up and Darius's pitiful whimper.

"Poor baby." Jacki massaged his little back. "He's suffering."

Darius was six and a half weeks old, and he hadn't slept for more than two consecutive hours yet. Thankfully, his wife and he were immortals who didn't need much sleep, or they would have been exhausted.

Shamash had turned out to be a pretty good babysitter, but neither Kalugal nor Jacki were comfortable letting him take care of the baby for more than a couple of hours.

"How much longer is this reflux thing going to last?" he asked, more out of frustration than hoping for a different answer than the one Bridget had given them.

According to the doctor, most babies got over reflux at four months, but some suffered from it much longer. The good news was that they all eventually outgrew it.

"I hope it will get better soon." Jacki walked around him and checked his back. "You're good. He didn't get you this time."

"I'm not ready to give him back yet." Kalugal rocked Darius until he fell asleep and only then handed him to Jacki.

"Did you hear from Phinas this morning?" She cradled their baby in her arms, holding him close to her chest.

"Not yet. He said he would call if anything interesting happened, so I guess nothing did."

"No news, good news, right?"

"Perhaps it's the calm before the storm." Kalugal leaned to kiss Jacki on her lips. "I won't be gone for long. If my meeting with Kian drags on for more than an hour, I'll skip the office today and come back home."

Jacki smiled. "I'm so glad that we are rich and can afford for you to stay home as much as you please. I feel sorry for all those parents who can't do that and have to leave their babies in daycare."

"I'm glad that I can afford to do it too, but it's not like all rich parents want to stay home with their babies. Amanda is not exactly destitute, but she leaves her daughter with the babysitter while she's at work."

"That's different. Her babysitter is right there with her at her lab at the university. She gets to see Evie whenever she wants." A smile spread over Jacki's beautiful face. "Maybe we can do that too. We could hire a babysitter to come to your downtown office or take Shamash with us, and we could both work from there. Bridget said that we need to get

Darius among humans so he can develop immunity to viruses."

"Not yet. He's too miserable as it is to get a cold or some other human disease on top of that. I'll consider it once he's over the reflux."

She arched a brow. "You will?"

His wife knew him too well. "Probably not. I like knowing that he's safe in the village."

9

KIAN

"*H*ello, cousin." Kian waved a hand, motioning for Kalugal to come in. "Can I offer you something to drink? The options are bottled water or whiskey, but it's too early for alcohol."

He should have gotten coffee and pastries. The idea was to make Kalugal feel welcome, and Kian was doing his best to look and sound pleasant, but that was probably not enough.

"That's a shame." Kalugal cast him a tight smile as he pulled out a chair next to the conference table. "It has been a while since we enjoyed cigars and whiskey together."

"Indeed. If it weren't so early in the morning, I would invite you for a drink and a cigar on the roof."

"I've heard of your rooftop retreat, and I was hoping to get invited, but I thought I never would."

As always, Syssi was right, and Kalugal had been waiting for more than one invitation from Kian.

"If you don't mind the early hour, we can go up there right now." Kian walked over to his desk to get his whiskey bottle and box of cigars.

"What about the rest of your team? Aren't they supposed to be here with you?"

His cousin was definitely feeling left out.

"Turner and Onegus are in the war room."

"How come you're not with them?"

"Nothing urgent is happening at the moment, and I figured it was a good time to talk with you."

Kalugal cocked a brow. "About what?"

"It occurred to me that you might be interested in joining us in the war room. After all, your men are more than half the force on the ship, and the decisions we make here affect them."

"I appreciate the invitation, but I don't know how much time I can devote to the operation. I don't like leaving the house for too long." He smiled. "First, it was the mate bond, and now it's the baby bond. Whenever I leave the house, I feel like two tethers are pulling me back."

"I know precisely what you mean." Kian sat down next to his cousin. "It's easier for me because Syssi and Allegra are gone most of the day. If they were here, I would have a hard time staying at work."

Kalugal tilted his head. "I don't know how you can tolerate having your mate and daughter away from the protection of the village. It would drive me insane to know they are an hour's drive away and unprotected."

Kian smirked. "Who said they are unprotected? I have the entire place rigged with surveillance cameras and Guardians on standby within a two-minute drive from the lab. My wife, my daughter, my sister, and my niece spend their days in that place. I would never have agreed to that without taking all the necessary precautions to safeguard them."

"Does Syssi know?"

Kian grimaced. "She knows some of it, but she doesn't know

the extent of the security measures and the resources I'm dedicating to the security detail. If she had known, she would have quit her job, and she loves it. Besides, I only beefed up what was already in place before Amanda and Syssi decided to take the babies with them to work."

Kalugal eyed him with curiosity mixed with suspicion. "That's more like you. What is not like you is to invite me to your war room or share details about operations and security measures with me. Usually, I need to probe and sweet-talk you into giving me crumbs of information. What happened? Do you need my help financing the Kra-ell relocation project?"

Kian shouldn't be surprised that Kalugal was wary of the sudden change in his attitude.

"I don't need financial help. We seized Igor's money, or rather the money he stole from Jade's tribe and the other tribes he'd robbed." He steepled his fingers. "I just think it's time you took a more active part in what's going on in the village, and this is a good place to start. Your men are on the *Aurora*, and the journey is fraught with peril."

"Oh, now I get it." Kalugal leaned back in his chair and crossed his arms over his chest. "You don't want to assume responsibility for the lives of my men. You want me to take part in the decision-making, so I won't be able to blame you if anything happens to them."

Evidently, the suspicion cut both ways, but Kian knew the blame rested squarely on his shoulders. If he had been more inclusive from the get-go, Kalugal wouldn't be so wary now.

"It's not about that. I've been assuming responsibility for people's lives for so long that it didn't even occur to me. If you're too busy or you don't have the stomach for it, that's fine. I just wanted you to know that the door is open, and you are welcome to join."

Letting out a breath, Kalugal uncrossed his arms. "I need to understand your motives. What brought this change about?"

"Syssi," Kian admitted. "She said that I tend to see things in black and white and that I've been judging you unfairly."

"Judging me? For what?"

"Let's face it, Kalugal. You made your money using insider information. That's dishonest."

"Are you always honest?"

"I try to be. I never take advantage of humans by using mind manipulation. I always try to even out the playing field and use the same resources available to my competitors, meaning smarts and business acumen. But Syssi pointed out something that I was too obtuse to think of myself. I was raised differently than you were and given where you grew up and who your role models were, it's astounding that you got to be as decent as you are." Kian shook his head. "I'm probably botching this speech and offending you left and right while trying to compliment you. What I'm trying to say is that I think you are a good man despite your shady dealings."

Kalugal snorted a laugh. "Diplomacy is not your strong suit, cousin, but your heart is in the right place. I understand what you are trying to convey, and I appreciate it. We each try to do the best we can with what we have, but I don't strive for saint-hood, and I admit to quite a bit of shady dealings. That said, I've never ruined anyone financially or otherwise unless they deserved it."

Kian nodded. "Shades of gray."

"The movie? What does that have to do with what we are talking about?"

"Nothing. When Syssi said that I tend to see things in black and white, she described you as slightly gray. I guess that's a fitting description."

Kalugal chuckled. "Despite your sanctimonious disposition,

you're not pristine either. There are some gray splotches at your edges."

"I guess you are right." Kian sighed. "All I can say in my defense is that I always try to do my best, but sometimes my best is not good enough."

KALUGAL

"*P*erhaps we should take a break on the roof after all." Kalugal pushed to his feet. "It might be too early for whiskey and cigars, but I want to celebrate this break-through in our relationship, and getting invited to your rooftop man-cave is symbolic."

Grinning, Kian got up and walked over to his desk. "I don't have a big selection here, but I have good stuff." He pulled out two cigars and handed one to Kalugal. "Opus-X is unbeatable." A small bottle of whiskey came out of the drawer next. "Royal Salute." Kian showed Kalugal the label. "Perfectly complements the cigars."

"Excellent." Kalugal waited as Kian pulled two glasses out of the same drawer.

The truth was that he didn't care whether the cigar, whiskey, or both were plain or superb. What he cared about was finally getting invited to Kian's roof and enjoying it with his cousin.

They had an odd relationship that had started out on the wrong foot, gotten better over time, and ended up as a tenuous friendship. They liked each other and enjoyed chatting over whiskey and cigars, but they were also suspicious of each other.

It reminded him of one of Jacki's romance novels, subtitled *Enemies to Lovers*. Perhaps his and Kian's relationship was a bromance. They'd started as enemies, with Kian sending a spy to trap him, and him turning the tables on his cousin and taking a Head Guardian hostage. He'd also taken Jacki along with Arwel and had fallen in love with her, so perhaps the Fates had orchestrated that.

Not that Kalugal was a great believer in the Fates, but Kian was, and the Fates provided a convenient excuse.

Somehow, he and Kian had managed to come to an understanding, and they had signed an accord. It should have been smooth sailing from there, but life was not a movie, and nothing ever worked as smoothly and seamlessly as planned.

Kian kept things close to the vest, and so did Kalugal, both for good reasons, but they were family, and despite their very different characters they liked and respected each other.

It would be nice to break the final barrier and demolish the invisible wall between them.

Was he ready for it?

"What are you smirking about?" Kian asked as he opened the office door and stepped into the hallway.

"Our bromance."

"Our what?"

"You heard me." Kalugal followed him up the stairs. "We are an enemies to lovers story just without the sex, therefore a bromance."

Kian shook his head. "We are not lovers, platonic or otherwise, and calling our relationship a bromance is so wrong that I'm starting to regret inviting you over and having this conversation with you."

"You're such a prude." Kalugal kept the banter going.

Teasing his sanctimonious cousin was too much fun to give up just because Kian's conscience had suddenly started troubling him.

When Kian opened the door at the top of the stairs and they stepped out onto the roof, Kalugal regarded the setup. The two foldable outdoor loungers and the small table between them were the kind people took with them to the beach. The sun umbrella shielding the seating arrangement from rain and shine was slightly more upscale, but the entire arrangement was unbecoming of someone of Kian's caliber.

Kalugal clapped his cousin on the back. "Nice man-cave, but it's quite plebeian. I would spruce it up if I were you."

"What's wrong with it?" Kian looked offended. "It's comfortable, and it serves its purpose. I don't need it to impress anyone but me." He put the bottle and two glasses on the table and sat down. "Are you going to join me, or is the furniture not good enough for your royal ass?"

Huffing out a laugh, Kalugal sat down on the other lounger. "I like to surround myself with luxury. Maybe that has to do with how I grew up as well." He cast Kian a sidelong glance. "Being Navuh's son got me the best tutors, but other than that, my living conditions were just as basic as those of other kids."

Kian shook his head. "That excuse will not work for you in this case because I didn't even have the luxury of tutors. My mother and Alena taught me everything they could. Our only so-called riches were the seven Odus my mother got as a wedding present from Khiann. They were a great help, erecting a shelter for us every time we moved, planting a vegetable and medicinal garden, and so on, but it was up to me to hunt and fish and bring game home for the Odus to cook. I did that since I was twelve years old."

Kalugal hadn't known that.

He'd assumed that Annani had thralled humans to give her

what she needed and provide her with free labor. She could have also traded her knowledge or used the gold and precious gems she must have taken with her when she ran away.

The goddess was too wise to have run off with nothing.

"Your mother could've easily provided for you and your sister by manipulating humans to serve her. Why didn't she do that?"

"Because it wouldn't have been right." Kian unscrewed the cap and poured whiskey into the two glasses. "She did that when she had no other choice, but she always preferred for us to survive by means that didn't involve taking advantage of others. That's the code of conduct she instilled in her children and the rest of the clan."

Kian pulled a cutter out of his pocket, cut off the tip of his cigar, and handed it to Kalugal.

"Thanks." Kalugal chopped off the top and waited for Kian to hand him the lighter. "You shouldn't assume that I didn't learn any morality in my youth because of who my father is. Navuh was never a significant influence because he simply wasn't around. I had excellent tutors, and I also read a lot. One of the only privileges I had growing up as Navuh's son was access to books. Naturally, once I joined the warrior ranks, I was exposed to all the propaganda, and Navuh's presence loomed larger than life, but I was immune to his compulsion, and I wasn't easily impressed either." He smiled. "I'm not the type who succumbs to peer pressure."

"I guess being a conceited bastard has its advantages." Kian finished lighting his cigar and handed him the lighter. "I wondered how you managed to turn out a decent person despite your father's teachings, but I assumed it was the result of your mother's good genes. After all, science has proven that nature trumps nurture."

Kalugal grimaced. "Given my family's history, I would like

to believe that we have more free will than being slaves to our genetics. My grandfather was a lunatic and a murderer, and my father is not much better. I don't want that in my future, and even less so in Darius's. I hope to prove that nurture can trump nature."

KIAN

"I hope you can prove it too, and not just for the sake of your son." Kian cast Kalugal a wry smile. "On some level, we are all a little anxious about you showing the first signs of insanity, but I'm not too worried. Lokan shares the same genes, and he has managed to stay sane for over a thousand years, so you have time."

Even Rufsur was on alert, monitoring his boss's behavior with an eye for suspicious signs of megalomania or murderous inclination, and apparently, so was Jacki.

She had mitigated her mate's megalomaniacal plans by convincing him to allow Kian and Annani to monitor him. With the Kra-ell crisis in full bloom, Kian hadn't had time to investigate Kalugal's Instatock application and how it was manipulating young minds to fit Kalugal's agenda. It was one more thing on his to-do list as soon as things returned to normal, or as normal as things ever got for him and his clan.

Leaning back, Kalugal released a puff of smoke. "It's never far from my mind. That's why I agreed to Jacki's suggestion to put checks and balances on myself." He tilted his head toward Kian. "The thing with insanity is that the insane are the last ones to realize that their minds are compromised. Frankly, it's terrifying."

"Indeed. Especially for someone as smart as you." Kian couldn't imagine losing control of his mind or living with the fear of that happening.

"Thank you." Kalugal grinned. "Coming from you, that's a great compliment."

"It's a fact." Kian took a puff from his cigar. "I don't know how you always manage to find out about things I'm trying to keep a secret. When you guessed what my birthday present was, I had the Guardians search the place for listening devices."

Kalugal affected an offended expression. "I would never do such an underhanded thing as planting listening devices around the village. We are allies."

There was also the fact that Annani's compulsion should have prevented him from doing anything of that sort, but there were ways around compulsion, and as a compeller himself, Kalugal probably knew every trick in the book.

"Then how did you find out?"

"You forget that my hobby is archeology and how passionate I am about it. I have a lot of experience piecing together information from mere fragments."

That sounded like a bullshit explanation, and Kian had no problem letting Kalugal know what he thought of it with a not-so-subtle arch of his brow.

His cousin frowned. "Don't give me that face. I told you the truth. I'm very good at solving puzzles, and your people are not as good as you think they are at keeping secrets. I overheard Amanda and Syssi talking about the incredible present you got from Okidu, then in another conversation, someone said something about how wonderful it would be to have more Odus in the village, and the look on Syssi's face was not one of wistfulness but of fear. Those clues were enough for me to figure out what your present from Okidu was."

"Incredible." Kian shook his head. "What about all the other things?"

"I don't know what things you are referring to, but I probably figured them out the same way."

It was a logical explanation, but it was still bullshit.

"I might have been inclined to believe it if you were in the habit of spending your time sitting in the café and listening to gossip, but you are in your downtown office most of the day, and when you come home, you leave your house only to go to a restaurant in town. When do you get to hear all those clues?"

"Jacki fills me in on the village gossip, and sometimes my men also hear things. They spend a lot of time with your clan ladies, and not all of it in bed."

Kian made a mental note to discuss that with Onegus. The Guardians needed to be more careful about what information they let leak.

His relationship with Kalugal was entering a new stage, and he might not wish to continue keeping secrets from his cousin, but leaks needed to be stopped, or they could find their way to other unintended ears.

Then again, security leaks had never been a problem before. Perhaps others weren't as good at piecing clues together, or maybe they didn't have the extra help Kalugal might have gotten from his wife.

"I don't want to sound offensive, but I still don't buy it." Kian tapped the cigar to dislodge a chunk of ash into the ashtray. "Are you using Jacki to spy for you?"

She could see events from the past by touching an object related to them, but she could also see the future. Kian had heard her story about predicting her friend getting into an accident with her new car.

Kalugal shook his head. "If Jacki's had any visions recently, she hasn't told me about them. Her last vision was at the ruins near Lugu Lake."

Kian wasn't sure he believed that, but he'd pushed Kalugal enough, and it was time to change the subject. Besides, he'd forgotten about the ruins and was curious to hear about Kalugal's progress with them.

After the tunnels had collapsed, Kalugal hadn't wanted to endanger lives by continuing the excavation. He'd entered a joint venture with a couple of scientists who'd invented a device that analyzed sediment composition to modify it so it could be used remotely.

"What's new with your investigation over there? Did you manage to alter that contraption to be able to dig its way in?"

"I did, but it got stuck, and my people couldn't retrieve it. They are back to doing it the old-fashioned way, which is taking the whole place apart one stone at a time. I have to find out what's hiding under those ruins. Especially now that we have confirmation that the Kra-ell arrived in escape pods. I'm willing to bet I will find one of those there."

Kian regarded his cousin with an amused smile curling his lips. "Let me guess. You pieced together the information about the Kra-ell ship as well."

"That was easy." Kalugal waved the hand with the cigar. "We suspected that even before Jade told Toven about the pods. But I have no problem admitting that I learned the rest from Phinas, who learned it from Jade."

So that was Kalugal's angle. By volunteering his men and sending Phinas to lead them, he'd hoped to get more information about the gods and the Kra-ell—information that Kian might have chosen not to share with him.

For that, Kian couldn't blame his cousin. They were all

eager to solve the mystery of their origins and why a small group of gods had gotten stranded on Earth.

"If there is a pod under those ruins, it couldn't have come from the ship Jade arrived on. It must have belonged to an earlier scouting expedition."

Kalugal looked offended. "I know that, but it doesn't matter which pod I find there. Just think about all the things we could learn from it. The technology alone is worth the effort, but perhaps it also has information stored in its computers that we can retrieve. If Jade's ship managed to survive for thousands of years while traversing the universe, that pod might still be operational."

That got Kian excited. "Perhaps we can find some of the pods Jade and her people arrived on. It will be interesting to compare the technology of the older pod to the newer ones and how much it progressed."

Kalugal eyed him from under lowered lashes. "If you want to get your hands on my pod, or rather get William's hands on it, you will have to share whatever you find. I'm no longer willing to be kept in the dark about whatever you choose to keep to yourself and be forced to scavenge for scraps of information."

Leaning forward, Kian offered Kalugal his hand. "Full cooperation in everything. I want to know everything you are working on, not just Instatock, and I'll share with you everything that we are doing. Are you willing to shake on it?"

Kalugal hesitated. "I keep all my profits. I'm too greedy to share them with the clan."

"I don't need your money, but I want to know what you're working on, and not after the fact. Full transparency."

"If we do that, I also want three seats on your clan's council. For me, Rufsur, and Phinas."

They had discussed creating a special council to supervise

Instatock, which was supposed to include Kian, Annani, all current council members, and an equal number of representatives from Kalugal's side. But what Kalugal was asking now was much bigger than that. He wanted to be included in every decision that Kian posed to the council.

"One seat, and I need to have the council approve it first. I suggest that you prepare a speech that will impress them."

"Two seats. If you do the math, my people represent fourteen percent of the village population. Your current council has fourteen members. Even two additional seats are less in percentage than our share in the population."

Kian wondered whether Kalugal had calculated all of that on the spot or had been planning to ask for seats on the council for a while.

"Two it is. Again, it's not solely my decision, and you will have to convince the council to accept two new members. You can choose either Rufsur or Phinas, but in my opinion, Rufsur is a better choice because he's mated to Edna, who is a council member. She'll vote to include him."

"Don't be so sure. Edna does not vote with her heart. She votes with her mind."

"True, but I'm sure you'll deliver a speech that will wow even Edna."

"You can bet on it." Smirking, Kalugal put his hand in Kian's. "To a bright future for all of us." He shook it firmly.

TOVEN

"You're quieter than usual." Mia turned to look at Toven over her shoulder. "Do you want to take a break?"

After leaving Valstar to wallow in his memories and joining Mia and the sisters on their explorations of the ship, Toven's mind had been churning with what he had learned and the questions he still needed to find answers for.

He leaned down and kissed her forehead. "Are you tired, my love? We can take a coffee break and continue later."

"I'm not tired. I'm sitting in a chair and being wheeled around. You're the one doing the pushing."

"I'm fine. I'm just preoccupied with thoughts of my conversation with Valstar. There are still so many questions that I didn't get to ask him."

"What did you talk about?" Jin asked.

"I asked him mostly about Igor and what he knows about him. Turns out that even Valstar doesn't know Igor's Kra-ell name. The settlers were chosen by lottery and weren't introduced to each other. They just loaded them into the pods and sent them on their way."

"That's weird." Mey leaned against a wall. "Didn't they get briefings about where they were supposed to settle? Instructions about what they were supposed to do? How could they have sent all those people across the universe with no guidance?"

"I think I know the answer to that." Mia adjusted the blanket, pulling it a little higher so it didn't drag on the floor, and at the same time scanning the area before lowering her voice. "Jade said they were sent to Earth to serve the gods, so they didn't need instructions. They were supposed to get them once they got to their destination."

Jin looked at Toven. "Did you know about the Kra-ell?"

He shook his head. "The gods who were born on Earth weren't told about them, and that's the biggest hole in that story. If the older gods knew about a ship of Kra-ell workers heading their way, we should have been told to expect them."

"Someone lied." Mey pushed away from the wall and resumed walking. "But who and why is anyone's guess. You should ask Valstar what he thinks about that."

"That's one of the things on my growing list of questions."

"What else did you talk with him about?" Jin asked.

"The trackers. Like Jade, he didn't remember getting implanted, but what threw me off was that he seemed not to know that all the Kra-ell had trackers in them. Valstar only knew about the Kra-ell who got implanted with them before leaving on missions, and the humans who had been sent to study at the university. But if we assume that all the settlers were implanted before boarding the ship, and that Igor cut the sophisticated trackers out of the Kra-ell he murdered, then Valstar must know about it because he went on those missions with Igor. So either our assumption about the trackers is wrong, or Igor made Valstar and everyone else who was there forget about cutting the trackers out of the victims before setting their bodies on fire."

Jin snorted. "Valstar is playing the victim game so you'll feel sorry for him and protect him from Jade. Don't fall for that."

"He can't lie to me, and he's not trying to absolve himself by blaming Igor's compulsion. He's also not faking being sorry for what he did. Given that he was compelled and couldn't disobey the order even if he wanted to, a human court would not have given him the death penalty. They would have given him a lighter sentence. I don't feel right about letting Jade execute him without a trial."

"You gave her your word," Jin said. "If you go back on it, she will never trust you again."

"I know. But now that I've talked to Valstar, I would feel like an accomplice to murder if I let her kill him. I need to talk to her and convince her to allow Valstar a trial."

"You can try it this evening." Mey turned into another hall-way, and they all followed. "We invited Jade to our cabin so Jin and I can ask her questions about our parents. You and Mia are welcome to join. Maybe after hearing our story, Jade will be in a more receptive mood."

"She won't," Jin said. "Do you think she feels bad about giving up the children of the hybrids for adoption? She does not."

Mey shook her head. "You haven't exchanged more than one sentence with Jade, and you're already an expert on her character?"

"I don't need to talk to her to know the kind of person she is. It's written all over her face, posture, and salty attitude."

Mey cast her sister a fond smile. "Takes one to know one."

Jin huffed. "I might be salty, but I would never have taken children from their parents and given them up for adoption."

Jade wasn't the cruel and unreasonable female Jin thought

she was, but Toven didn't offer his opinion. She wouldn't take his word for it anyway.

"I guess we will find out later this evening." Mey glanced at her watch. "I suggest we end our tour now to prepare for the meeting. I want to jot down my questions."

"Good idea." Mia lifted her eyes to Toven. "Do you want to talk to Valstar again? Maybe you could put together some arguments in his favor before the meeting. Something that would convince Jade to allow him a trial."

"Do you want to come with me?"

Mia shook her head. "Unless you need me there to enhance your compulsion, I'd rather not. Whether willing or not, Valstar is a murderer, and I don't want to be exposed to his bad energy. I'm not as strong as you are."

"You're right. I don't want you to be exposed to it either."

"Go. Come get me when you are done."

"Are you sure?"

Her portable chair wasn't motorized, and its wheels weren't comfortable for her to move over distances longer than getting to the bathroom and back. She needed to be pushed, and it was no trouble for him to take her back to their cabin before seeing Valstar again.

"I'm sure." She took his hand and gave it a loving squeeze. "Mey and Jin will help me."

13

PHINAS

"*I*'m surprised at how fast the pool is filling up." Phinas cast a sidelong glance at Karl, the assistant to the chief engineer. "I thought it would take a day or two until I could teach my first swimming lesson. Thankfully, the *Aurora* has plenty of outdoor lighting because the days are so damn short out here."

It was only six in the evening, but it had been dark for over two hours and the cold air was biting even for an immortal, and yet the human didn't seem affected.

Karl wore a coat and a scarf, and his cheeks were ruby, but he wasn't stomping his feet and rubbing his hands like Dandor was doing on Phinas's other side.

The engineer regarded him with a smug expression on his face. "We don't have a shortage of water or depend on the size of the supply pipe. We get as much as we can pump, and we can pump a lot."

"Is that unique to the *Aurora*? Or is it like that on all cruise liners?"

"It's like that on all the new ones. The water needs to be replaced every night."

Phinas arched a brow. "Why so often?"

The assistant engineer leaned over to get closer to Phinas's ear. "Because passengers pee in the pools."

"Gross. But they probably pee in public in-ground pools as well, and I know that they don't change the water in those on a daily basis or even monthly."

"Most pools don't have as many daily users, and their filtration system can handle the contamination."

"Disgusting." Dandor made a face. "I'm never going into a public pool again."

Phinas chuckled. "As if you've never pissed in a pool."

"I didn't. I pissed in the ocean, but that doesn't count."

His phone buzzing with an incoming message put an end to the discussion.

"Excuse me." He pulled the phone out of his pocket.

The message was from Kalugal:

Call me after you find a private spot.

"I have a phone call to make." He offered Karl his hand. "Thank you for helping us with the pool."

"You are most welcome." Karl shook his hand. "But I suggest heating it up. Otherwise, your swimming students will end up with hypothermia."

"We need to conserve fuel, so we can only heat it minimally."

Karl nodded. "You should keep the lessons short and have towels and blankets ready for the students."

"Of course." Phinas left Karl with Dandor and headed to his cabin to make the call.

Five minutes later, he was on the couch with a glass of water in one hand and the phone in the other.

"What's up, boss?"

"You go first. Do you have any juicy tidbits for me? Any conversations you overheard?"

"I know Toven talked with Valstar again, but I haven't heard what he learned from him."

"Keep your ear to the ground. Did anyone mention me in any way?"

"Not today. Why?"

"I just had a fascinating and entirely unexpected talk with Kian. He offered me two seats on the village council, pending the council's approval, of course. One will go to me and the other to Rufsur or you. You can also rotate the position, with each of you serving six months of the year or some other arrangement that works for you."

"Is the position that demanding?"

Kalugal chuckled. "Not at all. Kian rarely remembers to consult his council, and he only does so when it's a major decision that affects the entire clan. I don't think the council meets more than once or twice yearly."

"Then why do you need Rufsur and me to rotate?"

"I don't want to choose one of you over the other. You are both equally dear and important to me, but each brings different qualities to the table."

Phinas rubbed the back of his head. "Did you talk with Rufsur?"

"Not yet. I called you first."

Did that mean that Kalugal believed he was the better man for the job?

Phinas had always been the cool-headed one, while Rufsur had been the fun guy Kalugal liked to go clubbing with. That didn't mean that Rufsur wasn't suited for the job of a councilman, though. Perhaps his charm was precisely what was needed.

"What about Jacki? Did you consider offering the seat to her?"

"I did, but then decided against it. Kian was very gracious by offering me two seats, and I didn't want to repay him by getting him in trouble with his wife. If I offered the seat to Jacki, Syssi might get upset that he didn't offer her a seat as well."

"Maybe he has?"

"But what if he hasn't? I don't want to chance it."

"Then perhaps you should suggest nominating both ladies for the council. I'm saying that not because you are mated to Jacki, and Kian is mated to Syssi, but because the council needs more balance, and I'm not talking about gender. There are three males and three females on the core council. The balance shifts when the Guardians and Onegus are added, but that can't be helped until more females join the force and make it all the way up to Head Guardian. Jacki and Syssi bring more than just their gender to the table. They are both seers, and up until recently, they were both human. I think it's important to consider the impact on humans when making important decisions, and they can authentically represent that side of the equation."

"Bravo." Kalugal clapped. "I'm impressed. The seat goes to you."

"It wasn't my intention to impress you so you'd offer me the seat and not Rufsur. I don't want it, and if you don't want to offer it to Jacki, offer it to him."

"Why not? You seem to have solid opinions about things, and I like how enlightened you are. Frankly, I didn't expect that from you or from Rufsur."

Phinas chuckled. "Now I'm offended. Neither of us is a simpleton, nor are we influenced any longer by what we were fed in Navuh's camps. In fact, neither of us believed in his propaganda even then, which is why you selected us for your unit."

"I know that, and I didn't mean it that way. It's just that all of us are busy with our day-to-day responsibilities, and we seldom stop to think about the big picture."

It was nice of Kalugal to include himself in the 'we,' but he was the consummate big-picture guy, always thinking a few steps ahead of everyone else.

"Usually, you are right, but I'm in a unique position to observe a mini social reform."

"Are you referring to the Kra-ell and the humans they enslaved?"

"Yeah. Jade is a traditionalist, but she's a smart lady, and she listens. She's ready to make changes."

"I'd be most interested to hear about those changes."

"I'll keep you posted."

"Thank you." Kalugal let out a breath. "I'll give the council seat more thought, and I'll consult with Jacki. If she declines, would you be interested?"

"I'll give it some thought as well."

"Excellent. Good day, Phinas."

14

JADE

*J*ade walked into the kitchen and scanned the place for Isla. When she spotted her next to one of the workstations, she strode toward the woman. "Can I have a word with you?"

The human lifted a hand to her chest. "Did something happen?"

"I just want to discuss something with you. Is there a quiet place we can talk?"

Isla's hands started shaking. "What is this about?"

Jade needed to dial down her aggression or the human might faint from fright. She might be less terrified with her brother at her side.

Forcing her shoulders to relax, Jade affected a smile. "It's about our community's future. I want to understand the issues the humans in our community are concerned with."

"Oh." Isla let out a breath. "Perhaps you should talk with Jarmo. I'm not good at things like that."

Jade looked around the busy kitchen. "I disagree. You are good at organization, and people follow your lead, but if you are more comfortable with Jarmo present, I would welcome his input as well."

How was that for diplomacy?

Jade was proud of the polite words she'd chosen to put the woman at ease. She would never have spoken like that to a Kra-ell, and if she had, they wouldn't have taken her seriously. There was no beating around the bush in the Kra-ell culture or being mindful of hurt feelings. It was much better than the nonsensical way humans interacted, but when in Rome and all that. If she wanted to lead a contemporary mixed community, she had to adapt.

Her many years of interacting with humans during her business dealings had taught her a thing or two about their various cultures and accepted speech patterns. She wouldn't need to start from scratch and learn from her mistakes like she'd done back in the day.

"Maybe Sofia and Marcel should join us as well?" Isla asked.

"Since Sofia will most likely choose to live with Marcel, I don't expect them to be part of our community for long, and they shouldn't have a say in how it will be run."

Wording her reply in a way that wouldn't offend or frighten Isla had felt like a tongue-twister, and Jade's patience was starting to wear thin.

Despite her efforts, Isla didn't look happy with her answer, but she knew better than to push for a different one. "Jarmo is down in the animal enclosure. We can go to him." She looked around the kitchen. "I just need to get Helmi to take over for me."

"Very well. I'll meet you down there in ten minutes." That would give her time to calm down.

"Yes, sir."

That was the address that Igor had demanded. 'Yes, mistress," was the proper way to address a tribe leader, who traditionally was a female. But traditions were changing, and she was attempting to build a community where everyone was comfortable and felt respected.

Besides, it would be odd to be addressed as mistress again. It would also be painful, reminding her of what she'd lost.

"I don't require an honorific. A nod will suffice in most cases, and in others, you can just call me Jade."

Looking surprised, Isla nodded.

Jade used the ten minutes to walk through the deserted corridors of the crew quarters, and when she arrived at the animal enclosure, she was calmer and ready to go through another tongue-twister with Isla and Jarmo, who were already there.

Other than the animals and the two humans, there was no one else in the cargo, which was perfect.

"Let's sit over there." She pointed at the crates separating the goats from the sheep.

"What is it about?" Jarmo asked.

Jade was sure Isla had already told him, but he might have found it unbelievable that she wanted the humans' opinion.

Turning to Isla, Jade got straight to the point. "You told Phinas that the humans wouldn't mind continuing to work for us if they got paid and if the interbreeding stopped. The breeding is essential to us, and if the females are willing, I don't see the problem."

"The females are not willing," Isla said. "They agreed to do it out of fear, and so they would be allowed to marry a human once they had done their duty and produced a hybrid child. Those were Igor's rules, and they were coercive. Our young females didn't have a choice."

Perhaps Isla was projecting her own preferences on the other females of her community.

"You've never produced a hybrid child," Jade pointed out.

Isla nodded. "I was never allowed to marry a human male, but I was still blessed with wonderful children, so I consider it a fair trade. Luckily, I'm plump and short, and the purebloods don't find me attractive."

Jade shifted her eyes to Jarmo. "What about you? Did Joanna force you into her bed?"

"She didn't. I went willingly and more than once. I was young and naive, and I thought that we could be together despite who her father was. But she got tired of playing with the human pretty quickly, or maybe she got what she wanted, which was to get pregnant with a human child and get a rise out of her father."

That wasn't why Joanna had bedded Jarmo, but it was Joanna's story to tell, not Jade's.

"Still, you were willing, and so were many of the females who produced hybrid children for us." She shifted her gaze to Isla. "It would seem that not everyone is against the interbreeding."

Isla's plump lips twisted. "Those who agree do it for something, not because they find the purebloods appealing."

Jarmo cleared his throat.

Isla glared at him. "Besides you, that is, and you were infatuated with a hybrid, not a pureblood."

"Some of the young ladies find the pureblooded males attractive," Jarmo said. "That doesn't mean that they want to get pregnant with a hybrid child, though. They just want the sex."

Jade stifled a chuckle.

As a female, Isla should have been more attuned than her brother to the needs and wants of other women in her community, but she projected her own preferences on others and colored everything through the prism of her own beliefs.

"How do you know that?" Isla frowned at Jarmo.

"I have eyes. I see how they flirt with them and vie for their attention. I don't know how you don't see that."

Isla waved a dismissive hand. "They all want the benefits that come with bedding a pureblood and giving him a child. They are basically whoring themselves out for peanuts."

Jarmo winced. "That's harsh, Isla."

"But true."

Jade lifted her hand to stop the argument. "The women are free to do as they please with their bodies and bed whoever they want. I will prohibit any negative consequences for refusal and will harshly punish any pureblood or hybrid who threatens a woman with retribution for refusing to have sex and/or breed with him. But I will allow incentives for acquiescence. Hybrids are essential to our continuation, and if the ladies are willing to produce them for a price, I see no harm in that."

15

PHINAS

"Ready to try the pool?" Phinas whipped his shirt over his head and tossed it on top of one of the lounge chairs.

Dandor's lips curved downward. "Are you nuts? It's freezing."

"I can't tell the Kra-ell to get into the water if my own men are unwilling to get cold."

"What Kra-ell?" Dandor waved his hand around. "There is no one else out here."

"They are coming. I texted Yamanu and asked him to corral a couple of dudes. I want them to see us in the water when they come up here."

Dandor shook his head. "If I knew the things I would have to endure on this mission, I wouldn't have volunteered."

"Liar." Phinas kicked his boots off and unbuckled his belt. "You were chomping at the bit to get out of the village." He pulled down his pants and folded them on top of the shirt.

"We don't have towels or blankets." Dandor crossed his arms over his chest. "You heard Karl. We need those before we get in.

I don't know how long our bodies can combat the cold, and I don't want to accidentally go into stasis."

Phinas had never heard about any immortals going into stasis because their bodies couldn't keep generating enough heat to protect them from the cold, but he could imagine an instance where it could happen. Getting buried under an avalanche of snow or frozen inside a block of ice could do that, but getting submerged in cold water that was just a smidgen over freezing temperature should be fine for the hour or so he planned on dedicating to the swimming lesson.

"Stop being such a wuss." Phinas stretched, did a few jumping jacks, and ran in place to get his blood pumping. "The Kra-ell boys are bringing towels and blankets with them."

Letting his chin drop to his chest, Dandor released a resigned sigh. "Fine. But I'm waiting until they get here before I'm plunging into that water."

If Kagra were there, Dandor would have jumped into the pool without a single word of protest, but he had no one to impress.

"No pain, no gain, brother." Phinas cast him a reproachful look before jumping into the pool, feet first.

The shock was nearly paralyzing, but his immortal body was quick to adapt, increasing its inner temperature to compensate.

Floating on his back, he smiled at Dandor. "It's not so bad."

"Right." The guy still stood with his arms crossed over his chest and a pouty expression on his face unworthy of a warrior.

They had gotten soft over the years. Training in a gym and wrestling each other wasn't enough to keep them hard. They didn't push themselves, and after their training sessions they went to their comfortable homes, took showers in their luxurious bathrooms, and dried their bodies with soft towels.

Warriors were forged by surviving in harsh conditions and fighting in real battles.

Still, they had done well against the Kra-ell, even with the added difficulty of trying not to kill any of them.

Flipping to his front, Phinas started doing laps. By the time the two hybrids showed up with a stack of towels and blankets, he'd counted eleven.

They both looked familiar, but Phinas didn't remember their names.

He swam toward the edge of the pool and braced his arms on the concrete. "What are your names?" Not sure they understood English, he pointed to himself. "My name is Phinas."

"I'm Piotr," the one on the left said.

"I'm Tomos." His friend patted his chest.

Now Phinas remembered who he was. He was Sofia's cousin's boyfriend.

"Put the towels and blankets down and strip down to your underwear." He hoped they weren't going commando. "You'll be the first to receive cold water swimming and floating training."

The two exchanged glances, looked at him, and then followed his orders without arguing.

Phinas shifted his gaze to Dandor and lifted a brow. "What are you waiting for?"

"I was hoping the Russians would attack and save me from this torture." With a sigh, he took his clothes off and joined the two hybrids at the pool's edge.

As the three stood there and stared at the water, Phinas laughed. "Come on, boys. It's only cold for the first two seconds, and then it's warmer in the water than outside of it. The pool is not deep enough for a head dive, so jump in feet first."

It was still biting cold, but he and Dandor would survive.

The question was whether the hybrids' bodies possessed the same mechanism and would raise their inner temperature.

Uttering a battle cry reminiscent of Tarzan, Tomos jumped in, and his friend followed a split second later.

Their expressions telegraphed the initial shock, but as the seconds ticked off, the two relaxed.

"How are you feeling? Are your bodies regulating the temperature?"

Tomos nodded and translated for Piotr.

"Good. I was worried for a moment."

"What about you? How can you regulate yours?" Tomos asked.

Damn. He'd forgotten that they didn't know their rescuers were immortals.

"Navy SEAL training. Dandor and I trained for a very long time to learn how to do it."

"Oh." Tomos accepted the explanation without batting an eyelid. "So, what do we do now?"

"First, you learn to float on your back." Phinas demonstrated.

It took several tries, a lot of mutual teasing between the young men, and some help from Dandor before they managed to keep themselves afloat.

"How long do we need to do this?" Tomos asked.

"When you can hold yourself for five minutes straight, you can get out."

Phinas swam to the edge of the pool and hoisted himself out.

"Where are you going?" Dandor asked.

"To get Jade." He wrapped a large towel around himself. "I want her to get in the pool as well."

"It's not fair," Dandor whined. "You're leaving us here to freeze."

Reaching under the towel he'd wrapped around his middle, Phinas pulled his wet boxer shorts down. "If you get them to float for five minutes, the three of you will be done for today, and you can get out."

16

TOVEN

*W*hen Toven walked into Valstar's cabin, the guy's face brightened. "I wondered when you'd be back."

Was he so lonely that he was excited to see him? Or was he under the impression that his ploy to play on Toven's heartstrings was working?

Not that he was wrong. Toven would feel much less guilt if Valstar wasn't executed without a trial. The Kra-ell might be savages who lived by the sword, but the gods believed in due process, and despite their murky past, they still had the moral high ground.

Sitting in the same armchair as before, Toven crossed his legs. "I didn't plan on stopping by again today, but I realized that I didn't cover all the issues I wanted to go over with you. I still have many unanswered questions."

"You didn't answer my question either." Valstar tilted his head. "Were you among the original settlers, or were you born on Earth?"

Toven saw no harm in telling the guy the truth. Even if Jade agreed to let Valstar stand trial, Toven doubted the outcome

76

would be any different for him. The guy wasn't going to live long enough to tell anyone.

"I was born on Earth and didn't know that the Kra-ell existed. None of the original settlers mentioned you or the rebellion. The first I heard of it was from Jade."

That wasn't entirely true. Mortdh had thrown a few hints about the gods' dark past, but Toven hadn't paid attention to his brother's ramblings.

"Maybe they were forbidden to mention it," Valstar said. "Exile was probably a diminished sentence for their part in the rebellion, and a stipulation for being allowed to live was not ever mentioning it."

"Perhaps. Or maybe they didn't want the next generation to know that they had been exiled."

"That's possible as well." Valstar nodded. "The gods were a proud people, and they didn't like to acknowledge any wrongdoing."

Hearing the guy talk about the gods in the past tense had a trickle of apprehension slither down Toven's back. It probably didn't mean anything, and the planet of the gods was still out there along with its inhabitants—the gods and the Kra-ell.

"It is probably still as true today as it was then," Valstar added. "People don't change."

"Sometimes they do."

Toven still carried the burden of all of his misdeeds and failures. If he could have shed responsibility, he would have been a happier male. Even now, with a truelove mate at his side and surrounded by a big, loving family, he still suffered from bouts of melancholy whenever he reflected on his long life.

Uncrossing his legs, he leaned forward and looked into Valstar's black eyes. "I didn't come here to talk about me. I came here for answers, and I want you to tell me only the truth.

Did you see Igor or anyone else cut the trackers out of the males you slaughtered?"

Valstar's eyes momentarily turned green before going back to black. "I didn't. I was in charge of releasing the humans and searching for any Kra-ell who might be hiding among them. How do you know Igor did that? Did Jade tell you?"

"She didn't, but unless they had active trackers, Igor wouldn't have known where to find the other Kra-ell tribes."

"Maybe they did something to tip their hand?"

"Did he tell you how he found them?" Toven shoved his full power of compulsion into the question.

Valstar shook his head. "He just informed me when he found them and instructed me to conduct reconnaissance and plan the mission. He never told me how he found them."

"Unbelievable." Toven rose to his feet and started pacing. "Was there anyone else he confided in?"

"He didn't confide in anyone, and he used different people for different tasks, forbidding us from sharing what we knew with the others. Don't forget that none of us joined him voluntarily. We were compelled to follow his orders. Some had less of a problem with his agenda than others, and all of us liked having enough females, so no one had to go without, but I doubt everyone was okay with his methods. I wasn't, but I had no choice, and I couldn't confide my displeasure with the others either."

Perhaps Jin was right, and Valstar was playing the victim. He might have even convinced himself of that, and that was how he was able to circumvent Toven's compulsion.

"You were Igor's second-in-command. He wouldn't have chosen you for the position if he didn't believe that you were a hundred percent behind him."

Valstar sighed. "After Igor, I was the most capable and smartest male in our group. That's why he chose me. I learned languages fast, I adapted to human technology quickly, and I was a good administrator. He didn't care about my personal beliefs or whether I agreed with him or not. As long as I did my job well, I got to keep my position." He smiled. "Jade despised him and hated every moment she had to spend with him, and yet he chose her as his prime because she was the best at what she did, which was producing superior offspring. Unfortunately for him, she only gave him one daughter, and he wanted a son. But the moral of the story is that she did exactly what I did. To survive, she gave Igor what he wanted when he wanted it. The only difference was that her job was to spread her legs for him while mine was to kill the competition and make sure that the compound ran smoothly."

17

PHINAS

*P*hinas walked into the dining hall and scanned the tables for Jade, but she wasn't there. She hadn't been in her cabin or Kagra's either, nor had she been at the clinic or any of the other places he'd checked.

He stopped by a table with several hybrids. "Do you know where I can find Jade?"

"She went to the kitchen," one of them said.

Phinas's hackles rose.

The only reason for Jade to go there was to talk to Isla. She must have figured out that Isla had been the one who complained to him about the breeding, which was his fault for blurting out her name this morning, and she'd gone to give her a talking to.

When he turned toward the kitchen, Toven waved him over to his and Mia's table.

"Are you still coming to Yamanu and Mey's cabin after dinner?"

"I hope so." It depended on what was going on in the kitchen and if he and Jade would still be on speaking terms after he confronted her.

"Mia and I are joining as well," Toven said. "I spoke with Valstar earlier and learned a few new things."

That piqued his interest, but he was in a rush to get to the kitchen and protect Isla from Jade. "I would love to hear all about it, but there is something I need to attend to."

Toven nodded. "I will share my findings at the get-together."

"Good deal. See you there." Phinas cast a quick smile at Mia before turning away.

Striding toward the kitchen, he tried to calm down so he could plan his next move, but as he got in there and Isla wasn't to be found, he started to worry in earnest.

Finding Lana, he walked up to her. "Where is your mother?"

"She went down to the animal enclosure to talk to Jarmo."

Phinas released a relieved breath, but then it occurred to him that Isla wouldn't have left the kitchen during the busy dinner time just to go chat with her brother. "Do you know why she went there?"

"Jade wanted to talk to her, and Isla said that they needed to talk with Jarmo."

"Thank you." He forced a smile before turning around.

It was smart of Isla to suggest Jarmo should join. She would at least have him to back her up when Jade attacked.

Impatient to wait for the elevator, Phinas took the stairs down to the animal enclosure.

He walked in as Jade was finishing a sentence.

"—if the ladies are willing to produce them for a price, I see no problem with that."

He'd been right. She was talking with them about the breeding.

Jarmo noticed him first and gave him a tight smile, then Jade turned around and frowned.

"What are you doing here?"

"I was worried about Isla. I came to check that she was

alright." He didn't add that he had been worried about what Jade might do to her, but given the red flash of her eyes, she'd guessed it.

"Why?" She put her hands on her hips. "What did you imagine I would do to her?"

"I don't know. You tell me."

If looks could kill, he would be dead.

Jade looked like she was reining in her temper with much difficulty. "We are having a conversation about the future of our community, and it's none of your business."

Tilting his head to look at Isla, he asked, "Are you alright?"

She didn't understand the words, but she understood the tone and gave him the thumbs up.

Did he believe her?

Not really, but it didn't seem as if Jade was abusing her, and Jarmo was there.

Still, he was mad that Jade hadn't told him she was going to talk to Isla and that she hadn't invited him to join after they had discussed the matter this morning.

"If this is about the breedings, then it's very much my business. I was the one who promised Isla that the coercion would stop."

"I'm here to hear it directly from her and from Jarmo, and I don't appreciate you barging in on our private conversation and assuming the worst. Please leave."

Jade was holding her temper at bay and answering him as politely as she could, but Phinas knew that if he stayed even a moment longer, she would explode.

"Fine." He turned around and walked out.

Hovering just outside the entrance for a few moments, he made sure that all Jade did was talk, and when he was certain that Isla and Jarmo were safe, he walked away on silent feet.

JADE

When Jade stepped out of the elevator on her deck, she found Phinas leaning against the wall looking angry.

"Are you waiting for me?" she asked.

"Who else would I be waiting for? We are supposed to be at Mey and Yamanu's cabin in a few minutes, and you stink of animals. Are you planning to shower before we go?"

He was in a foul mood, and she knew why, but he had no right. If anyone should be angry, it was her.

Not only was her conversation with Isla and Jarmo none of his business, but his assumption that she would retaliate against Isla for talking to him was also insulting.

It was true that she was angry at the woman for turning to an outsider instead of talking to her first, but she understood why.

Isla's hands had started shaking when she'd approached her. The woman had been terrified of her, but she didn't know why. She hadn't exchanged more than a few words with her during the past two decades, and those words hadn't been angry.

With a slight arch of her brow, Jade pivoted on her heel and strode toward her cabin.

Uttering a growl, Phinas followed her. "You didn't answer me."

"I'm going to shower and change clothing, so I don't offend your people's delicate sense of smell."

As Jade opened the door to her cabin, she debated whether to close it in Phinas's face or let him come in. It would have been so satisfying to close it, but she was above such petty antics.

"Please, come in," she said in as polite a tone as she could manage. "Sit down and relax while I shower."

He closed his eyes and released a breath. "Why didn't you tell me that you were going to talk to Isla? And don't tell me that it's none of my business because it is. I was the one who brought the issue of the humans wanting a change to your attention."

Again, her knee-jerk reflex was to tell him that he had no right to butt in and that Isla should have come to her first, but she stifled the urge, and not just because she was above that. Phinas was an important asset, and she wasn't going to lose him over a nonsensical human-style childish drama.

"When I figured out that the human you spoke with was Isla, I wanted to hear her complaints first-hand and not through your filter." Heading toward the bedroom, she shrugged off her sweater and carried it into the bathroom to put in the laundry basket.

Phinas followed her inside. "What did you learn?"

She turned her head to look at him over her shoulder. "You should have started with that instead of growling insults at me."

"I just stated the facts. You smell of animals, and it's not pleasant."

"I'm not talking about that." She pulled her shirt over her

head and tossed it in the laundry basket. "I'm talking about your insinuation that I might retaliate against my people for speaking up. I admit that I was angry at Isla for coming to you instead of me, but I didn't lash out at her. We just talked."

"What did Isla tell you?"

"More or less the same she told you." Jade removed the rest of her clothing, stepped into the shower, and closed the glass door.

Regrettably, Phinas's eyes didn't blaze with desire upon seeing her naked, which meant that he was still upset over her talk with Isla.

What had he expected? That she would obey his wishes and implement changes without investigating the opinion of the people those changes affected?

Her talk with Isla and Jarmo was just the beginning. She would assemble all the human females and have the same talk with them.

"And?" Phinas leaned against the vanity with his arms crossed over his chest.

"Jarmo had a different perspective on the issue, and so did I." Jade started lathering her body with one of the fragrant soaps lining the shelf. "I agreed to disallow threats of negative consequences for refusal, and I promised that any instance would be severely punished, but I said that I would allow positive incentives. We have no choice. The pureblooded females don't produce enough children to keep our race from dying out."

"Did you address the issue of compulsion? What if the women cannot complain about being threatened because they've been compelled not to?"

"We didn't go into details, but I will address all those issues when I assemble all the adult human females and get their opinions on the matter. With all due respect to Isla and Jarmo, they weren't elected as the humans' representatives, and they have no right to decide for them."

"But you can?"

"If they want to stay under my leadership, the answer is yes. But I'm going to listen and try to devise a system that works for everyone. I don't have any illusions about creating a utopia, though. It's impossible to please everyone, but if I manage to prevent anyone from suffering, I will consider it a job well done."

"That's all I'm asking for."

When she turned the water off and opened the shower door, Phinas handed her a towel. "By the way, I bumped into Tom on the way. He and Mia are going to join us at Yamanu's cabin."

"Great." Jade finished drying off and hung the towel on the hook behind the door. "Anything else?"

"He spoke to Valstar again."

She turned to look at him. "Did he find out anything new about Igor?"

"He did. He said he would tell us at Yamanu's."

19

PHINAS

*P*hinas felt like shit for jumping to conclusions and flying off the handle before giving Jade a chance to explain.

Talk about presumptions.

He'd been sure that she'd berated Isla for confiding in him, but it seemed like they'd had a civilized conversation about their symbiotic coexistence and the future of their community.

But what if Isla and Jarmo had a different take on that conversation?

Jade was intimidating, and they might have said things they hadn't meant just to get her to back off.

He needed to have a talk with them and find out where things really stood.

"I'm ready." Jade zipped up her tight-fitting leather jacket. "Let's go."

"You look good." He put his arm around her.

She didn't brush his hand off until they were at the door. "You know my stance on public displays of affection."

"Yeah, you made it abundantly clear." He dropped his arm.

On the one hand, it was good that Jade didn't beat around

the bush and communicated her wishes clearly, but on the other hand it took some getting used to.

He'd always been attracted to strong women, but the ones he'd been with were a little softer around the edges, a little more mindful of his feelings.

The truth was that Jade was mindful as well. She wasn't aggressive with him, and he knew that she held back because of how much stronger she was. She believed that his male ego would suffer if he was overpowered by a female.

Was she right about that?

They wouldn't know until she let loose and had her way with him. The thought had him excited more than it should, and he needed to get rid of the evidence of his excitement before he knocked on Yamanu's door.

Jade eyed him from the corner of her eye and smirked. "You must really like my leather jacket."

"I like everything about you." He gripped the back of her neck and planted a kiss on her lips.

Turning into him, she wound her arms around him and returned the kiss.

When she licked his fang, he groaned into her mouth and cupped her bottom.

"Do you want to get a room?" Toven's voice cut through the haze of desire.

He was wheeling Mia down the corridor, and he wasn't trying to be stealthy about it. If he were an attacker, he would have caught both of them unprepared.

Closing his eyes for a brief moment, Phinas let go of Jade's mouth and turned around. "We have a room, and I plan to get back there as soon as we can."

Given her irritated expression, Jade didn't appreciate getting caught kissing in the corridor, and she didn't appreciate his answer to Toven either.

After nodding hello to Mia, she shifted her hard gaze to Toven. "I heard that you talked with Valstar again and didn't invite me to join you. I think we established already that I'm not going to kill him until we catch Igor."

"It wasn't that kind of an interrogation. I wanted him to feel at ease with me."

"What did you learn?"

"That even Valstar doesn't know Igor's Kra-ell name. I'll tell you more when we get inside. I don't want to have to repeat the story."

She nodded. "As the humans say, all good things come to those who wait. Let's go inside and get it over with."

As Phinas pressed the intercom button, Yamanu threw the door open. "Good evening, ladies and gentlemen. Please come in." He waved his hand in a grand gesture.

"Who said I'm a gentleman?" Phinas murmured.

Jade cast him a wry smile. "And who said that I'm a lady?"

"That's right." He took her hand and gave it a squeeze. "We are both warriors."

"You can be genteel warriors." Yamanu motioned for them to follow him to the sitting area. "I am."

"Hi." Mey got up and offered Jade her hand. "I'm so glad you came. My sister and I have a few questions we would like to ask you."

Yamanu wrapped his arm around his mate's middle and leaned to kiss her temple. "We should get a few drinks in us before we start."

Phinas agreed.

He had a good idea about what the sisters wanted from Jade, and she would need a few drinks to prepare for what was coming.

20

JADE

"*H*ere's your vodka cranberry." Yamanu handed Jade the glass. "Taste it and tell me if I mixed it right."

It was difficult to go wrong with such a simple drink, but she obliged him and took a small sip. "It's perfect, thank you."

Yamanu grinned. "Good quality vodka is the key. The cranberry juice is from concentrate, but that's the best we had on board."

Phinas sipped on the whiskey all the men seemed to prefer. "So, Tom, what new things did you learn from Valstar?"

"He didn't know Igor before boarding the ship. He said he found it odd that no activities had been organized for the settlers to get to know each other, and I agree with him that it's strange." He shifted his eyes to Jade. "After all, you were supposed to build a new community on Earth. How did your queen expect a bunch of strangers to do that once they landed? No command chain was established, no experts were introduced, and you had no bonding activities. If it were an evacuation, I could understand there was no time, but that wasn't the case."

Jade suspected that it had to do with the royal twins who'd been smuggled on board, but since she had no proof of it actually being them, she could hide it from Tom even if he chose to use compulsion, which he wasn't right now.

"It was the first settler ship, so maybe the queen hadn't figured out all the details yet. But since the gods were in charge, they should have thought of that."

Tom tilted his head. "You haven't mentioned that it was a first ship. I was under the impression that they'd been going on for hundreds of years by the time yours was sent."

"Prior to our departure, there had been several scouting expeditions to locations the gods indicated as suitable for us. The scouts were Kra-ell, but the gods provided the ships and programmed their destinations."

"Did your queen receive reports from Earth?" Mia asked.

"Supposedly she did, and the reports were positive, but I doubt that. The allure of coming to Earth was the compatible females our males could breed with, but the scouts must have realized that they weren't really compatible and that the second generation was born human. I'm sure they reported it, and our queen hid that information."

"Why would she do that," Mey asked, "if the idea was to establish a self-sustaining colony, and it wasn't about getting rid of undesirables? From what I've heard so far, the Kra-ell didn't seem to have a problem executing criminals or rebels."

Why did everyone assume that the Kra-ell were savages? They were aggressive, and in the distant past they might indeed have been savage, but so were the humans.

Hell, they still were, despite the gods' attempts to civilize them.

Jade glared at the female. "We only executed the worst of criminals. Those who harmed children or murdered innocent victims. Other transgressors could redeem themselves in several ways."

"Like fighting to the death?" Jin asked. "That's the same as execution."

"It is not when the opponents are equally matched. Can we please change the subject? I don't appreciate having to defend the Kra-ell traditions and way of life to someone who knows nothing about them."

"I might know more than you think." Jin flashed her a smile that revealed a pair of canines that were long enough to be considered fangs.

Jade leaned forward. "Female gods don't have fangs. Did their immortal descendants mutate?"

"They didn't." Mey put a hand on her sister's shoulder. "We suspect that we are hybrids. Part Kra-ell and part immortal. One of the females in your old compound must have been a dormant immortal, and she had us with one of your hybrids."

"What nonsense is that? You couldn't have been born in my compound or fathered by one of my hybrids."

After Mey and Jin exchanged glances, Jin frowned at Jade. "How do you know that we weren't? You gave the children of the hybrids up for adoption when they were babies. We probably looked a lot different back then."

"There was only one girl ever born to a hybrid male and a human female, and she stayed in the compound. I would have never given a girl up for adoption."

"Why not?" Jin asked. "Because you considered girls superior? Not that I disagree, but I admit that it's sexist."

Jade's lips twitched with a smile. Jin reminded her of Kagra. She was gutsy and irreverent.

"Well, there is that. But my reasons were more pragmatic. Humans are not like Kra-ell, and for their community to function properly, they need the ratio of males to females to be nearly equal. Since our males, purebloods as well as hybrids, produce predominately male children, I had no choice but to give the human boys up for adoption. Back then, China had a one-child policy, and since their society was highly patriarchal, families wanted sons who could carry on the family name. There was an abundance of baby girls in orphanages. Baby boys were highly prized and snatched immediately, while baby girls could only hope for adoption by foreigners. At first, it seemed like a reasonable solution, but when I realized that it caused undue suffering to the mothers, I forbade the hybrid males to produce children at all and solved the imbalance problem that way. Human children were fathered only by human males, ensuring an equal gender distribution in their population."

21

PHINAS

*P*hinas observed the sisters, curious to hear their response to Jade's pragmatic and cold solution, but they seemed too stunned to say a thing.

Yamanu was the one to break the silence. "I hate to admit it, but what you did makes sense. Once those boys reached maturity, you couldn't release them, and having too many human males for the number of human females within the compound would have caused unrest. There was already too much competition for their favors from the purebloods and hybrids. You could have abducted more human females for them, but that would have been even worse. On the other hand, though, you created unrest among the hybrids. Having no hope of ever producing offspring was depressing, and they must have disobeyed your orders with women outside the compound." He turned to Mey and Jin. "That's the only explanation for how you were born. One of Jade's hybrids must have had relations with a woman outside the compound, something happened to the mother, and that's how you ended up in an orphanage."

"I doubt that," Jade said. "The hybrids didn't roam free and do whatever they pleased. The only two who had such an opportunity were Vrog and Veskar. Vrog was working in Singapore on my behalf, and Veskar ran off. Vrog was lucky enough to find one of your females and produce a long-lived child, and Veskar might still do that with his mate, but they are the only two exceptions."

"The other hybrids must have found a way to dally with local women." Mey handed Yamanu her glass for a refill. "It's too much of a coincidence that we were given up for adoption in the same area your tribe was located."

Jade cast her an indulgent look. "The Beijing area is enormous. It's possible that the survivors of another pod were located there, and we didn't know about each other."

Phinas put his glass down and turned to face her. "Statistically speaking, Mey's scenario is more likely than yours. The odds of another pod landing in the same area as yours are negligible, but the odds of desperate hybrid males finding a way to procreate is significant."

Jin shook her head. "So why were we given up for adoption? If our father was so desperate for children, wouldn't he want to keep us even if our mother died?"

"Maybe they both died?" Yamanu offered. "Did you lose any of your hybrid males?"

Jade's lips twisted in a grimace. "I lost all of them, but not before Igor's attack. Your father wasn't one of mine."

"Could it have been a pureblood?" Mia asked. "Both of you display Kra-ell characteristics."

"We didn't have them before our transition," Mey said. "But we were born with very special talents." She shifted her gaze to Jade. "Were any of your hybrids able to watch and listen to echoes of past conversations embedded in walls?"

Jade frowned. "I've never heard of anyone with such a talent. Can you do that?"

Mey nodded. "I did it in your old compound. I saw you and

Kagra get into a fight. You nearly demolished the storage room."

A smile bloomed on Jade's face. "I remember that fight." Then her smile turned back into a frown. "That's an amazing ability to have. You probably got it from your Dormant mother because no Kra-ell can do that."

Yamanu handed Mey her refilled glass. "None of ours can do that either. Mey and Jin's abilities are one of a kind."

Jade shifted her attention to Jin. "Is your talent the same as your sister's?"

"Mine is better." Jin smiled fondly at Mey. "I can tether a string of my consciousness to anyone I touch and hear and see what they hear and see. I'm the perfect spy."

Jade recoiled. "Did you do that to me?"

"I didn't touch you, did I?"

"And you're not going to."

"I don't tether people just for kicks and giggles. It's draining and often disturbing. I might tune in while the person is on the toilet or when they are having sex. I only keep a tether to loved ones whom I worry about, and I only tune in once in a while to check that they are okay."

Mey put her glass on the table and leaned over to take her sister's hand. "Jin keeps our adoptive parents tethered at all times. They are both healthy, but they are elderly, and they live far away."

"Did you ever use your talent for spying?" Jade asked.

"I did, and it cost me dearly. I'm not going to do it again unless lives are at stake and my tether can help save them."

Arwel, who'd been quiet the entire time, put an arm around his mate's shoulders. "It turned out great, though. Kalugal and Jacki found each other, and Kalugal and his men joined the clan." He shifted his eyes to Phinas. "Aren't you glad that Jin tethered your boss?"

"I am. Moving in with the clan was mostly an improvement."

Yamanu arched a brow. "Mostly? In what way was it not?"

"Privacy, for one thing. Your village is a hive of gossip, and everyone is in everyone else's business."

Letting out a sigh, Mey lifted her glass to her lips and took a sip. "Jin and I thought we had the mystery of our origins figured out, and now we are back to square one."

Next to Phinas, Jade shifted so she was facing Mey. "Your father might have been a descendant of one of the scouts. The scouting missions were a one-way ticket, so to speak. The scouts had to survive wherever they landed and report back using the gods' communication satellites." She looked at Toven. "The Earth satellites must have been destroyed before you were born because you said that your people had lost the ability to communicate with home thousands of years ago."

Toven looked surprised. "I thought that the gods had a ship orbiting Earth and that the ship was the relay, but now that I think back, I remember seeing a depiction of satellites."

"A ship could be a relay, but they probably had satellites too. Otherwise, how did the scouts report to the queen?"

"Makes sense," Mey said. "We suspect that the scouts lived in the area of the Mosuo people and influenced their culture. One of their descendants could have found his way to the Beijing area and met our mother, who just happened to be a Dormant." She smiled. "Apparently, the special affinity immortals and Dormants feel toward each other extends to the Kra-ell. We shouldn't be surprised by that. After all, we originated from the same root species on the same planet."

22

JADE

"We should do what I first suggested," Mey said. "We should start with the orphanage. Yamanu can thrall the bureaucrats to provide us access to our files. We are not that old, so they should still have them."

"How old are you?" Jade asked and regretted it as soon as the words had left her mouth.

She didn't really care how old they were, and asking for their age would only lead to more talking when she wanted to be done and leave.

"I'm twenty-eight," Mey said. "Jin is twenty-four."

They were so young and mated to immortal males who were centuries older. Not that Jade knew for a fact that Yamanu and Arwel were that old, but she had a feeling that they were.

As she listened with half an ear to Jin and Mey come up with several more ideas for investigating their past, none of them promising, Jade glanced at Tom and noted the faraway look in his eyes. He wasn't listening either and seemed preoccupied. Throughout the get-together, Jade had caught him looking at her as if he wanted to ask her something and then changed his mind and looked away.

Maybe he thought she had more secrets to impart about the gods?

The truth was that she'd told him most of what she knew. She could have gone into more detail about the stages of the Kra-ell emancipation, but she doubted he was interested in their side of the story.

He wanted to find out more about his people's history, but she could only tell him the Kra-ell's version of it, which wasn't complimentary and probably wasn't accurate either.

When the sisters finally ran out of ideas, Tom rose to his feet. "It's getting late, and Mia and I are tired. Thank you for inviting us and for the lovely evening."

Jade could have kissed him for that.

Pushing to her feet, she murmured her thanks and added a goodnight.

"Goodnight, everyone," Phinas said.

Once they were finally alone in the elevator, Jade sighed in relief. "That was intense."

"It was." Phinas reached for her hand and pulled her to him. "We are alone, so there's no reason for you to brush me off. There is no public here to witness our display of physical affection."

Jade lifted her eyes to the camera, but the truth was that she didn't care if what happened in the elevator was recorded or if someone was monitoring the live feed.

Maybe it was the alcohol's fault.

Yamanu had kept refilling her glass, and Jade had kept drinking long after she should have stopped.

She hadn't appreciated the sisters' accusations even though they were justified. She might not have given them up for adoption, but she'd given up several boys before forbidding the

99

hybrids to father children. She still felt guilty about it, even though it had been the logical thing to do.

She couldn't have risked releasing the women with their babies and everything they'd known about the Kra-ell. Compelling them to keep it a secret would have kept their tongues tied for a while, but not indefinitely, and if they'd started talking about vampiric aliens, they would have been committed to mental institutions.

Besides, even if she could do that, the women had nowhere to go.

They had a life in the compound, they were safe, and at the time, life outside of its walls had been much harsher than inside of them, especially for single mothers.

Leaning into Phinas, she pressed her lips to his and kissed him. The taste of the whiskey he'd drunk wasn't unpleasant, and as it mingled with the taste of the vodka and cranberry in her mouth, it became sweeter. "Mmm," she murmured into his mouth. "You taste good."

His eyes turned into a pair of projectors, and his fangs made an appearance. "You promised to take from me tonight. Are you hungry?"

The elevator door opening delayed her answer for a brief moment. "I seem to be always hungry for you, but not in the way you think."

A smirk lifted one corner of his mouth. "Are you hungry for my hunky body?"

His physique was very appealing, and although he was much bulkier than the slim-built Kra-ell purebloods she was used to, she didn't mind that his body was different or that he looked so much like his godly ancestors, whom she'd despised.

Frankly, her view of them had changed after meeting Tom. He was not terribly conceited, and unlike his ancestors he was an honorable male who stood by his word and kept his promises.

As Jade opened the door to her cabin, Phinas didn't follow her inside. Instead, he stood at her doorway with one hand bracing on the doorjamb and the other on his hip. "You didn't answer me."

She reached for his shirt and tugged him toward her. "You are very handsome, and you know that. So why do you ask?"

He kicked the door closed behind him. "You know that you're beautiful, and you still like it when I tell you that."

"I don't always feel beautiful." She wrapped her arms around him. "But you always make me feel like I am even when you don't say it. I can see it in your eyes and smell it on your skin." She sniffed the spot where his neck met his shoulder. "So male and so virile. It's hard to believe that your fertility is so low."

If he were a Kra-ell pureblood, she would have invited him to her bed based on his smell alone. It was intoxicating to her, which in the Kra-ell culture was believed to indicate that their bodies were well-matched to produce a child.

He lifted her by her bottom and carried her to the bedroom. "Miracles do happen from time to time." He put her down on the bed and sat beside her. "Would you want to have a hybrid child with me, though? I thought that breeding with gods was a big no-no and that a child resulting from such a union was considered an abomination in your world."

"We are not in my world, and you are not a god." She unzipped her jacket, shrugged it off, and put it on the night-stand. "Besides, it's not in the cards. I'm not in my fertile cycle."

"Good. I want to ravish you tonight."

She liked the sound of that.

"I thought that you wanted to be the one to get ravished tonight." Whipping her shirt over her head, she tossed it on top of the jacket and lay back on the bed to unzip her leather pants.

23

PHINAS

The sight of Jade's dark turgid nipples straining toward him had Phinas's mouth water and his fangs punch all the way down over his lower lip.

Without any conscious thought, he shifted his body over hers.

Bracing on his forearms, he looked down at her gorgeous face and the smile that was more than just a lifting of her lush lips. It was in her enormous eyes and the softness of her facial features, and if he didn't know better, he would have thought that she was looking at him lovingly.

Right. The best he could hope for was lust and companionship, and that was enough.

Perhaps Jade was right, and love was an elusive and misleading term, a romanticized expression that described a combination of survival instincts that were hardwired into the human and humanoid psyche.

Spreading her legs, she made room to accommodate his body. "Shouldn't you get undressed?"

"I need to do this first." Tugging off the elastic holding her ponytail, he spread the long, black tresses over the white duvet. "Beautiful."

She chuckled throatily. "You needed to play with my hair?"

"I want to play with all of this." He cupped her cheeks and took her lips in a soft kiss.

Banding her arms around him, she kissed him back, her long tongue pushing into his mouth and doing wicked things to his fangs.

With a groan, he drifted his hand down and palmed her breast, rubbing the stiff nipple in slow, gentle circles.

When Jade arched up and pushed her pants down, he lifted a few inches off her to give her room to maneuver, and when he heard her leathers hit the floor, he let go of her mouth and slid down her body while trailing kisses on her neck, her shoulder, her collarbone, and finally taking a nipple between his lips.

The moan that left her throat was a feral growl he'd only ever heard from her and wouldn't mind hearing for the rest of his life.

As the realization stunned him, he pushed that thought into a corner of his mind to examine later. Right now, his hormones were in charge of his brain, and he wasn't thinking clearly.

Smoothing his hand down her body, he noted the differences between her and every other woman he'd ever been with. She was slim and muscular, her body long and hard, but her skin was silky soft, and she was all female to him.

When his hand reached her center, and he found her bare and moist, he hissed and plunged a finger into her wetness. "I need some of that." He shifted down until he was kneeling on the floor between her spread legs.

Jade didn't object when he lifted her legs over his shoulders and started feasting on her. Sucking and rubbing, he brought her to an orgasm in mere moments, and while she lay languid from her release, he got rid of his clothes and got on top of her.

The moment he was in position, Jade dug her fingers into his buttocks and thrust up with her hips, impaling herself on his length.

They both groaned, and as he started moving, she lifted her hand, clamped it around the back of his neck, and twisted them over, so she was on top of him.

With her eyes blazing red and her fangs on full display, Phinas knew what was coming next and nearly climaxed just from the anticipation. Holding back with an effort, he turned his head sideways and offered her his neck.

The moment her fangs struck his vein, his eyes rolled back in his head, and his shaft spasmed. When he thrust up into her, the wild sound she made had him shoot his load into her welcoming heat, but he wasn't done, not by a long shot.

Hard as if he hadn't released a moment ago, he thrust up into her again and again, and still she drank, the sucking noises and the sensation of pulling bringing him to another orgasm in minutes while pulling one out of her as well.

When her tremors subsided, Jade retracted her fangs, licked the puncture wounds closed, and then lay on top of him, warm, spent, and satiated.

Leisurely caressing her slim back, her rounded bottom, and the silky strands of hair strewn everywhere, Phinas felt himself drifting away on a cloud of bliss.

Was that how Jade felt when he bit her?

Her venom wasn't nearly as strong as his, so he was probably feeling only a fraction of that, but it was still incredible.

She kissed the spot she'd bitten. "I still think I like it better when it's you doing the biting. Your venom is addictive."

He chuckled. "Give me a moment to recuperate, and I'll return the favor. Right now, I'm floating."

She lifted her head and looked down at him. "Do you like the floaty feeling?"

He laughed. "Are you kidding me? This is the best I ever felt." He tightened his arms around her. "How did my blood taste to you?"

"Amazing." She pushed up and kissed him, thrusting her tongue into his mouth.

The coppery taste wasn't as offensive as he'd expected, and thinking of Jade at his throat had him harden again.

He flipped them over and looked down at her. "Are you ready for another round?"

She lifted her hips and rubbed against his erection. "Are you?"

"What does it feel like?"

"It feels like you are. Give it to me, lover boy."

"Just lover." He pushed into her in one long thrust. "It's been a very long time since anyone called me a boy."

A smirk twisted her gorgeous lips. "Give it to me, my immortal lover. Is that better?"

"It still needs work." He pulled out and surged back in.

"Give it to me, lover mine."

"That's perfect."

24

SYSSI

"Ah." Allegra pointed at the spoon in Syssi's hand.

"Yes, I know. It's so yummy." Syssi scooped up more cereal and lifted it to her daughter's mouth.

Pressing her lips closed, her baby girl shook her head. "Ah!" She pointed at the spoon again.

Understanding finally dawning, Syssi asked, "Do you want to hold the spoon?"

"Poon." Allegra nodded.

"Okay." Syssi put it in her little hand.

Smiling her thanks, Allegra gripped it tightly, and with a determined look dipped it in the cereal, but she didn't have the coordination to actually scoop anything up. Undeterred, she lifted the spoon to her mouth and licked whatever cereal had adhered to it.

The sound of the door opening had them both turn to look, and as Kian entered the kitchen, Allegra lifted her spoon triumphantly.

"Dada! Poon!"

"My big girl is eating with a spoon!" He walked up to her

and kissed her cheeks despite the cereal smeared all over them. "I'm so proud of you."

"Dada." She dipped the spoon in the cereal and lifted it to her mouth.

"I see. Good job, sweetie." He turned to Syssi. "Will she manage to get any food down like that?"

"I've already fed her mashed carrots and peas. The cereal is her dessert."

Kian chuckled. "I'm surprised that she's not demanding you-know-what."

Allegra loved cookies, but Syssi was trying to limit how many of them she ate a day.

"I'll let her have one later."

"Master! You're home." Okidu rushed into the kitchen as he did every day around the time Kian usually came home for dinner, but lately he'd been disappointed a couple of times when Kian stayed in the war room. "I shall serve dinner expeditiously."

"I'll just wash my hands." Kian went over to the kitchen sink to do that.

"How did your meeting with Kalugal go?" Syssi asked.

"It went well. I offered him two seats on the council. Naturally, it's not final until the council approves the additional seats, but I don't anticipate any objections."

"Oh, wow. I didn't expect that. How did it come to pass?"

It wasn't the first time that Kian had rushed to implement a suggestion she made without thinking it through, and she should have learned her lesson to be more specific.

When she'd suggested that he should talk with Kalugal, she hadn't expected it to go as far as inviting him to join the council.

"As we talked, I realized that Kalugal didn't want to remain an outsider and wished to become an integral part of the clan.

We promised each other complete transparency, with him allowing the clan full access to his business dealings and us allowing the same to him, but he keeps his profits and we keep ours. That's the only separation remaining, at least for now. Perhaps the next generation will decide to combine resources." He smiled at Allegra. "Right, sweetheart? When you mate Darius, you will combine us into one big family."

"Kian," Syssi assumed her admonishing tone. "I don't want you to say that even jokingly. Kids are impressionable, and Allegra might grow up thinking she's expected to mate with Darius. I want her to feel free to choose whomever she pleases."

He reached for her hand. "I want my daughter to find love as formidable as ours. Nothing less than a truelove mate will do for our princess. I was just teasing, but if you think my teasing might influence Allegra's future decisions, I'll either never do that again or change the name of her future mate so many times that she would know for sure it wasn't serious."

"Thank you." Syssi squeezed his hand. "Back to Kalugal, though. I'm surprised that both of you made such huge concessions in a few hours of negotiations. Perhaps you went too far too soon?"

Kian frowned. "I thought that was what you wanted me to do."

"That's the end result I was hoping for. I just thought it would take more time and involve a transition period. You know that I don't like rushing into things."

"I know." He leaned over and kissed her cheek. "I, on the other hand, like to move things off my to-do list as quickly as I can."

"I hope it will work out well for all of us." She sighed. "What's new with the Kra-ell situation?"

"Not much. That's why I'm home for dinner. We are waiting for Igor to make his move."

"Did you decide what to do with them?"

"Dada." Allegra held out the spoon to him.

He shifted his gaze to her. "Do you want me to give you the cereal?"

She nodded.

Kian moved to the chair on her other side, took the spoon, and fed their daughter. "I'm waiting to see what will happen with Igor. If we eliminate him, the Kra-ell can return to their compound."

"Didn't Turner advise against leaving them where you can't keep an eye on them?"

"He did, but I don't want them in the village, and I don't know what else to do with them. Along with the humans, there are over three hundred of them. That's a lot of people. If we were talking about one or two, I might have offered them sanctuary here, but I can't bring in a group of people almost equal in size to ours. Even if it wasn't a huge security risk, they would still drastically change the demographics of the village and our way of life. I don't want that. I'm happy with how things are now."

Syssi had a different opinion, but she was afraid to voice it lest Kian rushed to implement it like he had done with Kalugal. She needed to be careful about what she said to him.

25

KIAN

*S*yssi looked like she wanted to add something, but she was hesitating for some reason, and Kian didn't like it. She should feel comfortable saying anything to him, and the idea that he might still intimidate her in some way soured his mood.

He thought they were long past that point.

Then again, Syssi only appeared timid to those who didn't know her because she was soft-spoken and preferred to avoid confrontations. But he knew better. If she wanted to say something or effect a change, she simply waited for an opportune moment when she knew that her suggestions would be received with an open mind.

Except, he didn't understand why she thought now was a bad time to bring up whatever was on her mind. Perhaps she thought he was too busy? Or maybe he'd voiced his position on the Kra-ell too decisively, and she figured out that he needed more time to mull it over before bringing it up?

Kian waited until Okidu served them dinner to ask her.

"You don't seem to agree with my stance on the Kra-ell issue."

"I think we need to evaluate the pros and cons and come up with several alternative solutions. But first, we need to know more about these people. Vrog, Aliya, and Emmett integrated easily into our community, so maybe inviting the Kra-ell to join us wouldn't change things too much. Instead of discussing it with Turner, you should talk with the people who are actually spending time with the Kra-ell and ask their opinions. Also, I'm curious about the humans that came with them and what they want to do once they are free. They already know about aliens, and they can't be thralled to forget them. They can be compelled, but we know that compulsion needs to be reinforced from time to time, so it's actually safer to keep them contained within the village than to let them loose somewhere."

As usual, Syssi distilled the problem to its essence and addressed it both logically and compassionately.

Kian leaned over the table and clasped her hand. "You are so wise, my love."

"Mama," Allegra said in a tone that sounded like confirmation.

Kian smiled at her sweet little face. "Our daughter thinks so too."

"She understands every word we say." Syssi leaned over and kissed Allegra's cheek.

"I believe she does."

Leaning back in her chair, Syssi wound a lock of hair around her finger. "To be frank, I have an ulterior motive, and I'm not thinking only about the Kra-ell plight. I'm thinking about a group of two hundred warrior-like people who can shore up our defenses. If we can trust them, and if they learn to trust us, we will be stronger together. Of course, Igor has to be dealt with first. It would be too dangerous for us to bring them here if he's still around."

"You realize that along with the humans they would outnumber us. Where would we even house them?"

"They would have to be satisfied with living two to a bedroom." She chuckled. "After getting used to the luxury of the cruise ship, it would be an adjustment for them."

"Most of the village homes have only two bedrooms, so that's four to a house. To house three hundred and twenty people, we need eighty houses. We don't have that many available."

"What if you add a bedroom to each of the available ones? The lots can accommodate an addition of even two bedrooms."

"It would take time, and it would be messy, but it's doable. I could move whoever is still living in phase two back to the original village, fence phase two off, and add two bedrooms to each of the houses. Then I could annex phase two to Kalugal's section like Turner suggested and make them Kalugal's headache. Instead of one village, we would have two, and then I only need to worry about security and not about changing the way we live."

Syssi arched a brow. "We were talking about establishing trust. That won't happen if you try to keep them contained."

"It would have to do in the beginning, but we are getting ahead of ourselves. I haven't talked with Yamanu and Toven yet, and even if they are in favor, it's not a decision that I can make without the council's approval. In fact, this requires the unanimous vote of the big assembly."

"Not if you declare it a security issue." Syssi smirked. "You've used that loophole successfully many times before."

His sweet wife had a devious mind, and she wasn't wrong, but he couldn't use that loophole to cram the Kra-ell down his people's throats without earning their resentment, and rightly so.

"It is definitely a security issue, but given the massive

impact on our community, not putting it to a vote wouldn't be fair. I would have a rebellion on my hands."

"Dada." Allegra nodded in agreement.

"You see?" He waved a hand at their daughter. "Even the baby agrees that it should be a clan-wide vote."

Syssi regarded Allegra with a smile. "Our daughter is an old sage housed in a baby's body. We'd better heed her advice."

"I'm going to make the calls from my office. Do you want to join and have Okidu watch Allegra?"

Syssi pushed to her feet and pulled a wet wipe from the box. "Perhaps we should let her listen so she can offer us her opinion." She wiped Allegra's cheeks and hands. "Do you want to go to Daddy's office, sweetie?"

"No." Allegra pointed her finger at the television.

Kian laughed. "She knows that Okidu will let her watch as much as she wants."

"Du!" Allegra called.

Okidu dropped the plate he'd been washing into the sink and rushed over. "Yes, Mistress Allegra. How can I serve you?"

"Ah." She pointed at the television.

"Of course." He pulled her out of the highchair and carried her to the couch. "What will it be? *The Wiggles*? Or *Paw Patrol*?"

"We-we." Allegra bounced her bottom on the couch.

"*Wiggles* it is." Okidu clicked the television on.

"Come on." Kian took Syssi's hand. "Let's seize the opportunity that we have a few minutes alone to play footsie in my office."

She laughed. "You're incorrigible."

"But you love me despite that."

"I think I love you because of that. If you are still playful at your advanced age, you'll always be."

When Kian closed his office door behind them, Syssi

stretched on her toes and kissed his cheek. "Phone calls first. Footsie later."

Kian grinned. "I've just realized that it's four in the morning over there." Cupping her bottom with both hands and hoisting her up, he flattened her against his chest and straining erection. "Do you think Allegra knew that when she said no?"

Syssi laughed. "I think she knew all along that you wanted to play with Mommy, and she graciously bowed out."

26

TOVEN

"I haven't had breakfast yet." Yamanu cradled the cup of coffee Toven had made for him. "I'm good for nothing on an empty stomach."

"It must be important." Toven sat between Yamanu and Arwel on the couch. "Kian texted me an hour ago and asked to speak with the three of us first thing in the morning." He positioned the tablet on the coffee table, so the camera got all three of their faces. "I told him we would be ready for him at six in the morning, so he wouldn't have to wait for us to finish breakfast first."

Mia was still asleep in the bedroom, and he planned to return to her as soon as the phone call was over.

His tablet rang at precisely six in the morning, and as he accepted the call, he was surprised to see Syssi next to Kian instead of Onegus and Turner.

"Good evening," he greeted them.

Arwel nodded.

"It's morning here," Yamanu said. "What's so urgent?"

"There is no real urgency. I need to hear your opinion of the

Kra-ell in general and Jade in particular. What kind of people are they?"

"They are people." Yamanu shrugged. "Despite their spartan proclivities, they are just like any other community. Some are nicer than others, some are friendlier, and some are less so, and they are all anxious about their future."

Kian shifted his gaze to Arwel. "What's your take on them?"

"They are guarded and don't show emotions, but that doesn't mean that they don't have them." He smiled. "They are more like the Klingons than the Vulcans, but they are better behaved and not as hot-headed. I'm still not sure about Jade, though. She might have some Ferengi in her. She's a good negotiator."

The names sounded familiar to Toven, but he didn't remember where he'd heard them. Obviously, the Klingons, Vulcans, and Ferengi must be fictional people.

"*Star Trek*," Yamanu whispered in his ear.

"Oh. Now I remember where I heard those names before."

Toven wasn't a fan of the show, but it had become such an integral part of Western culture that most people got the reference even if they'd never watched the show or the movies.

Syssi leaned forward. "What we are trying to find out is whether the Kra-ell are trustworthy and whether bringing them to the village is an option. You've been around them for a while now, and we hoped you could give us an assessment."

Arwel shook his head. "I don't feel comfortable recommending one way or another. Perhaps Edna should run a probe on each individual and find out their motives."

"You should talk with Phinas," Toven said. "He's gotten very close to Jade, and he probably knows her better than any of us."

"Yeah," Yamanu seconded that. "We had a get-together in our cabin last evening, and the two of them seemed very cozy with each other, which is strange since the Kra-ell don't commit to just one partner. I've been watching them, and they really don't form couples. The males hang out with each other, the females do the same, and the young children split their time between their mothers and fathers like children of divorced parents."

"Except for Drova and Pavel," Toven said. "I've seen them sitting together in the dining hall, sipping on coffee and talking quietly. I think they are plotting something."

"Plotting what?" Kian asked.

"Probably a rebellion against Jade." Yamanu chuckled. "Either that or they are just two young people finding comfort in each other's company. By the way, we found out that Mey and Jin were not born in Jade's tribe, and she doesn't think they were fathered by any of her hybrids. The hybrids breed predominantly boys, and there was only one girl born in her compound to a hybrid father and a human mother, and Jade didn't give her up for adoption. She only gave up the boys to prevent gender disparity among her human subjects, which she knew would have led to problems, and when she realized how terribly the mothers suffered as a result, she forbade the hybrids to father children with the humans at all."

"So, who could their father have been?" Syssi asked.

"We speculated about it for hours." Yamanu took a sip from his coffee. "The only logical assumption is that he was a descendant of the scouts, and he made his way from Lugu Lake to the Beijing area. Mey and Jin want to check out the orphanage they were adopted from, and they want me to thrall the people in charge to release the files to them. Do I have permission to do that?"

"Of course, you do." Kian waved a hand. "It's crucial that we find out whether their parents are still alive and whether they have other relatives. We might find more Dormants and more hybrid Kra-ell, but it will have to wait."

"Naturally." Yamanu took another sip from his coffee.

Leaning against Kian's arm, Syssi said, "It's interesting how our view of Jade changes the more we find out about her. She's not the terrible and ruthless person we believed her to be. She seems to have always done what she believed was best for her community. It's a lesson to be learned not to prejudge people before getting to know them."

"I agree," Toven said. "But I think that in Igor's case, the mountain of evidence against him is decisive. I'm not sure about Valstar, though. He and the other males of Igor's pod didn't know Igor before getting on board the ship, and no one appointed him the leader. The moment he and his pod members woke up from stasis, he took over and compelled them to obey him. None of them had a say in it. The bottom line is that I think he and the others deserve a fair trial before we let Jade execute him."

"It's not our call," Kian said. "It's Jade's. If you can persuade her to give Valstar a fair trial, that's great. But if she's adamant about executing him, it's her prerogative."

Toven shook his head. "We are in charge, and if we can stop it, we should. We have a moral obligation."

"No, we don't." Kian regarded him with a hard look. "Unless the Kra-ell become part of our community, accept clan law, and vow to keep our rules, we shouldn't intervene in their affairs."

"But we already did," Toven insisted. "Without us helping to free the compound, Valstar wouldn't be facing his execution."

"It's a difficult call," Syssi said. "We should discuss this with Edna."

It was kicking the can down the road, but Toven was fine with that. His gut instinct was to intervene on Valstar's behalf, but his gut had steered him wrong in the past, so it wasn't all that reliable.

"I have no problem letting Edna decide." Toven put his cup down on the coffee table. "In any case, it's not an urgent matter because we don't have Igor yet, and Valstar enjoys a stay of execution until we do."

27

JADE

*O*nce again, Jade woke up with Phinas's body wrapped around hers, but this time they were in her cabin and not his. Not that it made much of a difference.

It felt just as good and just as sinful.

Spending every night with Phinas was a dangerous habit, and she should stop before she got so used to it that she couldn't fall asleep without him.

Except, it was too damn good to give up.

She liked falling asleep in his arms after he left her satiated and languid, and she liked waking up pressed against his big, warm body.

There must be something wrong with her that she was enjoying such an un-Kra-ell connection with a male. He aroused her with such surprising ease and without fighting for dominance that she was starting to suspect that it had some- thing to do with his inherited enhanced genetics.

There had been rumors about the gods manipulating their genes to produce powerful pheromones and increase their libido to compensate for their low fertility. It would have been simpler to change their genetics to increase their fertility, but she had to admit that their solution was more fun. They'd just made themselves constantly horny.

Gently untangling their limbs, she slid away from him, but she didn't get far.

His eyes popping open, he shot an arm around her and pulled her back against his chest. "Where do you think you're going?"

"It's time to get up." She pushed on his pectorals, copping a feel while she was at it.

"Today, you are getting your first swimming lesson, and I don't want to hear any arguments about why you can't make it."

She grimaced. "Not now. I need to see how Merlin is doing with the implant removal. I assigned Morgada to assist the nurse with tending to the patients after the removal, and Pavel to help Merlin with the MRI and the detection. I need to check on their progress."

Phinas frowned at her. "We are running out of time, and your people need to learn to swim or at least float. As soon as we leave the Baltic, Igor will attack, and he might succeed in sinking the ship. I hope it will not happen and that the sub will get him before he gets us, but we need to be prepared."

"Fine. I'll have Kagra arrange our people in shifts. How many can you teach simultaneously, and how long will each lesson take?"

"I can probably fit twenty people in that pool, and the lessons will be forty minutes long. I'm going to run the first one, and then my men will take over. Since you are their leader, you should go first, not Kagra."

Jade stifled a wince. "They don't need me to lend them the courage to get into a pool that's less than two meters deep."

"Perhaps that's true, but you need to get into that pool sometime today."

She wasn't looking forward to her dunking in the freezing

water, and the longer she managed to postpone it, the better. Phinas was right about the need to teach her people to float and swim, but it was more important that the others learn first.

If she got lucky, by the time her turn arrived the submarine would take out the Russian cruiser, and she wouldn't have to set foot in that pool.

"I don't have a swimming suit," she tried another evasive tactic.

"Neither do the others. You can go in a bra and panties."

Jade smirked. "I don't have a bra. Do you want me to swim topless? I have no problem with that."

He pulled her tighter against him. "So wear a T-shirt. No one gets to see my woman naked but me."

"I'm not your woman."

He squeezed her bottom. "Yes, you are."

"I'm not."

"You are. You're just too stubborn to admit it. I want you at the pool at four o'clock. That's enough time for you to do everything you had planned for today."

"It will be dark by then."

"So come earlier."

"I can't."

"Then you'll swim in the moonlight. Besides, the top deck has outdoor lighting. Enough with the excuses. If you are not there by four, I will come to get you, and I'll haul you to the pool if I have to carry you over my shoulder."

"You can try," she issued a challenge. "You can't make me."

"I'll find a way. I'll rope you in like a bull in a rodeo, tie you up, and throw you over my shoulder."

She'd heard about the so-called sport. Bulls were stronger than people, but they were dumb. Did he think she would be as easily overpowered as a bull? She was a well-trained warrior.

"Good luck with that. I'm not a bull."

"You're stubborn like one, and you are afraid of water."

"I'm not afraid of it." She pulled out of his arms and got out of bed. "I just don't like it."

Smiling, Phinas patted the spot she'd vacated. "I was just teasing. I know that the formidable Jade is not afraid of anything. Now come back in here and show me how strong you are." He spread his arms, his muscular chest and bulging biceps an invitation she found hard to resist. "Take me, use me. I'm yours."

Damn. How could she say no to that?

How did he manage to get under her armor and obliterate her resolve with such ease?

"You're such a smooth talker." She pounced on him. "Kiss me, lover mine."

28

PHINAS

"*S*ee you later, gorgeous." Phinas stole a quick kiss from Jade before exiting the elevator on the dining hall level.

"You're so bad," she said when the elevator door was closing, but she did it with a smile.

He blew her an air kiss and headed toward the kitchen.

Jade being occupied in the clinic was the perfect opportunity to check on Isla and see how traumatized she was after her talk with her leader.

He found her chopping carrots while chatting with another woman and sounding perfectly fine, but then she'd had enough time to calm down since yesterday.

Instead of approaching her and risking startling her, he looked for the young interpreter, Lana, and when he spotted her, he waved her over.

"Good morning." She wiped her hands with a dish towel. "How can I help you?"

"I want to speak to your mom, but I don't want to startle her while she is chopping things with a big knife. I don't want her to chop off a finger."

"Don't worry." Lana motioned with her head. "She heard you, and she's coming."

As he turned around, Isla offered him her hand. "*Hei*, Phinas."

"Hello, Isla." He turned to Lana. "I want to ask your mom if she's okay after her talk with Jade."

When Lana translated, Isla smiled, gave him the thumbs up, and said something in Finnish to Lana.

"My mom says that Jade is much more reasonable than she expected her to be. Jade promised the same thing you did, which my mom thanked you for. She knows it was because you talked with Jade."

Phinas didn't deny but didn't confirm either. "What did Jade promise you?"

He waited for Lana to ask and for Isla to answer, which took a while.

"Jade said that the purebloods would be allowed to offer the human women incentives for agreeing to breed with them, but they would not be allowed to threaten them in any way or harm them if they refused. What my mother is worried about is the males using their mind tricks to prevent the women from complaining about being harassed. Jade did not have a solution for that, but she promised to think about it."

She could make the male vow it, but the problem was that those young males grew up under Igor's influence, and they didn't follow the Kra-ell traditions. They might not take their vows seriously.

Nevertheless, he was glad to see that Jade hadn't terrorized the woman for voicing her complaint.

As his phone buzzed with an incoming message, he pulled it out of his pocket. It was from the big boss himself, so he needed to respond quickly.

"Thank you." Phinas patted Lana's shoulder. "I have to make

a call." He turned to Isla. "Thank you again for the fabulous meals you and the others prepare for us."

When Lana translated, she smiled. "*Ole hyvä*."

Out in the hallway, Phinas leaned against the wall and made the call. "Hello, Kian."

"Good morning, Phinas. Thank you for responding so quickly. I want to know your opinion of Jade. I was told that the two of you have gotten very close and that you know her better than any of the others."

A smile lifted Phinas's lips. "She's awesome."

Kian chuckled. "I need details."

"Why?"

"I'm contemplating allowing the Kra-ell and their humans into the village. It's not my idea, and I'm not keen on it because I don't know these people and because of their sheer number. Turner thinks that we should keep a close eye on them, and Syssi thinks it's a good idea to have two hundred or so additional strong warriors to protect the village. What's your take on that?"

The question was unexpected, and Phinas didn't have a ready answer to give. All he could do was think out loud.

"Jade is an honorable person, she cares about her people, and she is open to suggestions." He told Kian about Isla's complaint and Jade's response to it.

"That's a good start," Kian said. "She's willing to adapt."

"Up to a certain point, and I don't think she will accept your invitation. After living so long under Igor's thumb, she craves independence. There is also the issue of hunting. I don't think the Malibu mountains have enough wildlife for so many Kra-ell. They are fine with domesticated animals, but from time to time, they need to hunt. Even Igor allowed that, and he wouldn't have if it wasn't a necessity."

"I don't think it's a major consideration. If lions can live in

126

zoos and be satisfied with steak dinners, the Kra-ell will be satisfied with having access to domesticated animals."

"They might not go hungry or thirsty, but will they be happy?"

"Good point. Do you have another suggestion?"

Phinas closed his eyes for a moment. "How large is the plot around the cabin the clan owns in the mountains? Is it big enough to settle over three hundred people?"

"It might be large enough for very modest accommodations, and by that, I mean dormitory-style sleeping arrangements and communal everything. But to build there, we would need to employ the same camouflaging tactics as in the village, and those are costly to install and need trained operators. Besides, if we allow them to roam the area to hunt, we will not be able to monitor them as closely as we would like. I don't think it's an option, but I'll give it some more thought. What about the other Kra-ell? Did you get to know any of them?"

"Kagra is a fine female. She's an exceptional warrior, has a good sense of humor, and is less rigidly traditional than Jade. I like her. I also interacted with two young hybrid males yesterday when I taught them to swim. They were fun, full of mischief, and up to no good, but no more so than any other young men their age. Bear in mind, though, that I only spent an hour or so with them, so my impression is very superficial."

"Of course. I'm not going to make any decisions based on your testimony alone. I'm collecting information, and I'll probably have Edna probe each of them before making my final decision."

Thralling didn't work on the purebloods, not even Toven's. Phinas didn't know how Edna's probe worked, but if it was related to thralling or shrouding, it might not be effective on the Kra-ell.

"Edna might not be able to penetrate the mental shields of the purebloods."

"Good point," Kian agreed. "Perhaps we will need to do that the mundane way and get Vanessa to do a psychological assessment of them."

29

JADE

*J*ade entered the clinic and nodded at Merlin. "How is the removal of the trackers progressing?"

"It's going well." He motioned for her to follow. "We've removed sixteen trackers." He opened a drawer and pulled out three plastic bags. "I found three different types of trackers." He lifted a bag with a tiny thing that was no larger than a puffy grain of rice. "I suspect that this little fellow is the most sophisticated because I took it out of a pureblood." He lifted another bag with a much larger device. "This is second best. I removed two of them from hybrids." He lifted the third bag. "I assume this one is the least sophisticated one because it's the largest, and I removed this type from three humans."

"Didn't we agree that you would remove the trackers from the purebloods first?"

"We did, but I wanted to test my hypothesis, so I asked for two hybrids and two humans, but three humans showed up, so I figured why not?"

"How is Morgada doing? Is she helpful?"

"Very. We wouldn't have been able to remove as many without her help."

129

It was still too slow.

"Is there any way we can speed this up? What if we get one more person to help the nurse and another one to help with the machine?"

Merlin smoothed his hand over his white beard. "I can ask Marcel to help me with the scanning. I could use someone capable of replacing me, so I can concentrate on the removal. It will be crucial when we start removing the trackers from humans. Inga is not experienced enough to perform the extraction or to sew them up, and Morgada is even less so. I'll have to do that."

"What about the Kra-ell? Is Inga good enough to take care of them?"

He smiled sheepishly. "They heal fast, and they don't scar, so I let her sew them up. But I still remove the trackers myself because the little buggers are hard to find and to dig out."

It seemed to her that he could use two operators for the MRI and three nurses.

"Who else can operate the machine? I want you to delegate all the scanning to others."

"I can't. I have to see where the small trackers are hidden. Some are embedded so deep that I almost missed them."

"Then Marcel and whoever else is operating the machine can call you once they locate it, so you can see it and proceed right away to remove it."

He nodded. "That's doable. I'll ask Marcel to find another Guardian who can be taught what to do."

"I'll talk with Sofia," Jade said. "Since Marcel will be spending his days in the clinic, she might want to be the third nurse to be close to him."

Merlin looked around the room and sighed. "I don't know where everyone will work, but we will figure it out."

"What's in the rooms adjacent to the clinic? Maybe we can use one of them."

Merlin shrugged. "I don't know."

"I'll find out."

Jade walked out of the room and opened the door to its right. It was a small storage room filled to the brim with boxes.

If they took everything out, they might be able to get a cot or two to fit there, but that wouldn't solve their problem.

She closed the door and headed the other way, opening the door to the left of the clinic.

It was nearly as large as the main room of the clinic where the MRI machine was, and the only thing inside was a stack of chairs. It was probably meant as a waiting room that no one had bothered to organize.

"We can use the room next door," she told Merlin when she returned. "Do you need beds in there?"

"I need a couple, but we don't have more hospital beds. They will have to be regular beds."

"The beds are too big." The ones in her cabin, Kagra's and Phinas's were queen-sized.

"Check the staff quarters," Morgada said from the other room. "The beds in there are single-sized and should fit. If we find something to put under the legs to raise them up, they will do nicely as recovery beds."

"Good idea." Jade pivoted on her heel and headed for the door. "I'll get right on it."

30

KIAN

"*T*hank you for agreeing to see me at this ungodly hour." Kian took the coffee cup Shai handed him. "And thank you for the coffee. I need it." He took a thankful sip as he sat down.

Despite it still being dark outside and despite all the work Shai had been shouldering while Kian had been dealing with the Kra-ell crisis, his assistant managed to look as fresh and well-groomed as ever.

Still, there was a limit to what Kian could delegate to him.

Since the operation had started, Kian's neglected workload had been stacking higher with every passing hour, and some of the open items on his agenda were becoming urgent. He could no longer postpone addressing them in the hopes of a quick resolution.

Two days had passed since the *Aurora* had left Helsinki, and so far, they hadn't identified a pursuing ship. It might take many more days until Igor made his move.

"I don't think we've ever met at five-thirty in the morning before." Shai put down a stack of files on the conference table. "But we did meet in the war room before." He lifted his eyes to

Kian. "I don't know why you choose to do everything from here rather than from your office. It's depressing down here." He looked at the bare walls. "I should order some pictures for the place to liven it up."

"It's partly out of habit and partly out of practical considerations. Onegus's office and the lab are right here, and it makes it easier for them to come and go as needed without having to trek to the office building."

"Makes sense." Shai set his coffee cup down.

"I wanted to carve out some time to interrogate the two hybrids when they get to the keep, but I will probably have to delegate that to Anandur."

Shai nodded. "Anandur can be very intimidating when he wants to be. Do you think his terrifying monster illusion would work on them?"

Kian chuckled. "It has been so long since he used his red demon to scare his opponents that I'm not sure he can even summon it. But it wouldn't help him with the hybrids. After the experiments we conducted with Vrog and Aliya, we concluded that they can see through shrouds because they don't look substantial to them. The purebloods don't see them at all."

"That's a shame." Shai flipped his laptop open and got ready to take notes.

"Let's start with the most urgent item." Kian pulled the stack of files toward him.

Shai pointed at the file on top. "They are stacked according to urgency and importance. The one on top is naturally the top priority."

As Kian dove into the familiar territory of business dealings and read through the file and Shai's notes, he felt the muscles in his shoulders loosen and the tension in his chest abate.

He hadn't realized how much he'd been bothered by all the things that were falling by the wayside while he was dealing with the crisis. It had been gnawing at his gut and contributing to his disquiet. He didn't have to address all the issues in order to relax, but he at least needed to know what they were and whether anything was on the verge of collapse.

As qualified and reliable as the people managing the various clan businesses were, to stay in line they needed to know that someone was watching over them.

By the time Turner walked in, they'd managed to go over nearly half of the pile.

"Am I too early?" Turner glanced at his watch. "We were supposed to meet at seven-thirty, right?"

Kian was surprised at how fast the time had flown. "That's correct. Onegus should be here at any moment, and Kalugal will join us later." He cast an apologetic look at Shai. "I hoped that two hours would suffice, but I'm afraid we will have to continue either later today or tomorrow at the same hour."

Shai pulled the files toward him. "We've actually gone over most of what I needed your feedback on. I will send you a summary at the end of the day on where things stand and whether anything else needs your attention."

"Very well. We can address that tomorrow morning."

Shai nodded. "I'm at your disposal at any time you can spare." He put the files under his arm, picked up his laptop, and headed for the door.

"Thank you," Kian called after him.

"My pleasure." Shai tucked the laptop under his arm and reached for the door handle.

Reminded of Syssi's coaching about the power of positive feedback, Kian added, "Great work, Shai. I think that I could retire soon and leave all the day-to-day work in your capable hands."

Shai smiled. "I doubt that, but I appreciate the compliment."

Kian mentally patted himself on the back. He was making progress.

As Shai opened the door, Onegus came in, and as the two exchanged greetings, the sound of pounding footsteps had the three of them look at the doorway.

A moment later, Roni rushed in with his laptop partially open. "You will want to see this," he said as he put the laptop on the conference table, flipped it open all the way, and swiveled the screen toward Kian.

It was the same screen he'd shown them two days ago, and Kian recognized the blue dot representing the *Aurora*, but instead of the myriad of other dots previously littering the screen, there were only two aside from the *Aurora*, and both were flashing red.

Kian suspected that they represented possible pursuers, but he didn't want to make assumptions.

"What am I looking at?" he asked.

Looking cockier than ever, Roni grinned. "Captain Olsson's erratic course was more effective than I expected. The course he chose to follow was ingenious. It was so out of whack that the algorithm had no problem identifying the pursuer. The number of potentials hovered above ten for a while, and then it counted down to this." Roni pointed at the screen.

"There are two pursuers?" Onegus asked. "Or is one of them tailing the other?"

Roni smirked. "It looks like we have two vessels following the *Aurora*. Igor is not taking any chances. He wants his people back."

31

ONEGUS

*A*s Roni touched the flashing red dot closer to the *Aurora*, an information bubble popped up, and he read it out loud. "The *Marshal Anatolov*, a Parchin class Russian, is an anti-sub naval cruiser commanded by Captain Sergey Gorshekov." Roni glanced at Turner before continuing. "It's a 1972 ship that received a systems' upgrade in 1997. It has been keeping a constant distance of twenty nautical miles from the *Aurora*, and it has been adjusting its course, heading, and speed to match every move Captain Olsson was making. The *Anatolov's* maximum speed is twenty-four knots. It's slower than the *Aurora*, so I assume it will try to get closer to its target before the *Aurora* clears the Baltic into the North Sea and speeds up. The Russian has to attack before the *Aurora* has a chance to widen the gap between them."

Pointing at the second flashing red dot, Onegus asked the question on everyone's mind. "So, who or what is this?"

"That is the million-dollar question, isn't it?" Roni leaned forward again and touched the dot. "Allow me to introduce the *Grand Helena*, a Mangusta Maxi Open 165. That's a thirty-seven knots maximum speed luxury yacht owned by none other than Anatoli Zebneitski, an international weapons dealer oligarch. Since the *Helena* is keeping a significant distance, whoever is on board can apparently track both the *Marshal Anatolov* and the *Aurora* either with a radar system far more robust than what is typically found on a boat of this size, or they have access to the Russian navy's radar tracking system, which I think is more likely. The *Grand Helena* is trailing the Russian cruiser at a forty nautical miles distance, and it is more sophisticated than the *Marshal Anatolov* in how it is trailing both ships. Because of its far superior speed, her captain does not need to remain in lockstep with either of them. He can make assumptions as to their subsequent heading and correct course as needed. In fact, if not for the algorithm, I might have missed *Helena* tracking them altogether."

"Igor must be on board." Kian said what Onegus was thinking.

Turner nodded. "Based on Jade's account of his attack against her tribe, and based on everything else we've learned about him so far, he appears to be super careful, cunning, sophisticated, and tends to lead from behind. His MO doesn't lend itself to him being personally onboard the cruiser. There could be several reasons for that. First, the ultimate fate of the *Anatolov* might be one he wishes to avoid in person. While he has no reason to suspect that we have an armed sub protecting the *Aurora*, he must have considered that it's only a matter of time before the Russian navy will intervene once it realizes that the *Anatolov* went rogue. As soon as they realize that the cruiser is not where it's supposed to be, the Russian naval command will try to regain control of it, and when they fail to do that, they might decide to disable or even sink it. What's certain is that they will board it, and Igor wouldn't want to be anywhere near when that happens. There is also a chance of navies from neighboring countries coming to the aid of the *Aurora* and attempting to overtake the *Anatolov*."

"Maybe the *Anatolov* is supposed to cruise the Baltic," Onegus suggested. "If I were Igor, I would choose a ship that wouldn't be flagged from the get-go, and since he can access the Russian naval command, he must have known which ship to pick. In my opinion, naval command will not be alerted until the *Anatolov* leaves the Baltic. The further the Russian captain is from Mother Russia when he launches his attack on the *Aurora*, the better his odds of success are."

Turner nodded. "That's possible. But even if Igor doesn't expect the Russian Naval command to go after the *Anatolov* before it leaves the Baltic, he would still prefer not to be onboard. As someone who has existed in the shadows for so long, he would not want to take center stage among a large group of human sailors, in close quarters, and for days on end."

"What I can't figure out," Roni said, "is what the hell does he plan to do with a luxury yacht? Observe? Make sure that the Russian is obeying his commands?"

"It makes perfect sense." Kian got up and started pacing. "He believes that no one will suspect the yacht. It is keeping a significant distance and is not following the two ships in a readily recognizable pattern. But since the yacht is fast enough to close the distance in no time, he can take control of the situation and respond to changing circumstances as the need arises."

"What can he do, though?" Roni asked. "It's not like the yacht is carrying torpedoes that it can fire at the *Aurora* or sink the Russian to hide the evidence."

Kian sat back down. "His presence there is essential, either in person or via a short-range video feed that could not be traced to him. That's why he's following with the yacht. There would have been very little he could have done if he stayed behind in Russia, and it would have been a mistake that a sophisticated player like him wouldn't have made. Don't forget that the chess pieces he's moving are not his people, and he doesn't know how capable they are and what he can entrust them with. That's a lack of control that Igor wouldn't have been able to tolerate. Onboard the trailing yacht, though, he can observe, interject, and improvise as the need arises."

Onegus nodded. "There is one more thing that Igor couldn't delegate. Compelling a captain and likely also his top officers to hunt and sink a ship is one thing, but how will they know who to fish out of the water?"

32

TURNER

*K*ian lifted his gaze from the blinking dot on the screen to glance at Turner. "So what do we do about it? How does that affect our plans?"

"I hate to admit it, but the guy is more than just a powerful compeller, and he impresses me with every move he makes on the proverbial chessboard."

Igor was shrewd, calculated, inventive, and employed guerrilla tactics that kept surprising Turner. In fact, the Kra-ell was starting to undermine Turner's confidence in his ability to always see several steps ahead of his adversaries.

Then again, naval battles were not Turner's field of expertise, and neither were aliens with incredible compulsion abilities. Given those mitigating factors, the fact that he was still outmaneuvering the alien was impressive.

"That does not happen often," Kian said. "Should I be worried?"

Turner arched a brow. "He is certainly keeping me on my toes, but I'm still the better player. I anticipated most of his moves and deployed countermeasures." Turner let his lips tilt up in a smile. "That being said, we were hoping that Igor would take the bait, and he did. He has just handed us a way to finally bag him."

"How so?" Onegus asked.

It was Turner's opportunity to boast a little and lift his esteem in their eyes back to where it should be.

He lifted a finger. "First of all, we anticipated his move with the cruiser and deployed a submarine to counter it. We just got confirmation that our assessment was correct. Igor does not suspect that, and he does not have a contingency for it."

When he raised a second finger, Kian's phone buzzed with an incoming message, and as he read it, he lifted his hand. "Hold on for one second. I need to answer this." He typed up a quick text. "My apologies. My mother asked for an update, and I had to respond."

Turner nodded. "Of course. When the Clan Mother asks a question, it must be answered immediately." He lifted two fingers again. "While Igor probably assumes that we will at some point discover the Russian cruiser following the *Aurora*, he has no reason to think that it will happen before she crosses to the North Sea. In fact, he's banking on her not finding out until it is too late. And he certainly doesn't suspect that we know about the yacht."

Roni tapped his laptop. "It would never occur to him because no one has a program like this."

The kid was overconfident. He was a great hacker, perhaps even one of the best, but he wasn't the only one in the world.

Overconfidence was an issue for Turner as well, but he was aware of it and tried to counterbalance it with an abundance of caution. That was why he added, "Even though it's highly unlikely that Igor suspects we are on to him, I have no doubt that he has a contingency plan for escape in case things go sideways. His capture is not going to be easy, but it's possible."

Kian leaned forward. "I can see the wheels in your mind spinning. What's your plan?"

Turner didn't have one yet, but it was forming in his head as he was speaking. "It's obvious that Igor followed the trackers. With Olsson's erratic course, he wouldn't have been able to narrow his search and zero in on the *Aurora* so quickly otherwise."

Roni cleared his throat. "Not necessarily. The Russian vessel has access to the same networks I hacked into, and if Igor knows which ship his people are on, which he does, he has no problem following the *Aurora* on the screen."

"True," Turner confirmed. "But he knows which ship they are on only because of the trackers. And since he has a fast yacht and knows that his people are on the *Aurora*, he can follow the ship even after Marcel activates the scrambler when it leaves the Baltic. He can catch up to it and maintain a line of sight with it. So even if the *Aurora* disappears from the array, the Russian navy vessel could still follow the yacht to get to it."

"Clever bastard," Kian spat. "He knows we have a scrambler because his people's signals winked out for hours and then returned when they entered the port, and he knows that we will activate it the moment the *Aurora* is out of the Baltic and reaches the open sea. That's why he commandeered the yacht in addition to the Russian cruiser."

"That wasn't his only objective," Turner said. "He plans to use the yacht to fish his people out of the water after the Russian sinks the *Aurora*. He just doesn't know that we have a submarine to protect it."

Kian drummed his fingers on the table. "What if we employ the same tactic? We can split up the Kra-ell and put a few of those who still have trackers in them on another ship and send a small team of Guardians with them. We can equip all of them with earpieces and lure him into a trap while pulling him away from the Aurora. Is that what you have in mind?"

Lacing his fingers, Turner nodded. "I don't have clarity on all the details yet, but here is what I'm thinking." He pulled a pen out of his pocket, flipped his yellow pad to a new page, and started sketching. "We instructed Olsson to hug the coast all the way up to Bergen, from there to cross the North Sea toward the Shetland Islands, and the North Atlantic beyond. There are many ports along the way between the *Aurora*'s current location and Bergen. She can pretend to make a refueling and resupplying stop somewhere en route, and it wouldn't look suspicious because cruise ships typically do that every day or two." He marked several locations along the coastline he'd just sketched. "Depending on what we can find for hire in the area, we can rent a large yacht or a small commercial vessel, and while the *Aurora* will continue on its course toward the North Atlantic, the decoy vessel will sail northward along the coast or southward toward the English Channel, luring Igor away from the *Aurora*."

Roni looked doubtful. "If the Russian cruiser switches to pursuing the decoy, it might sink it because it will be defenseless. Your friend's sub will be too far away, protecting the *Aurora*. Unless we tell Nils ahead of time to follow the Russian, we won't be able to divert him because he can't maintain communications with us while submerged."

"We can tell him to float a buoy," Onegus said. "But that puts him at risk."

Kian looked at them with a deep frown. "I thought that Nils would need to maintain radio silence for security reasons. Are you telling me that he can't communicate with us at all? And what's a buoy?"

"Radio waves don't travel well through salt water," the Chief explained. "Only very low-frequency waves can penetrate through a few hundred feet of seawater, and the transmitters needed to do that are enormous. There are several specialized technologies under development, but nothing that we can get our hands on. Anyway, for Nils to communicate with us, he will have to either surface, raise an antenna above sea level, or float a tethered buoy carrying an antenna, but all three methods will make him vulnerable to detection."

Kian leaned back. "Then we need to decide on a course of action ahead of time. I don't want to risk exposing Nils."

Turner seconded that opinion. "We can't risk Nils, and given that the *Anatolov* is a submarine killer, as soon as they detect him, it will be game over for him."

KIAN

*O*negus leaned back and crossed his arms over his chest. "The question is whether Igor will send the Russians after the decoy. If the decoy is a yacht, I don't see him dispatching a Russian naval ship to follow it instead of the *Aurora*. Why would he? Taking over a yacht at sea is much easier than taking over a cruise ship, and he can do that with his boat. That way, he will avoid a high-profile incident involving a Russian naval vessel close to shore."

"What about manpower?" Roni asked. "We know that the *Helena* is fast, and we also know that Igor has two purebloods and a hybrid with him. Since the yacht belongs to an oligarch, he might even have some weapons on board, but he's a cautious bastard, and he might still send the Russian cruiser to pursue the smaller craft because he doesn't want to engage in person. He prefers for someone else to do the dirty work for him."

"You forget Igor's strongest weapon," Onegus said. "He doesn't need an army. He's an army of one. He believes that all he has to do is get close enough to the yacht to use a bullhorn and command everyone to stand down."

Exasperated, Roni threw his hands in the air. "How is that

different from the cruise ship? If he can get close enough to the *Aurora* to command everyone to freeze, he doesn't need to sink it either."

Onegus cast the kid a smile. "Igor doesn't know who is on the cruise ship and what weapons it has on board. That's why he's being so cautious and has a Russian vessel following it."

Roni shook his head. "I still don't see how a yacht is different except for its size. It can also carry hidden weapons or another powerful compeller."

"It's a probability and perception game." Kian put an end to the back and forth between the two. "That's why we need a small vessel that seems like a lesser challenge, either a rundown yacht that's not too fast or a very small commercial vessel. Anything larger than that is not suitable precisely for the reasons Onegus voiced. If it seems like too much of a challenge, Igor might be wary of going after it with his yacht, and he might send the Russian cruiser to disable or sink it. Also, the speed of his vessel gives him less of an advantage over larger ships, because even if he catches up to them and uses a bull-horn, chances are his voice will not be heard by all onboard. "

Staring at his notes, Turner nodded. "Let's break this newly-hatched tentative plan into bite-size action items. I will make some inquiries about the availability along the route." He turned to Roni. "I will need your help with that. Can you search for suitable vessels using your program?"

"I'll get right on it." Roni typed a note on his laptop.

Shifting his gaze to Kian, Turner continued. "We need to have a video meeting with Olsson and Yamanu and bring them up to speed. Hopefully, the captain can spare a few of his crew to operate the decoy. Yamanu will need to put together a team of Guardians to accompany the Kra-ell we will transfer to the other ship."

Kian nodded. "I want Kalugal to be here when we make the

call. I have to check with him when he'll get here and schedule accordingly."

"Do you think Jade should be included in the meeting?" Roni asked. "She knows Igor and might be able to anticipate his moves."

"Jade is still an unknown," Turner said. "I don't want her to get too familiar with our mode of operations. She's a smart lady, and she could use what she learns against us."

It was ironic of Turner to say that after pushing for inviting the Kra-ell to join the village. What did he expect, that they would keep them locked up in an enclosed area with a guard tower and armed Guardians to keep them from leaving?

Hey, maybe that wasn't such a bad idea. Perhaps not the tower and the armed Guardians, but some other form of careful supervision.

Despite what Syssi had said and Yamanu and Toven's positive opinion of Jade, or even Phinas's, it would take a long time for her to prove herself trustworthy enough to be included in their war room discussions, if ever.

"I agree." Kian typed a message to Kalugal. "It's difficult enough for me to include Kalugal and Phinas, whom I've known for a while and trust at least on some level. I'm not going to include a stranger until she has proven herself above and beyond a shadow of a doubt."

"We should supply our Guardians with better weapons," Onegus said. "We didn't have time to get anything fancy to the *Aurora*, and all we have on board are machine guns. Given that Igor's yacht belongs to a weapons dealer, it's safe to assume that it has the most sophisticated weapons one can load on a luxury yacht. If he has a premier shoulder-fired anti-armor system, he can disable or even sink the smaller decoy. The best of them are self-guiding, but I doubt he keeps a weapon of that caliber on board. We should equip the Guardians with hand-held rocket launchers or shoulder-fired missiles so they could fight fire with fire."

Kian looked at Turner. "Can we get our hands on one of those premier self-guiding missiles? That will give us a significant advantage if Igor doesn't have them on board the yacht."

"Not on such short notice," Turner said. "If I'd had a month, I might have been able to procure one. But not in two days."

Onegus nodded in agreement. "I'll put together a list of weapons and munitions that are easily obtained, but I will need you to find a local supplier who can deliver them to the port we'll get the decoy from."

"Maybe you need two decoys," Roni murmured. "If Igor sinks one, the second one can fish our people out of the water."

"That's not a bad idea," Kian said.

When his phone pinged with an incoming message, he glanced at the screen. "Kalugal will get here in forty-five minutes." He lifted his gaze to Onegus. "Schedule a meeting with Yamanu, Toven, and Phinas in an hour and fill them in on what we discussed, so we can get right to it. I'll use the time to brief Kalugal."

34

JADE

*J*ade inspected the new clinic room when Tom came in. "I was told I would find you here." He closed the door behind him. "I want to speak with you."

She arched a brow. "About?"

"Please, let's sit down." He pulled out one of the two chairs for her and sat in the other. "It's about Valstar."

She had a feeling it would come to this. Tom had been spending time with the manipulator, and Valstar must have convinced him that he'd been innocent of wrongdoing and that it all had been Igor's fault.

"I hope you don't intend to go back on your word. The moment Igor is captured, both of their heads are mine. One for each of my sons they slaughtered."

Tom winced. "When you put it like that, it's really difficult to come up with an argument against it."

"Then don't." Jade smiled. "Are we done?" She started to rise.

"We are not. Please, just hear me out."

The pleading tone in his voice made her uncomfortable.

Gods didn't plead. They issued directives. But Tom wasn't like the gods back home, and he'd helped free her people.

She owed him.

"Fine." She sat back down. "But you are not going to convince me."

"Then at least I'll have a clear conscience for having tried."

"When you put it that way, I have no choice but to hear you out."

"Thank you." As he looked into her eyes, she braced for the compulsion that never came. "Valstar didn't have a choice. He didn't know Igor before boarding the ship, he wasn't in cahoots with him on some grand plan to kill off all the other Kra-ell males and take the females in order to create a new Kra-ell society on Earth that was patriarchal instead of matriarchal. As soon as he and his pod members woke up from stasis, Igor took control of them, and they were enslaved to him the same way you were ever since."

She bared her fangs at him. "I did what I had to in order to survive and to help others, but I've never hidden my hatred for Igor, or that I would kill him the moment I could. In contrast, Valstar and the others were very cozy with him, and not all of them had the excuse of having weak minds."

"Maybe they do? How many aside from you and Kagra were able to resist Igor's compulsion? Not that you could really resist it. All the two of you could do was to remember what he had done to you and why you hated him. The others were unable to do even that. I've seen the grief the other females experienced when I freed them from the compulsion. They couldn't even feel it before that."

Jade shifted on the narrow chair. "It might have been true for most, but not for Valstar. He's smart and cunning, and he's not weak."

"Being smart and cunning doesn't make someone strong. He

feels true remorse for what he did, and he wants a better future for his daughter and granddaughter."

"Pfft." She waved a hand in dismissal. "He sent his granddaughter to be captured and possibly tortured for information. Sofia told me how he reacted when she faked a heart condition and pleaded with him to allow Jarmo to come to be at her side during the operation. Valstar refused."

"Did he have a choice? Would Igor have allowed it?"

"He wouldn't," she admitted. "But he might have allowed Valstar to go. If he cared so much about Sofia, he could have suggested it."

Tom nodded. "You have a point. Still, I think Valstar should at least get a fair trial before you execute him."

"Trial by whom? You?"

"The clan has a judge, and she's not a softie by any stretch of the imagination. In fact, she has a special ability that might prove useful, not as evidence for or against Valstar, but perhaps an opinion."

"What is her special talent?"

He smiled. "They call her the alien probe because she has the ability to reach into a person's mind and evaluate their inner core, their intentions. She can determine whether they are good or evil or somewhere in between. I'm told that Kian uses her ability often, and I'm also told that she's a very strict judge. She's not merciful."

"She's an outsider. If anyone should judge Valstar, it should be the people he harmed. All the females whose families he slaughtered."

Tom shook his head. "They could be witnesses and provide testimonials, but they shouldn't be the judges or even the jury. For the trial to be fair, those need to be impartial people."

"If the judge finds him guilty, will she sentence him to death, though? The gods didn't believe in a death sentence.

The worst of their criminals were only sentenced to entombment."

"Personally, I think entombment is a worse punishment than death."

"Perhaps," Jade conceded. "But it's not as satisfying to the families of the murder victims. For over two decades, I've dreamt of taking Valstar and Igor's heads off, along with everyone else who was there that day and either did the killing or stood by and did nothing to prevent it."

Tom's eyes were full of sorrow as he looked at her. "You couldn't prevent it either. Everyone there was a victim in one way or another. The only one who's guilty beyond a shadow of the doubt is Igor, and he's yours to kill."

She let out a breath. "So, what do you expect me to do? Tell you that I'm okay with Valstar standing trial and your judge determining the verdict?"

"I gave you my word that his head is yours, so if you refuse, I'll honor your decision. But I want you to give it some thought. If you want, we can go talk to Valstar together. You know that he can't lie to me, so if he tells us that he's sorry and that he cares about his daughter and granddaughter, it will be the truth, or at least the truth he believes in."

Jade crossed her arms over her chest. "You've just echoed what I was thinking. Valstar might be a pathological liar who believes in his own lies and therefore can lie to you despite being under your compulsion to tell the truth."

"That's possible. Nevertheless, will you do me a favor and give it some more thought?"

When put like that, she had no choice but to agree. She could promise him to think about it, but she wouldn't change her mind.

"For you, I will give it some thought, and I'll even consider talking to the bastard."

"Thank you. I appreciate it."

Jade rose to her feet and offered Tom her hand. "No one can accuse me of being unreasonable. I'm always willing to listen."

He took her hand and smiled. "I have to admit that you impress me."

Well, what do you know?

Should she bask in the praise?

If it were any other god, she would have sneered at the compliment, thinking that it was meant to manipulate her, but Tom had proven to be different, and she took him at face value.

"Thank you. You impress me too."

35

YAMANU

"*T*his was delectable." Yamanu rose to his feet and offered Mey a hand up. "I wish I could stay for coffee, but I have less than ten minutes to get to the meeting."

Onegus had texted him over half an hour ago with the news about two vessels following the *Aurora*, but he hadn't told Mey what the meeting was about.

There was no reason to worry her. Not yet, anyway.

The consensus was that Igor wouldn't try anything as long as they were in the Baltic, but knowing that he was pursuing them made Yamanu's gut churn with unease.

He didn't like having Mey and Jin on board, but he knew better than to say anything. Both would chew his head off if he suggested that they disembark somewhere on the way. Perhaps he could throw a hint Kian's way and have the boss command it.

Except if Mia stayed, and she had to, Kian couldn't demand that Mey and Jin get off somewhere. Besides, the ship was full of humans and children, and they couldn't leave for the same reasons they couldn't just fly out of Helsinki. They had trackers in their bodies and no passports.

Mey patted her stomach. "I could get used to being served delicious breakfast, lunch, and dinner every day. And to think that you warned me that we would have to make our own food."

"I didn't know that there were such culinary experts on board or that they would volunteer to cook for us."

She leaned closer to whisper in his ear. "I vote for bringing them to the village. Since Callie's is only open for dinner, they can serve breakfast and lunch in her restaurant."

He wrapped his arm around her. "You know what Kian's position on the subject is."

Even though he'd said he was considering allowing the Kra-ell and the humans into the village, Yamanu knew the boss too well to believe that. He might say that to appease Syssi, but he would never allow it.

"He might not allow the Kra-ell, but what about the others?" Mey asked.

They were careful not to refer to the humans as such because they were pretending to be humans themselves. The ruse would be up as soon as the fighting started, and the Guardians, along with Kalugal's men, would have to reveal their superior speed and strength.

"Kian won't allow them in either."

Sighing, Mey leaned her head on his shoulder. "Maybe once this is over, and Igor is no longer a threat, the Kra-ell can go back to their compound, and the others can stay on the ship as its serving crew. Kian is looking for staff, and they are looking for jobs. It could be the perfect solution. The ship is amazing, and living on board is not a hardship." She lifted her head off his shoulder. "Is there a chance that Onegus would allow you to switch positions and become the security detail for the *Aurora*?"

Yamanu laughed. "Only temporarily, and only when I'm escorting the clan's royalty."

"Careful," Mey whispered. "People are looking at us."

His booming laughter must have drawn their attention, or maybe they were looking at his beautiful mate, but in either case, he didn't mind.

"Let them look." Walking Mey out of the dining hall, he tightened his arm around her. "I have to admit that being here is a treat. We are staying in a luxurious cabin, your sister and Arwel are here with us, and so are many of our friends. On top of that, we are being served three gourmet meals a day."

It felt like the honeymoon they'd never gotten to have, provided that they could ignore the looming danger of an attack by the Russian cruiser, the powerful and potentially lethal Kra-ell and hybrids on board, and the worry about the well-being and survival of the humans and the children of both species.

When they reached the elevators, Yamanu turned to Mey and dipped his head to kiss her. "I hope the meeting will not take long. Are you going to be at the cabin?"

"I'll be at Jin's. She wants to go over a few ideas for next year's collection."

"You are supposed to be on vacation."

Mey smiled. "When you are a business owner, you can never unplug."

The sisters weren't making any money yet, but as long as Mey was enjoying it, Yamanu had no problem with her and Jin working long hours and making no profits. But it surely wasn't worth sacrificing personal time for.

"I don't see why not, but I can't talk about it now because I need to go." He leaned and kissed her forehead. "Have fun."

When he got to the cabin they had designated as their war room aboard the *Aurora*, Phinas was already there, pouring himself coffee from a pot.

Since when did Phinas attend their meetings? Not that

Yamanu had a problem with that. On the contrary. It was about time.

"Good evening." Phinas lifted the cup. "Do you want some coffee?"

"I'd love some, thanks." Yamanu sat down on the couch and flipped open the tablet, positioning it just so.

"Here you go." Phinas handed him a cup and sat down next to him on the couch.

"Thanks, but you'd better pour one for Toven as well."

"Sure."

Was it his imagination, or did Phinas seem annoyed by the suggestion? Maybe something about the meeting had upset him?

"Did Kian tell you what the meeting is about?" Yamanu asked.

"Onegus filled me in." Phinas rose to his feet. "And half an hour later, Kalugal texted me the same information."

As Phinas poured coffee into the third mug, the door opened, and Toven walked in. "Good evening, gentlemen."

"Here is your coffee." Phinas thrust the cup at him.

"Thank you." Toven regarded him with a puzzled expression. "Did I miss anything? Have you already started the call?"

Had Phinas been offended by Yamanu's request to pour coffee for Toven?

It wasn't likely.

Yamanu had gotten to know Phinas well during the trip to China and on the mission, and the guy wasn't the type who got his feelings hurt over nonsense like who was making coffee for whom.

Phinas had excellent fighting instincts, he was decisive in battle and in his command style, he treated his men with respect, and he was attentive to the humans, which earned him the most points in Yamanu's esteem.

Phinas returned to his spot on the couch. "The call should come in right about now." When the ring sounded, he pressed the green circle on the tablet. "Perfect timing."

"Good evening," Onegus said.

He was seated in his regular spot at the round conference table in the underground war room, with Turner on one side and Kian on the other. Surprisingly though, Kalugal was there as well, seated to Kian's left, opposite Turner.

That was also a first.

The question was what had brought this about. Had Kalugal demanded to be included or had Kian decided that Kalugal needed to be there since his men were on the *Aurora*?

Perhaps that had been Kalugal's plan all along and the reason he had volunteered his men. Maybe he was tired of observing from the sidelines whenever something big was going down, and he'd bought his ticket in by offering his assistance.

"Let's get started," Kian announced without much preamble. "We have both the *Marshal Anatolov* and the *Grand Helena* following the *Aurora*. We assume that Igor is on the *Helena* rather than on the *Anatolov*. It fits his objectives and his mode of operation." He paused to take a drink of water and give the others a chance to jump in and add their comments.

"Why do we assume that Igor is on the *Helena*?" Phinas asked. "Wouldn't he be safer on a Russian warship? It would make more sense for him to be where he can direct the Russian captain and his crew."

36

KALUGAL

*A*s Phinas voiced his unsolicited opinion, Kalugal smiled smugly. His guy was intelligent and confident, and he wasn't intimidated by Turner or Kian.

Unlike Phinas though, Kalugal preferred to sit back and listen first. It had been decades since he'd last participated in any military operation, and he didn't want to appear less capable or brilliant than Turner, which meant that he would probably have to stay quiet throughout this meeting and the ones that followed.

Besides, Kalugal wasn't even ready to formulate an opinion, let alone voice it. Once he was fully briefed on all the details and heard all the arguments behind the assumptions and decisions that had been made so far, he would be in a better position to throw in a few remarks that wouldn't reveal how little he had to contribute in comparison with Turner.

The guy was a hard act to follow, but given enough time, Kalugal was confident that he could outsmart and outmaneuver even the renowned strategist. Except, he didn't have the time or the inclination to immerse himself in military strategizing to such an extent.

He was much more interested in making money and seeing how far he could manipulate humanity through the clever use of social media.

Turner raised his eyes from the screen. "We assume that Igor's plan is for the Russian to sink the *Aurora*. Once that's done, he will need to collect its passengers, or rather just the Kra-ell, load them onto another vessel, and disappear with them before the Russian navy comes after its rogue ship. He doesn't want to be anywhere near the destroyer when that happens."

"Makes sense." Phinas picked up his coffee cup. "That means that he can monitor the Russian cruiser from the yacht and also control the captain, telling him what to do."

"Correct." Turner glanced at his laptop screen. "The *Helena's* top speed is thirty-seven knots, the *Aurora's* is twenty-seven knots, and the *Anatolov's* is twenty-four knots. The yacht's superior speed is an advantage that Igor will make good use of. Once the Russian cruiser hits the *Aurora* she will issue a distress call, and Igor will want to collect his people as quickly as possible and get out of there before the responders arrive. A speedy boat that's faster than any navy vessel in the area is essential for that." Turner shifted his focus to Toven. "If at some point during the battle Igor reveals himself, do you think you can compel him?"

That was something that Kalugal wanted to know as well, but it was anyone's guess.

Toven needed Mia's boost to overcome Igor's compulsion, so he might not be able to compel Igor when pitted against him face to face.

Igor might even be more powerful than Navuh, which would be both remarkable and scary. In Kalugal's opinion, it would be best to kill him and eliminate the threat and not try to capture him, but he wasn't ready to suggest it yet.

"I am not sure," Toven admitted. "I'd rather not base our strategy on the assumption that I can overpower Igor."

Kalugal appreciated the god's honesty.

It was remarkable how little of his prodigious ego Toven injected at times. Growing up on Navuh's teachings, Kalugal had believed that the gods were aloof, arrogant, and condescending. And yet, the three remaining gods on Earth were not that bad.

His mother was loving and kind and never demonstrated the larger-than-life persona he'd associated with the gods.

Annani was not lacking in the diva department, but even though she definitely appeared larger than life, she was never arrogant or condescending. Her palpable power was mitigated by her loving nature and sense of humor. She cared deeply for humans and dedicated her long existence and that of her clan to humanity's advancement.

And then there was Toven. A powerful god who was older than both Annani and Areana, a god who possessed a fortune so vast that his net worth equaled or exceeded that of many of the world's top economies. And yet there he was, comfortable with being a team player and not the one calling the shots.

Perhaps it was Toven's innate nature not to assume the lead. Not everyone was a born leader like Annani or Kian.

"I agree." Kian nodded, echoing Toven's sentiment. "Not necessarily with the part that you can't compel Igor when the need arises, but with your advice not to plan on getting to where it will need to be tested. I would much rather engage with Igor on our terms, at a time and place of our choosing, and where we can have an overwhelming force to ensure the outcome. I don't want to rely on compulsion to apprehend him. We need, however, to make sure that he can't compel any of ours. No one engages with him without earpieces."

"Naturally." Kalugal smoothed his hand over his freshly

trimmed beard. "What are your objectives, though? Do you want to capture Igor or do you want to eliminate him?"

"I'm conflicted," Kian admitted. "On the one hand, I want to get out of him whatever we can about the gods' planet, the Kra-ell's mission to Earth, and the fate of the Kra-ell ship and its missing escape pods. But on the other hand, I want to kill him on sight so that the threat is neutralized once and for all."

"Tough call," Kalugal said. "In my opinion, neutralizing the threat is more important. Although, don't get me wrong. I'm just as curious about what we can learn from Igor as you are."

Happy with his cleverly worded remarks, Kalugal sat back and sipped on his coffee. He'd managed to sound smart and involved without actually saying anything.

Maybe he should go into politics. The ability to talk big without actually saying anything seemed to be the most important talent required to win an election.

KIAN

*K*ian was surprised that his cousin chose caution over gain, preferring to eliminate the threat rather than learning from Igor about the gods.

Kalugal had gone into archeology in the hopes of finding out more about their ancestors, and yet he was willing to give up on the chance to learn about them in exchange for safety.

Perhaps being a father had rearranged the guy's priorities, or maybe he'd always been cautious. After all, Kalugal had escaped discovery by his father for decades, and he wouldn't have been successful if he hadn't learned how to hide and fly under the radar, so to speak.

If he cared to be honest with himself, Kian had mixed feelings about inviting Kalugal to join their planning session, but he was starting to realize that Kalugal's swagger was misleading. When the stakes were high, Kalugal's approach was careful and levelheaded.

"Personally, I would love for Toven to compel Igor and get him to talk," Onegus said. "But only if we can do that safely. Otherwise, I would rather see him blown to pieces and sunk to the bottom of the ocean with all his knowledge."

Setting down his coffee mug, Toven turned to Kian. "As I said, I do not know if I can compel Igor even under ideal circumstances, but if we manage to capture him without exposing ourselves to too much risk, it's worth a shot. If I fail, Annani might give it a try. I don't know how strong her compulsion ability is, and neither does she, but I have a feeling that she's much more powerful than she realizes. After all, she's Ahn's daughter, and he was the strongest compeller among the Earthbound gods."

Kian's knee-jerk response was a vehement refusal to even consider letting his mother attempt that. "I am not letting Annani anywhere near Igor, not even via a video call. Even if we have him in chains and a muzzle on his mouth, I don't want him to know that Annani exists. It's an unacceptable risk for her and for the clan."

Phinas nodded in agreement. "I know this is above my pay grade, and I might be overstepping, but I feel I might be remiss if I don't, and this concerns all of us." He paused and looked at Kian.

Kian had no intention of overruling him. Phinas had good instincts, and his opinion was valuable. He had grown to respect the guy during this operation. Yamanu and Bhathian reported that his leadership and fighting skills were exceptional.

Successfully wooing the fearsome Jade was no small achievement either. He was also completely at ease during this meeting, twice now interjecting in a way that could be construed by some to undermine, or at least question, Kian.

That was not the case, of course. Kian welcomed discussion and appreciated all points of view, but most people were intimidated by him no matter how hard he tried to appear accommodating.

Not Phinas, though.

The credit was due to Kalugal, no doubt, who must have trained his subordinates to speak their minds freely.

"Go ahead. I might not agree with what you suggest, but I'm always willing to listen."

"Thank you." Phinas dipped his head. "It is true that as long as Igor draws breath, even while in custody, he could somehow get free and pose a threat to the clan or the Kra-ell or both. But the risk can be mitigated." Phinas paused and shifted his gaze to his boss.

Kalugal's nod was almost imperceptible, but it did not escape Kian's notice.

"What do you suggest?" Kian asked.

"When we capture Igor, we can keep him in chains and partially tranquilized, and while we interrogate him, we can keep all the Kra-ell quarantined and guarded. In addition to Guardians with earpieces, we can use Jade and Kagra as backup. They have their own earpieces, and they can be fully armed and in position right behind him. This alone will prompt him to cooperate with no need for compulsion. His life will depend on it, and if he refuses, Jade will cut his head off as she was promised."

The visual Phinas's words painted in Kian's mind was powerful, and given the expressions on Toven and Turner's faces, they liked that image as much as he did.

Even Yamanu, who wasn't particularly bloodthirsty, had a small smile tugging at his lips.

Encouraged by their responses, Phinas continued. "In the unlikely event that Toven could not compel Igor even with Mia's help, we can have the Clan Mother attempt doing so via an audio call. Igor might guess that she's a goddess, but he wouldn't see whose voice it is. This will not pose even an oblique threat to the Clan Mother. On the other hand, we could gain knowledge that otherwise might be forever lost."

38

PHINAS

So far, Kian had seemed semi-agreeable, but as soon as Phinas brought up the Clan Mother, Kian's shields went up and his armor locked in place around him.

"I don't want Igor to know that there are any gods left on Earth even when he's in chains with Jade holding a sword over his head. That is not negotiable."

Toven shook his head. "If I compel him, he will know about the existence of at least one god. He probably already suspects that a god is involved. Who else could have overpowered his compulsion and freed his people?"

"So what if he knows?" Phinas took a quick sip from his coffee and immediately set the cup down. "Igor's days are numbered. We promised Jade his and Valstar's heads, and she is very eager to collect on that promise. We question him and then she offs him."

Turner, who hadn't taken part in the exchange so far, looked up from his notepad, sat back, and tapped the pad with his pen. "We might be able to do that."

"What do you mean by that?" Kian asked.

Phinas wondered what that meant as well.

Was Turner referring to the discussion about Annani or to the previous one about capturing Igor and interrogating him while minimizing the risk?

Seemingly oblivious to the question, Turner picked up his notepad and glanced briefly at what he had written down. "While you were talking, I was thinking, and I came up with a twist on our previous idea. We know that Igor is tracking both the *Aurora* and the *Anatolov*, which means he has access to the Russian Navy's tracking system. We also know that he is tracking his people via the various devices implanted in them."

"Which are getting removed as we speak," Phinas said. "Regrettably, not fast enough."

"Correct," Turner confirmed. "The original plan was to dispose of the trackers in the ocean, shroud the *Aurora* by reactivating the signal disruptor, and basically use the big North Atlantic to pull a disappearing act from anyone tracking and following it. Then we came up with a plan to use a decoy ship, load it with the Kra-ell who still had trackers in them, and have Igor follow them. The problem with that plan was the shortage of earpieces. I assumed that the Guardians who remain on the *Aurora* could lend their earpieces to the Kra-ell, who would transfer to the decoy, but on further thought, I realized that it would have left the *Aurora* unprotected in case Igor decided to follow it instead of the decoy for some reason." He cast a quick glance at Onegus. "There was another problem with that plan that I wasn't aware of until I checked with William. He told me that once the earpieces mold to a specific person's ear, they can't fit securely in someone else's, and the compulsion waves might be able to pass through."

"I didn't know that," Onegus said. "William never mentioned it to me."

Phinas could already guess Turner's solution to the problem. "You want to load the trackers that were already removed onto the decoy vessel and leave those who still have them on the *Aurora*. That way, only Guardians or my men will be on the decoy, and all of them have properly fitting earpieces."

"Correct." Turner cast Phinas an appreciative look. "You're a fast thinker."

It was a nice compliment, especially when it came from someone of Turner's cerebral caliber.

"Thank you." Phinas dipped his head.

"I'm not complimenting you. I'm stating the obvious." Turner swiveled his chair toward Kian. "We need to choose the port where we will make the switch carefully. It needs to be large enough for the *Aurora* to dock, and it has to have a lot of traffic. The port of Copenhagen is perfect for that, but the question is whether we will find a suitable vessel available for rent in its vicinity. Since it needs to be a yacht or commercial vessel large enough to supposedly carry all of the Kra-ell and humans who have had their trackers removed, it might be difficult to find. So far, Roni hasn't found any suitable vessels, so we expanded the search to include ships for sale. The rest of the plan stays the same. Once the *Aurora* is back at sea it will continue as planned, heading toward the Shetland Islands and the North Atlantic, while the decoy vessel, with the trackers and a sufficient force on board, will head northward while still hugging the coast."

"This is a solid idea," Toven interlocked his fingers and set his hands on the table. "But I see several issues with it that need to be addressed. First, can we safely assume that the Russians will continue after the *Aurora* and only Igor will follow the decoy? If the Russian cruiser follows the decoy, the vessel will be defenseless. Second, can we reasonably guess what kinds of weapons Igor has on board the *Helena*? We will need to equip our guys with sufficiently superior firepower. Third, do we know if the *Helena* has a compelled human crew on board and any other collateral targets? We should not plan on shooting at or sinking a vessel with innocents on board. Fourth, Igor seems to have a plan B for every move. Could we reasonably rule out a plan B for this situation, and if not, can we guess what that would be? And lastly, if we miscalculate and get any of these answers wrong, what is our backup plan, and how do we get our guys safely out of there?"

Phinas regarded the god with renewed appreciation. He'd been a warrior most of his life, and he hadn't thought of half of the issues Toven had brought up.

Then again, the god was as ancient as human civilization, and he had seen it all play out in one way or another over and over again.

The weapons and the vessels changed, but people were people no matter what species or culture. They were all motivated by the same things, namely fear and greed.

Turner appeared a little less smug than usual. "We have already come up with answers to most of the issues you've raised, but I have to admit that none of us has thought of the human crew aboard the *Helena*."

39

KALUGAL

Kalugal stifled a smile. The indomitable Turner had been humbled by Toven's list of issues, and the guy's ego had suffered a blow. Kalugal could think of several solutions to what bothered Toven, but he preferred to leave it to Turner and give him a chance to save his reputation as the guy who thought of every possible angle.

"Let's break for lunch," Kian said, probably thinking along the same lines. "Obviously, we need to spend more time developing the plan." He turned to the camera and addressed Toven. "I hope that by tomorrow morning your time, we will have answers for you."

Toven nodded. "If you need me, call no matter what time it is. We need to act swiftly."

"Same here," Yamanu said with much less enthusiasm.

The Guardian probably couldn't wait to return to his mate and wanted the meeting over.

Kian terminated the call and closed the tablet. "Do you want to get food from the café and bring it here, or should we get some fresh air and eat over there?"

"Let's get out of here." Onegus pushed to his feet.

Kalugal could eat, but he wasn't happy about discussing sensitive issues in public. He knew better than most what could be gleaned from casual eavesdropping.

"Are you sure that's a good idea?" He followed Kian up.

"No, but I'm tired of the basement. We will keep it down."

Kalugal shrugged. "As you wish. You're the boss."

Kian arched a brow. "Do you want to lead this mission? I'll gladly transfer the responsibility to you."

His cousin was just teasing, but even if he wasn't, Kalugal had no wish to take over command. He was only taking part in this and sacrificing time with his wife and son because his men were involved, and he wanted to have a say in the future of the Kra-ell.

"No, thank you. My job is to poke holes in the plans you and Turner come up with, but since Toven is doing that so well, I can sit back and enjoy the show. I'm just an observer."

That was only partially true.

He was glad to finally be included in the war room team, and he was enjoying the company, but those reasons were not important enough to take time away from his family. Given that he had to be there anyway, though, he could at least enjoy himself.

He was finally included in Kian's inner circle.

Turner was his least favorite, even though he was the smartest of the three. He was dry and humorless and despite his vast knowledge, kind of boring. Nevertheless, Kalugal admired him not only for his tactical instincts but also for his superb organizational skills, and most of all for his invaluable worldwide network of military suppliers and subcontractors.

Onegus was a fun guy, but he was also the consummate professional. He knew his stuff and ensured every move was carefully considered from all angles, especially the Guardians'.

Kian was Kalugal's favorite, though, and he found that he

enjoyed his cousin's company even more than he enjoyed Rufsur's, which was saying something.

Rufsur was his right-hand man, and until Kalugal had met Jacki, he was the person he'd been the closest to.

Thankfully, Rufsur was happily mated to Edna, or he would have felt neglected. Fates willing, the two would be blessed with a child soon, and then Rufsur's life would be complete. They were working on it, using the potions Merlin had prepared for them before leaving on the Kra-ell mission, and Kalugal was keeping his fingers crossed for them.

Phinas and he had never been that close, but he trusted Phinas just as much as Rufsur.

Still, he liked spending time with Kian more than either of his lieutenants.

It could be the familial connection or the fact that they were equals, or maybe it was the banter they enjoyed over whiskey and cigars, but the affinity was there.

"Igor's yacht is remarkably fast for a vessel of that size," Onegus said as they sat down at the table. "It won't be easy to find a yacht or boat large enough for the number of passengers we will supposedly be carrying, and fast enough to outrun Igor's boat."

"It doesn't need to outrun the *Helena*," Turner said. "In terms of size, any reasonably large yacht or small commercial vessel should do. There is no reason for Igor to think that we set his people up comfortably two-per-cabin. In fact, he would probably assume that we deliberately chose a small craft so he wouldn't suspect that we were using it to sneak his people away."

"What if Roni can't find a boat?" Kalugal asked.

Kian had told him that the kid had hacked into restricted naval systems that gave him access to information about any vessel at any location, but that didn't mean that any of them would be available for rent or even for sale.

Kalugal hadn't known that every ship, whether private or military, was being tracked in real time. Did that include fishing boats, though? Perhaps they could use one of those.

Turner shook his head. "We have a very specific set of pre-qualifiers we are looking for. Roni found several candidates, but they were not offered for hire. I have my people working on it as well. As to the boat's speed, a not-too-swift yacht might actually be an advantage. If our end game is to capture Igor, what better way to lure him closer than to make him think that we cannot outrun him? A boat that is just slightly slower than Igor's will have him speed up right into our trap."

Kalugal liked the way Turner's mind worked. "So, what you're saying is that we need to look for a vessel that can accommodate over two hundred people below deck and that is reasonably fast, but not as fast as Igor's boat. That may prove to be a tall order. Maybe it would be easier to get a couple of smaller vessels and split the people between them. That will further confuse Igor."

"Roni had the same idea," Kian said. "I'm starting to think that maybe we should do that."

As they sat down, Aliya approached their table, and the discussion halted.

"What can I get for you?" she asked.

Kian smiled up at her. "Coffees all around, and some sandwiches and pastries. You know what to get me."

She nodded. "The vegetable wrap. I always save one for you."

"That's so nice of you. But I don't come to the café every day, and I don't want it to go to waste."

"Don't worry, it doesn't. When Jackson restocks the café, Wonder eats your wrap if you didn't get it that day."

"I'm glad."

"Anything else?" She looked at Kalugal.

He cast her a smile. "Whatever you get us is fine."

Did she know that Phinas and Jade were an item? Should he tell her?

Nah. With how fast rumors rushed through the village, she'd hear about it soon enough.

Kalugal looked around at the other patrons. "How secretive are we supposed to be? It's not like we have privacy here. I could shroud us, but the Clan Mother forbade me from using my powers on clan members. If you approve, though, or ask me to do it, I might be able to circumvent her compulsion."

"Don't worry about it." Kian clapped him on the back. "No one here is going to warn Igor about what we are planning for him, and we are not discussing anything else."

"Right." Kalugal leaned closer to Kian. "How important is it for us to catch and question Igor? I still think that blowing him out of the water is the easiest way to get rid of him, while capturing him presents all kinds of risks, both during the operation and after, when he's in our hands." He chuckled. "Are we going to put a muzzle on him, Hannibal Lecter style? Or maybe cutting out his tongue is a safer solution?"

Kian winced. "Very funny."

"What?" Kalugal arched a brow. "Is killing him better?"

"If we can manage to do it safely, I'd rather capture him alive and interrogate him, but he will need to have a tongue for that. Jade and Valstar know a lot, and some of the other original settlers might have additional information, but I have a feeling that Igor was much higher up in the Kra-ell pecking order, and he knows more. Still, we can probably figure out most of it from the others. In other words, I am unwilling to risk anyone's life for what's in Igor's head. If we can capture him without additional risk, I am all for it. Otherwise, I'd rather see him blown to pieces."

"I agree." Onegus started but stopped when Aliya returned with their order.

"He doesn't need a tongue," Kalugal murmured. "He can write his answers."

The others chuckled, but he hadn't said that as a joke. It was a viable solution. Igor needed his tongue to generate the sounds that carried compulsion. Cutting it out would render him harmless, and he could still tell them everything he knew by writing his answers with pen on paper or typing them on a laptop or tablet.

After taking the paper cup marked with his name, Kian leaned back in his chair. "I suggest that we take a break from the planning and let our minds rest."

"I have a great idea." Kalugal unwrapped one of the pastries. "How about we continue the meeting up on your roof? We can drag a couple of chairs up there and smoke your cigars."

Kian grinned. "I like the way you think, cousin. After we finish our coffees and sandwiches, we can move our meeting to the roof."

40

KIAN

"How are the hybrids doing?" Kian asked Onegus. The topic was related to what they'd been discussing before, but it didn't require any cerebral effort.

Onegus shrugged. "Frankly, I don't know. I didn't check on them this morning. But if they were giving my guys any trouble, I would have heard about it."

Kalugal frowned. "What hybrids?"

Kian unwrapped his sandwich. "Igor sent two hybrids to follow Sofia around, but since we removed the tracker from her body and put it in a cat, they didn't know that she was no longer in Safe Haven and stayed in the area. Then they disappeared for about twenty-four hours, and we were afraid that Igor had retrieved them, but they returned, and our guys got them. They are in the keep right now, and I wanted to pay them a visit later today, but I'm too pressed for time, so I decided to send Anandur instead. I wonder if he'll get anything useful out of them."

"Like what?" Kalugal asked. "What can they know that we don't already?"

"Perhaps Igor contacted them. They were away for a whole

day, and they left their car in front of their Airbnb. Maybe they came back to collect their things and go to Igor. The Guardians tranquilized them and loaded them into the van without asking them anything, and they kept tranquilizing them along the way. It's not that anything they can tell us will help with capturing Igor, but I'm curious to know whether he contacted them."

Turner was holding the phone to his ear, but since he wasn't saying anything, Kian assumed that he was listening to a message. When he put the phone down, he asked. "Anything for us?"

Turner nodded. "Nils left me a message. He can meet the *Aurora* at Skagen."

"Where is that?" Kalugal asked.

Turner brought it up on Google maps. "It's the northernmost town and port of Denmark. It's right at the entrance to the North Sea proper. It's a good spot since we don't expect the Russian cruiser to attack before the *Aurora* is a day or so into the North Sea."

Kian frowned. "How many days will it take the *Aurora* to reach Skagen?"

Turner looked at the map. "Taking into consideration a stopover of several hours, probably two days."

Kian released a breath. "That's not too bad."

"Provided that our assumption about the Russian is correct," Onegus said. "If he decides to attack her while she's still in the Baltic, we have no way to protect it."

Kalugal rubbed his jaw between his thumb and forefinger. "She'll be close enough to the coast for rescue to arrive within moments. Our people will have their hands full thralling the rescuers not to see the passengers' peculiarities."

"I'm not worried about that," Kian said. "What worries me

are the humans and children on board who will not survive more than a few minutes in the cold water."

"A ship doesn't sink that fast even if it's been hit and takes in water." Turner took a sip of his coffee. "They will have time to load the humans and children onto the lifeboats, and the rescue will arrive quickly enough. So quickly, in fact, that Igor won't have time to get his people. By the time the lifeboats are in the water, the place will be swarming with helicopters. That's why I'm positive he won't make his move until she's out of the Baltic."

He sounded very sure about that, and since Kian didn't have much experience with ships, sinking or afloat, he had to trust the guy's logic.

41

JADE

"Are you serious?" Kagra looked at the water as if it was full of poisonous *Pogdas*. "Are we supposed to get in there?"

Jade let out a breath. "I'm as unenthusiastic about it as you are, but Phinas has a point. If the ship goes down, we need to be able to at least float until help arrives."

"We have lifeboats," Drova said. "And if he tells you that there aren't enough of them, it's a lie. I counted, and there were enough seats for every passenger on board. He's just a sadistic bastard."

Pavel pushed his hands into his pockets. "Tomos and Piotr had a swimming lesson earlier today, and they said it wasn't that bad."

"They lied." Drova cast him a baleful look. "They didn't want to be the only suckers who suffered."

"What if the ship capsizes before we can get into the lifeboats?" Jade asked. "People still die at sea despite all the cruise ships having them. Knowing how to swim can save our lives. Besides, the cold is unpleasant, but it's not going to kill us. Our bodies will raise their temperatures."

"That's another thing that bothers me about it." Drova huddled inside her coat. "Phinas and Dandor are human. How come they didn't get hypothermia after spending nearly an hour in this pool?"

Good question.

Jade was proud of her daughter for wondering about it, but she couldn't tell her the truth about the immortals. Not yet, anyway.

"Maybe it's not that cold. The pool is heated. Otherwise, it would have frozen over."

"Hello, everyone." Phinas strode onto the deck. "I wasn't expecting such a large turnout, but I'm glad to see you all here." He smiled at Jade. "Are you planning on swimming fully clothed?"

She glared at him. "We found a solution for the lack of bathing suits."

"I can't wait to see it." He gave her a lascivious look that she hoped Drova didn't notice.

Smiling, she pulled her sweater off, revealing the swath of fabric she'd cut out of one of his black T-shirts and wrapped around her breasts. "They say that necessity is the mother of invention." She pulled her pants down next.

The glow from Phinas's eyes could have illuminated the pool, but thankfully, Drova was busy getting undressed, and Pavel was busy watching Drova.

Jade frowned. Drova was too young to be of interest to an adult Kra-ell male. Even though she was already at her full height and had the hips of a grown female, she was still a child, and she was not ready to have sex yet.

For a moment, Jade considered having a talk with Pavel, but then she reconsidered. Drova was under a lot of stress, and Pavel seemed to make her happy.

Except, Kra-ell didn't do couples.

Or did they?

Whether Jade was willing to admit it or not, she and Phinas were a couple. They had been exclusive with one another, and others regarded them as a couple as well.

Still, Drova and Pavel were probably just friends or rather cohorts. Purebloods didn't flirt or formed exclusive relationships. The two were spending a lot of time together, though, probably plotting a revolution, but it was all good. There were a lot of changes in their future, and she needed to be flexible and listen to what everyone brought to the table.

Turning so she was facing Phinas and blocking him from Drova's view, Jade whispered, "Your blazing gaze should focus elsewhere."

"Damn." He turned to look up at the sky. "Look at all these stars."

"Beautiful, aren't they?" Max walked up to them, wearing a pair of boxer shorts and a towel draped over one shoulder. "I heard there is a pool party going on."

Kagra snorted. "You came even though you didn't have to? Do you enjoy torture?"

He grinned. "It depends on who's inflicting it. I'm willing to suffer if it's you."

"You're crazy." Kagra unzipped her jacket. "Let's just get it over with so I can return to my cabin and soak in a hot tub."

"Can I come with you?" Max dropped the towel.

"In your dreams, hotshot." Kagra shrugged the jacket off, revealing the same makeshift swimming top as Jade's.

Phinas frowned. "Is that my T-shirt?"

"It was." Jade grinned. "We needed a garment large enough to supply fabric for three tops, and your shirt was the only one that fit the bill."

"It was well worth the sacrifice." Phinas whipped his shirt over his head. "I'm going in."

As he pulled his pants off while walking toward the pool and jumped in, Jade stifled a chuckle.

Did he have something to hide?

Without giving herself time to reconsider, she followed him and jumped in as well.

"Dear Mother, it's cold." She wrapped her arms around herself, regretting that they had company.

Right now, Phinas's big warm body would have been a welcome reprieve.

Kagra jumped in next, and Max jumped right after her.

Drova put her foot in the water and pulled it out quickly. "I'm not going in there."

"Come on," Pavel said. "If I can do it, you can do it too." He sat on the edge of the pool and slid inside.

The water barely reached their upper chests, and after the first shock, it wasn't that bad.

"Okay, people," Phinas said. "First lesson is to float on your back. I'll demonstrate on Jade how it's done."

KIAN

*T*urner lifted his eyes to the sky. "It looks like it's going to rain."

"We have an umbrella." Kian put the chair he'd carried from his office next to one of the loungers.

It had been a beautiful sunny day up until about half an hour ago, and then swollen rain clouds had drifted over, hiding the sun. They weren't thick or dark enough to produce rain, but more were drifting over by the minute.

"It's Southern California." Onegus put the chair he'd carried next to the other lounger. "We might get a little drizzle, and then the sky will clear by evening."

"I wouldn't bet on that." Turner sat down on the chair and put his laptop on his knees. "I checked the forecast, and there is a storm heading our way."

After Toven had pointed out all the things he hadn't considered, Turner had gotten into a mood, and all during lunch he'd been either typing on his laptop or jotting notes on his yellow pad.

Not that he was ever cheerful, but now he had his own personal cloud hanging over his head.

"Storm." Kian snorted. "Every rainfall is called a storm in this desert. Where we come from, now, those are storms."

The comment didn't pull a smile out of Turner as he'd expected.

Onegus nodded. "Winters in the Scottish Highlands are brutal, but they are nothing compared to winters in Finland or Northern Russia. I don't envy our people out there." He chuckled. "Phinas decided that the Kra-ell and the humans needed swimming lessons, and he had the pool filled up. Imagine swimming in that freezing water."

"He has to heat it up," Kian said. "Otherwise, the pool water will freeze."

Yamanu had told Kian about Phinas's initiative, and he approved. It was a good idea in case the worst happened and the passengers ended up in the water, but heating up the pool meant an additional expenditure of fuel. If they weren't planning a refueling stop, that would have been a problem.

"He's only heating it up minimally," Onegus said. "He wants the Kra-ell to learn to swim in nearly freezing water, so they won't panic if the *Aurora* gets hit and starts sinking."

"It won't," Turner said. "Nils will sink the Russian before he can fire at the *Aurora*. Besides, the humans will be in the lifeboats. There is no need to torture them by having them take lessons in the freezing pool."

"Nevertheless, I applaud his initiative." Kian pulled four cigars out of his coat pockets and handed out three of them. "Even if the only thing the lessons achieve is entertainment, I'm sure that they all need a way to release the tension."

Onegus took the lighter from Kian and lit his cigar. "Back to our discussion from before. I still think that we should eliminate Igor rather than risk people just for a chance to learn more about our history. But before we rule out capturing him because of the added risks, we need to evaluate them." The Chief looked at Turner.

Leaning forward, Turner placed his hands on the table. "I see several possible scenarios. The most worrisome one involves Igor ordering the Russians to drop the *Aurora* and change directions to follow the smaller vessel. When Nils realizes that, he will need instructions from us, and he will be forced to either surface or float a buoy and break radio silence, risking the sub's discovery. Because of the confusion, he might also fall behind because the vessels will continue on their respective courses while he is surfacing and waiting for our input. Don't forget that the sub is the slowest of the vessels involved. This could lead to him not being where we need him when we need him. We can mitigate that by having the decoy boat progress slowly, but that might raise Igor's suspicion."

Kian didn't understand why that was a problem. "As Roni pointed out, we can still reach Nils, and if he knows the plan ahead of time, he will know what to do. He needs to follow the Russian cruiser no matter which vessel it is following. The yacht will not follow the *Aurora*, and if it does, the force on board can take care of it."

Turner shook his head. "We've just discussed how important it is to safeguard the *Aurora*. If it is sunk in the North Sea, where rescue will take too long to reach it, everyone on board will be at risk. That's why it's our top priority. Igor might have rocket launchers on board the yacht. A rocket might not be enough to sink a cruise ship, but it can disable it, and he can board it. We also don't have the specialty earpieces for the Kraell on board the *Aurora*, and Igor could command them using a bullhorn. They would have no choice but to strike against the remaining Guardians. True, we can lock them up in one of the steel storage spaces before the yacht gets close enough, but the fact remains that whatever we do, without the sub the *Aurora* is vulnerable. The only scenario where we will need Nils to follow the decoy is if Igor follows it along with the Russian cruiser and no vessels follow the *Aurora*. The bottom line is that we can't tell Nils ahead of time who to follow."

43

KALUGAL

*K*alugal was puzzled by the exchange and wondered how come the solution hadn't occurred to Turner. "If we can provide air cover to keep the decoy safe, we can tell the submarine captain to stick to the *Aurora*."

Having taken part in WWII and seen first-hand the importance of air superiority, Kalugal thought that should have been crystal clear to everyone. Perhaps the problem was getting the air coverage. Turner's contacts might not be as all-encompassing as he'd led everyone to believe.

Onegus nodded. "If we can contract a military helicopter armed with missiles and a powerful gun, it could work."

As all eyes shifted to Turner, the guy looked absolutely smug. "I have contacts in Europe that have the equipment, aircrew, and armaments." He smiled, his self-assured attitude firmly back in place. "They are going to be costly though, especially on such short notice, but I've contacted two of my best sources earlier today, and I expect to hear back from them this afternoon."

It was both annoying and impressive that the guy had

already thought of the solution. Evidently Turner had been waiting for them to catch up, or maybe he'd wanted to show off that he had thought of it first.

After all, he had face to save.

"I like it," Kian said. "Air coverage might prove essential in every scenario, especially if Igor has a plan B, which I suspect he does. I wouldn't be surprised if he thought of the same thing and planned to compel a military vessel or aircraft to join his attack. In case Igor once again pulls the proverbial rabbit out of the hat, having a helicopter on the scene as quickly as possible is vital to the security of our people. The question is how we can pull it off while the ship is progressing. Helicopters have a relatively short range. Will it follow the ship from one refueling station to another?"

Turner put his cigar in the ashtray and started typing on his laptop. "It can be done as long as the decoy follows the coastline but doesn't get too far north. There is a long stretch along the coast of Norway that doesn't have any nearby airports. Frankly, that's more than I planned to use this resource for, but I agree that this approach affords us a better margin of error. I am sending an expanded scope of engagement email as we speak."

"What if we trick him?" Onegus's eyes blazed with an inner light. "Igor's default is compulsion. It is reasonable to assume that this is the first thing he will try to do. When he attempts to compel our men, they could play along, leading him to believe that the decoy is no longer a threat. He will feel confident to board their vessel in order to take control of it, at which point we can take him and his cronies down with tranquilizer darts."

Kian's expression was skeptical. "Igor will not fall for that. As much as I have absolute confidence in the Guardians, and as much as Kalugal's men have proved themselves capable, they are not good enough actors to pull it off and fool him. Besides, he could order our guys to throw their weapons overboard to verify that they are responding to his compulsion. Would they? Of course not. He might order them to bring their passengers on deck, and they couldn't do that either because they will have no passengers. Hell, he could test his compulsion and order them to shoot each other."

Onegus's face fell, but the guy had no ego issues, and he had no problem admitting that his plan had huge holes in it. "Yep. You are correct. I did not think it through."

"Let's continue with the possible scenarios," Turner said. "I agree with Kian that it is not very likely that Igor will order the Russian to follow the decoy. After our tele-meeting with Toven, I asked Roni to do more research about the owner of the yacht Igor had commandeered and to confirm that the oligarch it belongs to is indeed an international weapons dealer. It's safe to assume that the yacht is not only equipped with very un-yacht-like defensive and offensive capabilities but has a security detail onboard, so Igor has additional trained killers with him. He will feel confident about his ability to take over the decoy and will tell the Russian captain to keep trailing the *Aurora*."

"In a way, that's good news," Kian said. "If the *Helena* is run by the Bratva, I have no qualms about blowing it up. I'll let Toven know that he has one less thing to worry about. There are no innocent civilians on board."

Turner lifted his head. "There might be. What about the cook, the maid, the mechanics? They are not all evildoers."

Kian let out an exasperated breath. "Then we will do our best not to blow it up but to disable it instead. But if it's a choice between saving our people and whoever is on board the *Helena*, our people come first."

"Naturally." Turner resumed typing.

The military helicopter idea was solid, but if the yacht was equipped with more than machine guns, it might score a hit before the helicopter arrived, and Kalugal didn't like the odds.

His men comprised the majority of the force on the *Aurora*, and many of them would be on the decoy, including Phinas. He wanted them armed to the teeth so they could protect themselves.

"Is there a way to get shoulder-mounted missiles for our guys?" he asked. "That would buy them time until the helicopter is within range and engages."

"We're already taking care of that," Onegus said. "I made a list of weapons we need, and Turner is getting them from his suppliers. We just need to know which port to deliver them to."

Turner nodded while typing. "I sent another inquiry to my contact. Assuming that he's available and willing to take on the mission, I will run by him what we are dealing with. He is an experienced navy helicopter pilot, and I have no doubt that he will have some suggestions and ideas for us."

44

PHINAS

*J*ade adjusted the blanket over her shoulders and lifted the cup of tea Phinas had made her. "I don't even like tea, but I'm chilled all over, and tea seems like a good idea."

He sat next to her on the couch and wrapped his arm around her. "I ramped up the heating. It should get warmer in a few minutes."

She leaned against his side. "Aren't we supposed to conserve fuel?"

"It's less critical with the new plan." He proceeded to tell her about the decoy idea.

Jade looked skeptical. "When I visited Merlin earlier today, he had only sixteen trackers removed. That's not enough to make the decoy attractive enough to lure Igor away from the *Aurora*. He needs to believe that most of the purebloods are on board the decoy to change course and follow it."

"We have two to three days, and Merlin told me that you arranged for two new assistants for him so he could work faster."

"Three." Jade took a sip from the tea. "Marcel promised to find another Guardian who can tackle the scanning."

"Ruvon is good with tech stuff. I can have him stop by the clinic to see whether he can handle the MRI."

"Who is Ruvon? Did I meet him?"

"You've seen him, but you probably don't remember. He's a tall skinny guy, with dark curly hair and smiling brown eyes."

Surprisingly, Jade nodded. "I know who you're talking about. Can you send him over tomorrow?"

"I can, but you should check with Marcel first. Maybe he's already found someone for the job."

"I will, and I'll also check with Pavel. He's a quick study." She sighed. "It would have been so much easier for me if my people and I had phones. It's a pain to track down everyone I need to talk to."

Was this a good opportunity to check with Jade about her thoughts about moving her people into the village?

It was important to find out if Jade would even consider it, but the subject should be broached as a hypothetical because Kian would most likely decide against it. The only reason he was collecting opinions about Jade and the other Kra-ell was to appease Syssi, who wanted them in the village to shore up its defenses. Turner also seemed to be pushing for it, but although Kian respected the guy's opinion, he had no problem over-ruling it.

He wouldn't overrule Syssi as easily, though, if at all.

In fact, Kian might invite the Kra-ell to the village despite his own objections just to make his mate happy.

Most mated males did everything they could to please their females, and Phinas had no problem with that. Peace and harmony at home were essential to mated bliss, and who did not want that.

Jade lifted her head off his arm. "What are you thinking about?"

"Mated couples."

She arched a brow. "What about them?"

"My boss found the love of his life about a year ago, and they got pregnant right away. They have a little baby boy who is the center of their lives. I've known Kalugal for many decades, but I've never seen him as happy as he is now, and that's despite sleepless nights and a colicky baby who is miserable most of the time and can barely hold any food down. Kalugal and Jacki didn't even leave the house until recently because they were afraid of exposing their baby to viruses. The clan doctor had to convince them that they were doing their son a disservice by overprotecting him. He needs to be exposed to germs so his body will develop immunity to them."

"That's a lovely story. Does it have a point?"

Chuckling, Phinas tightened his arm around her. "The ever pragmatic Jade. Sometimes a story is just a story, and it is not meant as a cautionary tale or encouragement to become more and do heroic things."

"Then it's not a good story." She brought the mug to her lips and took another sip. "If I told you a story about a woman traveling for business and sightseeing while she's at it, you would be bored unless something interesting happened to her. She could have met a mysterious man who turned out to be a spy, or she could have been the victim of a terrorist attack and its only survivor, or she might have been running for her life from an assassin. Those are the kinds of things that make a good story."

Phinas smiled. "I heard that you were a good storyteller, but I find that difficult to reconcile with the pragmatic, no-nonsense female who I've grown to like and respect."

He'd almost blurted out that he'd grown to love her, but that would have been a red flag that would have sent her running away. Besides, he wasn't sure that he was in love with her.

Jade was so different from him or anyone else he knew that it might not work out for them in the long term. Right now, they were still enjoying the novelty, but who knew how long it would last.

For a long moment, she regarded him with those huge, unblinking eyes of hers. "I've grown to like and respect you as well. I enjoy your company." She leaned over and smoothed a finger over his lips. "I didn't expect to enjoy our bed play so much. I'm used to rougher games."

"Oh, yeah?" Phinas cupped the back of Jade's neck. "I enjoy your company as well, in bed and outside of it."

He brought their mouths together for a kiss, but Jade didn't respond with her usual fervor, probably because she was still holding the teacup and was afraid it would spill over, but it was also possible that she was uncomfortable with the direction their conversation had taken.

45

JADE

*J*ade put the teacup down and shrugged the blanket off.

It was either getting much warmer in Phinas's cabin, or it was her response to the kiss and what he'd said as well as what he hadn't said.

She had too little experience with humans and immortals to read them as easily as she read other Kra-ell.

When Phinas had talked about his boss and his mated bliss, his eyes had shone with emotion, and she'd detected wistfulness in his tone. He wanted that for himself, a loving mate and a child to dote on, and she had a feeling he wanted it with her.

Except, she couldn't give him either of those things.

Or could she?

Jade had considered having a child by Phinas, but there were just too many reasons why it was a bad idea, not the least of them that Phinas would want to be part of that child's life, and that was not possible.

They came from different worlds, and their time together was precious but temporary. After Igor was dealt with, they would go their separate ways, and if they had a child together, that child would naturally have to go with her. A hybrid Kra-ell needed to be raised by a Kra-ell mother in a Kra-ell community and learn the Kra-ell way. They couldn't grow up among immortals who weren't as strong or as fast.

Unlike a pureblooded father, Phinas would never be satisfied with just visiting his offspring. He would want to be there every day and witness every milestone.

"What are you thinking about?" Phinas hooked a finger under her chin and turned her head toward him. "I hope it's about sex."

She chuckled. "In a way, it is." She shifted to face him. "You wanted to know why I like to tell stories."

He nodded, even though he hadn't asked that. He just had trouble reconciling her character with storytelling.

"People need something greater than themselves to believe in, heroes to worship, and adventures to crave. Everyday life is mundane, and it's not glamorous. We get up in the morning, work or do our chores, eat, sleep, and repeat the same thing daily. When we hear a story or watch a movie, we identify with the protagonists and live vicariously through them. Suddenly, we feel more important, more heroic, and more glamorous. Stories give meaning to our existence."

He tilted his head. "What about children? Their lives are full of wonder and discovery. The mundane existence is an adult affliction."

"Teaching children through stories is more fun for them and more effective. They might forget dry history lessons, but they will forever remember the fables I've told them." She smiled. "I was telling the children of my tribe stories long before I was captured, and in captivity, I used the fables to circumvent Igor's prohibition to tell them anything about the Kra-ell past or way of life."

He took her hand. "Perhaps you could write children's books."

Jade snorted out a laugh. "If you heard my stories, you wouldn't say that. Mine don't have a happily-ever-after or even a happily-for-now. My stories mimic life and rarely end well. The moral I try to impart is that a life lived well, honorably and courageously, is worth living even if the hero doesn't make it to the end. The journey is what matters."

Phinas grimaced. "Poor children. Why make them face the harsh realities of life at such a young age? They will discover them soon enough when they grow up."

She tilted her head. "You told me that your childhood was terrible. Would hearing happy stories have made you feel better about your life?"

"First of all, my childhood wasn't terrible. I had a loving mother, and life was good in the Dormants' enclosure. It turned bad when I transitioned and was taken away to the war camp. That was miserable. Back then, if anyone told me a happily-ever-after story, I probably would have punched them in the gut."

"See?" She waved a hand. "I was right."

Phinas picked up the blanket and draped it over her shoulder. "When I was a little boy, my mother told me fun stories that never ended badly, and I loved them. I think that those stories helped me through the bad times. They reminded me that there was decency in the world, and that not everyone was cruel. I don't think I would have been the male I am today without them."

It was a sweet sentiment, but he was wrong.

"Didn't your mother tell the same stories to your brothers?"

"She did."

"And yet they didn't turn out like you. They had different fathers and inherited different attributes from them." Jade closed her eyes. "I'm always watching Drova for signs of her father's character. She has some of it, like the bossiness and the condescending attitude, but I think she's good on the inside. I just hope that she stays that way."

"She seems like a good kid." He wrapped his arms around her and pulled her into his lap. "Do you think she suspects that we are together?"

"We are not together. We just happen to spend some time with one another, and I don't think Drova suspects anything."

"You're such a stubborn female." He cupped the back of her neck and took her mouth in a demanding kiss.

When they came up for air, he regarded her with glowing eyes. "One day, you will admit that you are mine."

"Don't hold your breath." She kissed him back to shut him up.

KIAN

*K*ian was startled awake as the war room door banged open, and William walked in.

Lifting his head off the conference table, he glared at Onegus. "You shouldn't have let me sleep."

"I didn't notice that you'd dozed off."

The guy was not even trying to sound sincere.

"I assume you are all curious and want to hear what I've found out about Sofia's tracker so far." William put his laptop on the table and opened it to display a close-up of a tiny pebble that wasn't really a pebble.

"We definitely are." Kian rose to his feet and walked to the rolling cart Okidu had brought earlier. "But I need some coffee before I can focus enough to understand your technical jargon." He turned to the others. "Anyone?"

The three shook their heads.

Onegus chuckled. "At the rate I've been gulping coffee lately, I'm surprised that it's not going straight through my system and coming out the same color on the other end."

Wincing, William pushed his glasses back on his nose. "You could have spared me that image."

He'd gone back to wearing them in the lab mainly because the glare from the computer irritated his eyes, but also because his mate thought he looked distinguished in them, or something to that effect. Kaia might have said that he looked sexy or hot, but Syssi had used some other adjective when she'd told Kian about it.

When Kian sat back down with his coffee in hand, he took a long grateful sip and waved at William to begin.

"It's alien technology," William stated.

"Are you sure?" Turner asked.

William nodded. "I didn't take it apart because it's a solid-state piece, but I ran a lot of tests on it and put it through various imaging devices. The materials it is made of didn't come from Earth, and neither did the technology. It's inert when not in a living host's body, emitting no signal whatsoever. It uses the body's electricity to work, but the signal it emits is so weak that it barely registers. To compensate, though, it doesn't get any weaker with distance."

Kian frowned. "Did you have it implanted in another animal?"

"I had to. It wouldn't have worked otherwise. Magnus let me borrow Scarlett for a day, and one of my guys drove her around so I could test the signal's strength depending on the distance. He drove all the way to Santa Barbara, and there was no change. I bet we could have flown Scarlett to Scotland, and the signal would have remained the same."

Turner leveled his stare at William. "I hope you didn't implant the tracker in Scarlett in the village or bring her back with it."

"Of course not." William looked offended by the suggestion. "Julian did it in our warehouse downtown, and once we were done with the experiment, he took it out of Scarlett and brought her back to Magnus."

Turner looked as if he was chewing on a lemon. "I'm embarrassed to admit it, but I didn't take that into account, and I should have. We knew that the tracker needed a living host." He looked at Kian. "We can't just take all the trackers that Merlin extracts and give them to the Guardians to put in their pockets when they transfer to the decoy. All trackers of this kind, which I assume are predominantly taken out of the purebloods, will have to be implanted in either the Guardians or the crew."

Onegus flashed him a grin. "Not necessarily. There are plenty of goats and sheep on the *Aurora*. I'm sure the Kra-ell can do without a few of them for a while. We can implant two trackers in each to minimize the number of animals we will need to transfer." He looked at William. "Will that work? Or will it look suspicious that the trackers are moving in pairs? Can he determine where the different signals are coming from when they are so close to one another?"

"He can, and it will look strange, but Igor won't suspect that we removed the trackers from some and implanted them in others, doubling up. Don't forget that he probably thinks that we took his people by force, so he would assume that we chained the purebloods in pairs."

Onegus looked at Kian. "Would that have been your assumption in similar circumstances?"

Kian let out a breath. "That depends on what Igor knows and what he believes."

He'd spent long hours thinking about it, and when he realized that Igor had no reason to believe that a stronger compeller had released his people, he tried to put himself in the guy's shoes and speculate about what had actually happened.

His first thought would have been that they had been taken by other Kra-ell by force. The gaping holes in the compound's wall would have reinforced that suspicion.

The other option was that they had been taken by humans

after being drugged, gassed, or incapacitated in some other way and imprisoned.

The one thing that wouldn't have made sense to Igor was the cruise ship they had been loaded onto. It didn't fit either scenario, which was probably why Igor was proceeding with so much caution.

Onegus arched a brow. "Care to elaborate?"

Kian turned to him. "Igor must have investigated what was loaded on the *Aurora* and found out about the MRI and the animals. He's either assuming that we are conducting experiments on his people or suspects that we found the trackers. Chaining the purebloods in twos doesn't fit either scenario."

"What's the solution, then?" Onegus asked.

"Smaller animals, of course." Turner looked at William. "Would gerbils provide enough electricity to power the trackers?"

William removed his glasses and put them on the table. "We know that the tracker worked when it was inside a cat, so I suggest we use a similarly sized animal. If you want, I can get a gerbil and a mouse and test it, but we don't have time. We need to get a hundred and fifty to two hundred cats delivered to the *Aurora* as soon as possible, so Merlin can implant them."

Could the doctor do so many in just a few hours?

The tiny trackers were easier to implant than to remove. Nevertheless, Merlin would have to organize an assembly line to get it done.

Kian groaned. "I can't believe how deep of a hole we've dug for ourselves. It's going from bad to worse. We have sheep and goats on our luxury cruise ship, and now we are going to add cats that will do their business all over the place. I will have to remodel it again."

William pushed to his feet. "I'll drive downtown right now, get a gerbil, and test whether the tracker works in its small body. If it does, it's going to be much easier to get a large number of gerbils to the *Aurora* than cats."

Turner lifted his hand. "We need to check with Merlin about how many of those alien trackers he expects to extract. Perhaps we won't need so many animals after all. The rest of the trackers do not require a living host to operate."

47

SOFIA

"We are cracking today." Sofia bandaged Gordi's thigh. "You are the fifth this morning."

His eyes shone as she tied the bandage and secured it with medical tape. "I like you taking care of me."

She lifted her gaze to him and smiled. "Careful. My boyfriend is in the next room operating the MRI machine."

"I don't mind sharing. Does he?"

Sofia put her hands on her hips and glared at him. "I'm not interested, Gordi. So lay off."

He opened his mouth to say something but thought better of it. Instead, he pulled up his pants and zipped them. "Thank you for the bandaging."

"You're welcome." She waited for him to leave the room before letting out a breath.

It was a difficult transition for everyone involved. Gordi wasn't a bad guy, but he wasn't used to not getting his way with the human females. He was making an effort to adjust to the new rules, though, and that was all she could ask for.

It wasn't easy for her either.

She was still gripped by anxiety whenever she had to deal

with pureblooded males, and since the purebloods were getting their trackers removed first, she'd had to deal with five of them just this morning.

A break would be lovely, but they were all pressed for time.

Merlin had organized a production line type of operation, and they were all working in a synchronized manner. Marcel operated the MRI, and when he found the tracker, he called Merlin to show him where it was. Merlin marked the spot on the body, and then the pureblood was moved to one of the beds in the other room to have the tracker removed. Morgada administered the local anesthetic, Merlin dug out the tracker, Inga sewed the incision up, and Sofia put the bandage around it.

"You look tired," Morgada said. "Take a coffee break. I can bandage the next one."

The Kra-ell could keep working for hours without rest, and so could the immortals, but Sofia was still human, and keeping up was impossible.

"Thanks." She smiled at the female. "I need to get off my feet for five minutes."

"Go." Morgada waved her off.

Isla and her father had set up a refreshments table out in the corridor, with coffee, water, and snacks for the humans and immortals, and Marcel had lined up the chairs they had taken out of the converted waiting room along the corridor on both sides of the snack table.

She poured herself a cup, grabbed a granola bar, and as she sat down with a relieved sigh, Isla walked out of the elevator on the other end of the hallway.

"Hello, my talented niece." She walked over to Sofia and sat down next to her. "You're just the person I wanted to see. What do you think about us organizing a dance party tonight after dinner?"

"Who are us? I'm going to be in the clinic all day, so I can't help organize anything."

Isla waved a hand. "Helmi, Lana, and Hannele are helping me, and I can get more people if I need to. I just wanted your opinion. Do you think the liberators would enjoy a dance when there are not enough ladies for them to dance with?"

Everyone loved dancing and needed some fun time to take their minds off the impending attack.

"You can organize line dancing. That way, no one needs a partner."

"That's a fabulous idea."

Marcel came out of the MRI room and poured himself a cup. "Did I hear you talking about dancing?"

Sofia nodded. "Isla wants to organize a party after dinner tonight, but there are not enough ladies for couples' dancing, so I suggested line dancing. Do you think your friends would like it?"

"Some of them know the Scottish sword dance. It's kind of like line dancing, and it's very entertaining, especially when they do it in kilts. Regrettably, we don't have any here." He sat on Sofia's other side.

"Do you know that dance?"

He winced. "I know a few moves, but I'm clumsy and not well coordinated. I'm not going to perform."

"That's a shame." She smiled. "I would have loved seeing you in a kilt." She leaned closer and whispered in his ear, "Is it true that the Scots don't wear anything under them?"

"Not anymore." He wrapped his arm around her. "What about the Kra-ell? Do they have war dances?"

"I think so. Not that I've ever seen them dancing, but I assume that they do."

As Boris arrived to have his tracker extracted with Jade

escorting him, Sofia overcame the spike of anxiety and asked, "Do your people have traditional dances?"

Boris shook his head. "We don't."

"Yes, we do," Jade said. "Back home and in my tribe, the males performed for the females. It was most pleasing, and it got everyone in the mood for the other kind of dancing." She clapped Boris on the back. "The problem is that the only ones left who know the steps are Igor's cronies, and they are all locked up."

Marcel grinned. "Perhaps we could let them out for tonight just to perform for us and teach the young males the steps. It could be a test of sorts to see how well they behave."

Jade looked doubtful. "Are you going to post Guardians with tranquilizer guns to shoot them if they misbehave?"

"I'm sure they are not stupid enough to try anything, but we are not going to take any chances."

"Learning the steps to the dance is not that important," Jade said. "It's not worth the risk of letting them out."

"Are you planning to execute them?" Marcel asked.

She shook her head. "Only Valstar and Igor are on my kill list. The others were not there when my people were slaughtered."

A shiver ran down Sofia's back. Did she care whether Valstar lived or died?

Perhaps she should talk to him.

Heck, she needed to talk to her mother.

They had been avoiding each other for long enough. Perhaps Valstar's impending demise was reason enough for them to finally talk and maybe go visit him while there was still time.

It might be their last chance.

48

JADE

"Are you sure this is a good idea?" Phinas adjusted his holster.

Jade let out a sigh. "Tom assured me that they are under such strong compulsion to obey that they can't go to the bathroom without asking first, and they are the only ones who can teach the young males the dance steps. It would be a shame to lose it."

He arched a brow. "What are your plans for them?"

"They will stand trial, and those they harmed will provide testimony. They weren't among the ones who slaughtered my people, and I don't know if they were involved in the other raids." She stopped in front of the prisoners' cabin.

As the Guardian at the door nodded his greeting and opened the way for them, Phinas put a hand on her shoulder to stop her from going in.

"How have they been behaving?" Phinas reached behind the Guardian and closed the door.

The male shrugged. "Docile as newborn calves. They've been mostly watching television and playing video games.

They asked for alcohol, but we didn't give them any. It might mess with the compulsion."

Jade snorted. "If alcohol had any effect on it, I would have been chugging down gallons to get rid of Igor's compulsion. I assure you that it doesn't."

The guy shrugged again. "My apologies, but my orders are not to provide them with alcoholic beverages."

"No apologies are needed. I was just correcting a misconception. Can we go inside now?"

The Guardian put his hand on the handle. "Let me make sure that they are all seated with their hands in their laps before you go in. Toven commanded them to obey my and the other Guardians' orders."

Jade frowned. "Toven?"

The Guardian's eyes widened, and he looked at Phinas as if asking for his help.

"That's Tom's other name," Phinas explained.

"Is it his nickname?"

"You'll have to ask him." Phinas motioned for the Guardian to get on with it.

When the guy ducked inside and closed the door behind him, Jade turned to Phinas. "Why does he have two different names?"

Phinas's lips curved up on one side. "Why do you call yourself Jade? I'm sure that's not your Kra-ell name. Were you given a shameful name like Emmett?"

"I have my reasons, and I'm not ready to share them with you."

"Why not?"

She was saved from having to answer when the Guardian opened the door and motioned for them to enter.

He followed them inside and took a post near the door that offered him a clear line of sight to all six of them.

Three purebloods sat on the couch, another two on armchairs, and the sixth one on a straight-back chair. They were all motionless, and their expressions were schooled to show no emotion, but she could see the trepidation in their eyes.

"Hello." She walked toward the dining table and pulled out two chairs, one for her and the other for Phinas.

He shook his head. "I'll be right here where I can get a clean shot at each one of them." He remained standing next to the Guardian.

It wasn't necessary, but she liked that he wanted to protect her.

Nodding, she put her chair with its back to the balcony doors and sat down facing the six. "I have a proposition for you," she said in Kra-ell. "The humans are organizing a dance tonight, and you are the only males on board who might know the steps to our traditional dances. I thought it would be a good opportunity for you to teach them."

Rovaj regarded her with defiance in his eyes. "Why? So the knowledge will not be lost when you execute us?"

"I'm not going to execute you. None of you slaughtered my people, and although I have other grievances with you, none of them justifies an execution. You will stand trial, and those you harmed will testify. If their testimony reveals that you partici-pated in the slaughter of other tribes, though, you will be executed." She gave him a cold smile. "I'm giving you a chance to do something nice for the community, which might earn you an honorable death instead."

Voplach lifted his chained hand and smoothed it over his long braid. "I don't know if I still remember the dance steps or the songs that went with them."

"I do," Mored said and started singing.

As the other five joined him, Jade had to fight the tears stinging the backs of her eyes.

It had been so long since she'd heard the song. Her firstborn son had been gifted with a beautiful, deep voice and perfect pitch. She'd loved hearing him sing.

Choking on the lump in her throat, she pushed to her feet, walked over to the bar, filled a glass with tap water, and took a few sips, slowly regaining her composure.

When the males were done, she clapped her hands. "That was very good. You should practice the other songs and the dance steps and get ready to perform tonight."

The consensus was that Igor and his Russian captain would not attack the *Aurora* as long as it was in the Baltic and close to shore. It might be her people's last opportunity to celebrate their freedom.

As all six turned to look at the Guardian, he nodded. "I allow you to practice singing and dancing in preparation for tonight's performance."

49

SOFIA

Sofia hesitated before ringing the doorbell to her mother's cabin.

She hadn't talked with her in years, and it felt awkward as hell to initiate a conversation with the hybrid female who had given birth to her and then abandoned her to the care of her human father and barely acknowledged her existence.

Joanna shared the cabin with another hybrid female, and she might have guests over as well, so they would not have privacy, but maybe they could go on a walk or find a quiet spot on the top deck. Unless Phinas or his men were conducting a swimming lesson, the place was mostly deserted.

Either way, it needed to be done, and she didn't have much time. She was using her lunch break to do this, and she still needed to grab a bite to eat before returning to the clinic.

Sofia took a deep breath and pressed the ringer.

The door opened a moment later. Her mother narrowed her eyes at her. "Sofia, to what do I owe the pleasure?" She looked pointedly at the bun on top of Sofia's head.

One of the few interactions they'd had involved Joanna commenting on Sofia's chosen hairstyle.

"I need to talk to you. Can I come in?"

Her mother opened the door all the way and waved her in.

"Where is your roommate?" Sofia sat down on the couch.

"Eating lunch in the dining room."

"What about you? Are you not hungry?"

Joanna flashed her a pair of fangs in a mockery of a smile. "I don't eat human food."

"I didn't know that." Sofia snorted. "That just demonstrates how little we have interacted over the years. I don't know anything about you."

"There isn't much to know." Joanna sat across from her on an armchair. "I heard that you got engaged. Congratulations."

"Thank you."

"I also heard that Igor sent you on a mission. Did you bring the so-called liberators?"

"So-called? Did you enjoy having your mind under Igor's control?"

"We were freed from one compeller and right away subjugated by another. I'd rather have my mind controlled by one of ours than by a human."

Sofia stifled the urge to release a relieved breath. If her mother hadn't guessed Toven's true identity, then the others hadn't either. As long as they didn't know who their liberators were, their options after Igor was captured were open.

"I prefer the human, and not because I'm human myself. Tom is a kind man. Igor is a monster who slaughtered the males of several Kra-ell tribes. They weren't given a chance to die honorably in battle. He froze them in place and ordered his cronies to cut off their heads. Valstar was one of those who did the killing."

Joanna's face twisted in a grimace. "I have no love lost for Valstar or Igor, but I don't know whether Tom is a good man or not. No one does what he and his friends did out of the goodness of their hearts. They want something from us, and it might be worse than what Igor wanted."

Sofia knew why they came. Igor was a threat to them, and they needed to eliminate him. But the fact was that they'd mobilized their forces to rescue the people of his compound instead of blowing it to pieces and getting rid of him without risking any of their own.

"What do you think they might want from you?"

Joanna regarded her as if she was mentally impaired. "Isn't that obvious? We are a long-lived alien species. They want to study us to find what makes our lives so much longer than humans and what makes us stronger and faster."

"That's not what they want. If that were the case, you wouldn't be enjoying a comfortable cabin on a luxurious cruise ship. You would be locked down in a cage and transported somewhere to be experimented on."

Joanna nodded. "I wondered about that. I figured that they wanted to study us." She waved a hand around the cabin's living room. "This place is probably full of surveillance cameras and listening devices, and they are recording everything we do and say."

"Did you find any?"

"No," Joanna admitted. "They must be very well hidden."

There was no point in continuing that line of conversation. Sofia had come over to talk about Valstar and not their liberators.

"I think that we should go talk to Valstar. It might be our only chance before Jade executes him. Whether we like it or not, he's our blood. Your father and my grandfather."

Joanna's eyes flashed red. "After I gave birth to a human child, he no longer acknowledged my existence. He doesn't think of me as his daughter, and I have nothing to say to him."

Sofia had known that Joanna and Valstar weren't on the

best of terms, but she hadn't known that he had disowned her mother. Perhaps that was why she resented the child that had caused the rift?

"Things that seemed important back in the day seem much less so when one is about to die. He might have changed his mind about it. Also, it's possible that he was ordered by Igor to disown you as a precautionary tale to warn the other females against taking human lovers. You know how important the females were to Igor. He wanted to create a Kra-ell society that was ruled by males, and to do so, he needed to solve the problem of the scarcity of females. That's why he slaughtered the males of the tribes he raided. He also stole their money, but our liberators got some of it back for us."

"I've heard." Joanna grimaced. "I doubt we will get any of it."

This was getting tiresome.

Sofia wasn't the clan's ambassador to her people, and it wasn't her job to defend them. It was Jade's.

"I'm sure we will, but I'm not here to defend the people who saved us. Do you want to accompany me to see Valstar or not?"

Joanna hesitated for a brief moment before nodding. "I'll come with you. He'll probably ask me to leave, but I'll give him one last chance."

50

PHINAS

"*T*he seating will be cramped." Phinas pushed the table further toward the wall. "But that's the best we can do if we want to clear a large enough area in the middle for dancing."

The ship had a club room with a dance floor and a bar, but it could accommodate only up to a hundred people, so it wouldn't work. It also had a theater and several conference rooms, but none of them were suitable. The dance had to be held in the dining hall.

Dandor adjusted the chairs and looked at the work the rest of the men had accomplished so far. "Not everyone will want to dance. We don't have enough ladies." He sighed. "It reminds me of the old days before we moved into the village, and I don't miss those days."

Phinas smiled. "Do you have someone special?"

Dandor grinned. "I have several someones."

That was surprising. Dandor wasn't the best-looking guy, and his charm could also use some work. He was intelligent but not well-read, and his fields of interest were race cars and football. He was also shy and awkward around women, but the clan ladies had no problem initiating, which seemed to work well for him.

Was he really that popular, though? Or was he exaggerating?

Perhaps he was an exceptional lover whose reputation preceded him.

The clan ladies were enjoying Kalugal's men and vice versa, but they weren't forming long-term relationships because none had found their true-love mates. Immortals were naturally promiscuous, and usually remained so even when married. The females didn't want to get addicted to one male's venom, and frequently changing bed partners was the best way to avoid that.

Still, it was odd that no one other than Rufsur and Edna had found each other and bonded. Perhaps it was because suddenly the clan females and Kalugal's men had a selection of potential immortal partners and did not want to commit to one before they sampled all that was available.

At least that was what Phinas had believed before meeting Jade.

He knew better now.

It was like the puzzle pieces had fallen into place, and he knew deep in his gut that she was the one for him. It didn't make sense, and it was probably one-sided, but Phinas wasn't afraid of challenges, even one as formidable as Jade.

It might take a while, and there might be obstacles the size of mountains in his way, but somehow he would make her his.

Regrettably that hadn't happened for his men, and none had found their fated mate among the clan ladies, which was disappointing.

When everything was done and all the tables were pushed away from the center, the dining room still didn't look much different or significantly more festive than it had before. The tables were covered in white tablecloths, and colorful cloth napkins were arranged to look like flowers and tucked inside wine glasses, but those were the only enhancements the humans had come up with from what they could find aboard the ship.

No one would be dressed up either, with the exception of Mey and Jin, who might have brought some evening attire with them, but Phinas doubted that.

Would Jade come up with something inventive like she had done with the swimming tops she'd made from his shirt?

If she used any more of his clothes, he would have to launder the shirt he had on every night and put it on the following day, but he was willing to endure that for her.

Hell, he was willing to endure much more, but for now that was all he could offer her.

When Jade strode into the dining room in her usual garb of cargo pants, a tight-fitting shirt, military boots, and her long black hair gathered in a ponytail, she couldn't have looked more beautiful to him if she had been wearing an evening gown and diamonds.

She was the most stunning female in the room, attracting everyone's attention as if she were the queen of the ball.

He waved her over to his table, and as she smiled at him, his damn heart skipped a bit.

What was he? A teenage boy with his first crush?

Hell, he'd never had the chance to have a teenage crush because his teenage years had been spent in a training camp, and when he was seventeen, he'd been taken to the brothel and lost his virginity to a woman twice his age or more.

He still smiled when he thought back on the clumsy boy he had been. The woman had been kind and patient with him, and he'd fallen in love with her as young men tend to do with the first female they have sex with.

Perhaps that experience had influenced his lifelong preference for mature, experienced women.

When Jade made it to the table, he pushed to his feet and pulled out the chair he'd saved for her, the one that had its back to the wall and faced the dance area and the entrance to the dining room.

"You know me so well." She gave him a brilliant smile as if he had greeted her with flowers. "Thank you for reserving the best seat for me, but I should sit with my people tonight."

"You are sitting with your people. Kagra, Drova, Pavel, and Piotr are going to join us."

He'd arranged it so she would enjoy her evening to the fullest without having to choose between those dear to her.

"What about your people?" Jade asked.

"There are four more seats at the table. Dandor and Chad reserved their spots, and the other two can go to whoever comes first."

51

JADE

*a*t precisely eight o'clock in the evening, the six members of Igor's pod entered the dining hall. They weren't in chains, but four armed Guardians escorted them.

Murmurs arose all around, mainly from the other purebloods and the hybrids who knew who they were. The humans might not have known the difference between these males and the purebloods who had been born in the compound, but they should have noticed that Igor's inner circle members hadn't worn collars on their necks, while the others had them unless they were going out on missions.

Given that they all had implanted trackers, the tracking devices inside the collars had been redundant, but the collars had also contained explosives. If anyone tried to run, Igor could have activated them remotely. Except, he hadn't attempted that even after he'd realized the compound had been compromised, probably because he believed he could get his people back.

Jade rose to her feet and walked to the center of the room. "Allow me to present tonight's entertainment." She waved her hand at the six males standing in a straight line. "Madbar,

Shover, Rodof, Berdogh, Mored, and Voplach will demonstrate several dances from our homeland. Traditionally, males performed these dances to entertain and entice females during festivals, but Igor squashed that custom the same way he did every other time-honored tradition of the Kra-ell. I encourage all the Kra-ell males to form lines behind the performers to learn the steps. Everyone else is welcome to join in singing the songs."

Drova raised her hand. "What if I want to learn the dance moves? Am I not allowed because I'm a female?"

Patience. Jade schooled her features to hide her annoyance.

She'd decided to be flexible and listen to what the people wanted, but it was difficult when her own daughter was challenging tradition.

Perhaps that wasn't a bad thing, though. Her people were at a turning point, and they could create new customs that would take all the positive things from the old ones and improve on them.

There was no reason to prevent females from learning the dance moves or even performing them for the males if they wished. Pragmatically, there was no need for the females to entice the males, but dancing was enjoyable whether it had a purpose or not.

Jade forced a smile. "It's not a question of being allowed or not. Traditionally, the dances are performed by males, but if you want to learn the moves, you are welcome to do so." She switched to English and repeated what she'd just said.

When she was done, Jade turned to the males. "You may begin."

Mored tapped his foot three times on the floor, and on the third tap, the six started singing, their deep male voices reverberating off the walls.

As the sound cut through her heart and reopened old

wounds that had never healed and were still bleeding, Jade sat down next to Phinas and kept her expression neutral.

He put his hand on her thigh under the tablecloth. "Are you okay?" he whispered.

"I'm fine. The song evokes bittersweet memories."

"I bet." He gave her thigh a gentle squeeze before removing his hand.

He probably thought that the song reminded her of home, which it had, but the pain he must have felt radiating from her had nothing to do with her missing the place of her birth. She missed her sons, and she missed the males who had fathered them and the other children of her tribe.

Perhaps she wasn't the strong Kra-ell leader she was pretending to be. Or perhaps the many years she'd lived on Earth had changed her. Kra-ell mothers were supposed to be proud of the sons they lost in battle. They were allowed to grieve for them and to seek revenge, but they were not supposed to dream of a world in which their children didn't have to fight at all.

They were also not supposed to choose one male over all others. It wasn't fair, and the right thing was for a female to rotate between the males she had selected for her tribe.

Jade hadn't selected hers, she hadn't even known them before they were put in the same pod, but she'd grown to care for them nonetheless.

What she felt for Phinas, though, wasn't what she'd felt for them. She wanted to be with him and no one else, and that was very un-Kra-ell of her.

It was shameful, disturbing, disquieting, and yet she couldn't bring herself to push him away. Her excuse was that she needed Phinas to get information on the inner workings of the clan, and she would cling to that excuse when challenged, but deep in her soul, she knew that wasn't the real reason she was still with him.

52

PHINAS

*T*he wave of misery that had leaked from Jade when the males had started their performance had been so intense that Phinas had gotten ready to shield her if she burst into tears, but his female was made from titanium alloy, and she'd pushed through the pain.

Her mood had gradually lifted, and now she was smiling, clapping, and stomping her feet to the beat along with him and everyone else who wasn't on the dance floor.

Nearly two hours had passed since the performance had started, and although the males' routine had lasted no more than fifteen minutes, they had spent the rest of the time teaching the steps and the songs that went with them to everyone who wanted to learn, and that included humans, Guardians, and his men.

The purebloods were either good sports or didn't want to go back to the confinement of their cabin.

The Kra-ell language reminded him of the imagined Klingon language, the melody was catching, and the dance moves were aggressive, mimicking fighting, but there was a certain grace to them. They also required agility and flexibility that the humans had a hard time accomplishing, even the young ones.

Still, everyone seemed to be having great fun.

He leaned toward Jade. "Do you want to get up and dance?"

Kagra was on the dance floor with Dandor, Drova, and Pavel, and when Max had joined their line, he'd gotten between Kagra and Dandor, which hadn't made Dandor happy.

"I'd rather stay here and supply the beat." Jade kept clapping and stomping. "Someone needs to do that."

"There are enough someones." Phinas rose to his feet and offered her a hand up. "Come on. It looks like fun."

"Females are not supposed to participate in these dances. I allowed the others to join if they wish, but I shouldn't."

"Why not?" He waved a hand at the dance floor. "Look at all the ladies enjoying themselves."

Yamanu was there with Mey, and so were Jin and Arwel. Toven had tried to persuade Mia to let him carry her and join the dance in his arms, but she had vehemently refused and was now watching her mate dance and clapping her hands to the beat.

"I'm not a good dancer." Jade lifted her drink and took a sip. "But you go ahead. You look like you're itching to join in."

"Not without you." He leaned to whisper in her ear, "You don't want your people to think that their leader is a dry stick. They need to see you having fun."

When Jade took the bait and took his hand, Phinas stifled a smile. He knew what buttons to push to make her do the things he believed she should.

"Finally!" Kagra said when the two of them joined the line.

She pushed Pavel toward Drova and pulled Jade next to her. "Watch my feet and follow my lead."

Phinas squeezed in on Jade's other side. After watching the steps for two hours, he had the routine memorized, and as he and Jade threaded arms to perform the kicks and flips, they moved in synchronized perfection.

The smile on Jade's face was priceless, and the longer they danced, the wider it got.

Somehow, Max got to the center of the dance floor and waving his hands shouted, "Everyone who knows the sword dance, please come forward. It's our turn to show them how it's done."

Yamanu, Arwel, and some of the other Guardians joined them, and as they started their Scottish sword dance, it took the Kra-ell males mere minutes to follow the complicated foot-work. It took the humans a little longer, and some were still fumbling the steps, but it just evoked more laughter and more mirth.

"This is nice," Jade said breathlessly. "All of our people joining to celebrate."

"Isn't that ironic?" Drova said. "The enemies of yesterday are leading today's fun."

Jade's smile vanished, but she didn't respond to her daughter's taunt.

Another hour passed before people started drifting back to their tables to get drinks from the open bar.

"What do you want us to do with the dancers?" Max asked Jade. "Can they be given drinks?"

She nodded. "They earned them. Let them sit at a table and bring them a couple of bottles to share between them. After they are done drinking, take them back to their cabin. Please," she tucked on at the end.

Max grinned as he saluted her. "Yes, ma'am."

"I like him," Kagra said. "Maybe I'll invite him to my bed tonight."

Drova clapped her on the back. "Why maybe? Go for it." She turned to look at Jade. "Right, Mother?"

Jade glared at her. "You are too young to make comments about things like that."

"I'm sixteen, not six."

Jade had told him that the age of consent for males was twenty, but she'd never told him what it was for females. Was it the same?

"You are not having sex until you are at least twenty!"

Apparently, it was the same.

As mother and daughter argued, Phinas hid his smile by turning to Dandor. "Did you enjoy yourself?"

Dandor made a sour face. "I did until a moment ago." He cast a look at Kagra, who got up and headed toward the bar, where Max was collecting bottles for the Kra-ell. "What does Max have that I don't?"

Phinas chuckled. "The question is what he doesn't have that you do, and that's fear of rejection."

"I'm not afraid of anything." Dandor pushed to his feet and headed toward Kagra.

53

ONEGUS

"We have a decoy vessel," Turner said as he put his phone down. "It's an old cruise ship for sale that's currently docked at the port of Copenhagen. As cruise ships go, it's small, with room for one hundred passengers and forty-eight crew. In other words, it's large enough to pass the plausibility test. Our aim is to make it look as if all the purebloods and some of the hybrids are on board."

Kian regarded Turner accusingly, pretending dismay, "You bought us another cruise ship, Victor?"

Onegus didn't miss *The Hunt for Red October* reference, and it pulled a chuckle out of him, but Turner didn't even smile, and it wasn't as if he was too young to have seen the movie. The guy was in his forties, so he was a kid when it first came out, but it was a classic, and people watched it years after its release.

At times, Onegus wasn't sure whether Turner was impervious to humor or was just having fun keeping a straight face. If so, he played the part pretty damn convincingly.

"I didn't buy it," Turner said. "I leased the boat for a month at a great price under the pretext that we represent a potential buyer who wants our professional opinion on the ship's condition and value. I should have the paperwork ready for review and approval within a couple of hours, and as soon as we wire the funds and bind insurance coverage, we can get it prepped for departure. We are even getting it fully fueled."

Kian grimaced. "I'm sure they are charging us for the fuel. It's so damn expensive to fill up the tanks on those things."

This time a smile lifted one corner of Turner's lips. "Naturally, but the price for the rental itself is symbolic. They really want to get rid of the old clunker."

Onegus could tell that there was an undertone to the delivery hinting of a 'but' to follow. "What's the catch?"

"There is no catch, but there is a disadvantage that might actually turn out to be an advantage." Turner glanced at his notes. "The ship's maximum speed is fourteen knots. That's a snail's pace compared to Igor's yacht, which can cruise at thirty-seven knots. So outrunning Igor is not in the cards, and neither is choosing the where and when of the battle. It's going to be on his terms, or rather what he thinks are his terms. We are going to outsmart him."

Kian shook his head. "The bastard is always one step ahead of us. We had the element of surprise, superior technology, and greater manpower, and yet Igor is still calling the shots in this cat-and-mouse game we are playing. I can't wait for you to explain how having a slow vessel is an advantage."

A shadow of a smile appeared on Turner's stoic face. "We have a helicopter, so outrunning Igor or choosing the time and location of engagement are not as important as luring him in and encouraging him to engage without raising his suspicions. And that is exactly what we will achieve with this boat. It can accommodate nearly all of his people, which would have been a hard sell with a yacht and would have given him pause. It is also a larger vessel, making it very unlikely that Igor will opt to take it over by forcing his way onboard. He will have to resort to firing on the decoy with the intent of disabling or sinking it."

"How is that an advantage?" Kian asked. "It's exactly what we were trying to avoid, and also the reason we were looking for a smaller vessel and not another cruise ship."

"I know that's counterintuitive, but it might work in our favor. His yacht might be equipped with hand-held rocket launchers, but it's doubtful to have torpedo capability. I assume he will have to slow down to align his yacht with the cruise ship for the kill shot, telegraphing his intent and timing. This will give our pilot an advantage by allowing him to approach Igor's yacht from the rear while Igor's attention is focused on the ship in front of him."

Kian regarded Turner with a doubtful expression on his face. "Since the trackers will move to another cruise ship, and Igor will assume that his people are on the decoy, he will command the Russian to leave the *Aurora* and follow it instead. That's good because we can get the Kra-ell safely away. But I'm worried about the risk to our people on board the decoy."

Turner's smug smile reminded Onegus of a cat that just ate a mouse. "He will not command the *Anatolov* to leave the *Aurora* and follow the decoy for two reasons. The decoy will hug the coast, so launching a torpedo at it to sink it doesn't make sense any more than launching it at the *Aurora* before it's in the open sea. If we could remove all the trackers before reaching Copenhagen and transfer all of them to the decoy, he might have commanded the Russian to stand down because it was no longer needed. But since we can't remove them all in time, and some will remain on board the *Aurora* before Marcel can activate the signal scrambler, Igor will not allow them to get away. If he can't get them back, he'd rather kill them along with the people who took them. He can't let them fall into the hands of other Kra-ell or humans who will experiment on them.

Thinking that the decoy has most of his people, he will go after it with the yacht and command the Russian to sink the larger cruise ship."

"Brilliant," Kian murmured.

"Thank you." Turner leaned back and crossed his arms over his chest. "Turning circumstances from disadvantageous into advantageous is very satisfying to me."

Onegus narrowed his eyes at the strategist. "You weren't looking for a yacht and settled on an old boat instead. You were actually looking for this type of vessel when you finalized your plan."

"Correct."

"Why didn't you tell us?" Kian asked.

Onegus snorted. "So you'd call him brilliant."

Turner's ego had taken several blows during the planning of this mission, and he needed to get it back to where it had been before, with everyone admiring him and calling him a strategic genius.

"I don't need ego boosters," Turner said. "I wasn't sure I'd be able to find the kind of vessel I was looking for, and I didn't want to get you two excited for nothing."

KIAN

*a*t first glance Turner's plan seemed brilliant, but the more Kian thought about it, the more his confidence in it wavered. A lot was based on assumptions and guesswork trying to anticipate Igor's moves, but the guy had been proven difficult to predict.

If the decoy hugged the coast, he would not choose to sink the vessel for the same reason he hadn't told the Russian cruiser to attack the *Aurora* yet. Rescue helicopters would arrive too quickly for him to collect his people.

On the other hand, he couldn't board the decoy and compel its passengers as long as the decoy was moving. Given his Kra-ell super strength, he could potentially leap onboard along with a couple of his cronies, provided that the vessels were matched in speed and course and provided that the decoy vessel's deck was not too high. But without knowing the force he'd meet onboard, that would not be wise, and Igor was not the kind of guy who made unwise decisions.

"I don't think Igor will attempt to sink the decoy. At least not initially." Kian proceeded to explain his reasoning. "Sinking the decoy vessel so close to shore would not give him enough time to do what he needs to do and would expose him to the risk of being shot at by the Norwegian Navy or Air Force. His likely initial move would therefore be to try and compel whoever is on board. If successful, and he should have no reason to suspect that he won't be, he could board the vessel at his leisure and assume command."

Turner tilted his head. "I agree that it would be his most likely first move. But if we are planning on luring him in and disabling his yacht, does it really matter what happens when he realizes that he cannot compel the crew?"

Turner's question was clearly rhetorical, but Onegus answered it anyway, "The effective range for him to compel everyone onboard the decoy, and especially those on the bridge, is limited. He needs to be close enough for the sound waves of his voice to reach them. My guess is that he will attempt to get within one hundred meters of the boat to do so, or even closer if the sea is rough or the weather stormy."

Kian drummed his fingers on the table. "Why do we need to wait for Igor to make his move, though? We can have the helicopter fire at him long before that and be done with it. We just need to lure him far enough up the coast of Norway, where there is barely any population so there are no witnesses." As the wheels in his mind kept spinning, he continued drumming his fingers. "I assume that Igor will issue a distress call, but even if he does, we can collect him and his cohorts from the yacht before the search and rescue parties arrive at the scene. Grabbing four people is not as time-consuming as grabbing nearly two hundred. I also suggest that we have the helicopter fire on the yacht as soon as it is safe to do so. I want us to choose the time and location."

"We don't know what weapons Igor has on board," Turner said. "If he has shoulder-mounted missiles as we suspect, he can shoot at the helicopter. Those rockets are not accurate, and it's hard to hit a moving target with them, but he might get lucky, and we can't risk that. The helicopter is equipped with superior guided missiles that are not going to miss, and our best bet is to keep Igor focused on the decoy while the helicopter approaches from his aft and fires a killing shot."

Kian groaned. "There are too many ifs for my liking."

"Nothing is ever guaranteed," Onegus said. "But we can improve our odds by not waiting for events to unfold and force the outcome we want. Igor either gets close to try and compel, and we launch a missile at him first, or he doesn't, and we fake a mechanical issue slowing the decoy to a crawl. That will lure him closer, and then we fire. It's great if we hit him, but not necessary. The idea is to keep him focused on the ship in front of him while missing the danger from behind."

Kian found a gaping hole in Onegus's logic. "How? Until he's ready to attack, he won't get close enough to be in range even if the decoy vessel slows down to a crawl. In fact, being as careful and paranoid as he's proved himself to be, he will probably suspect a trap and be more likely to keep his distance."

Onegus smirked. "We make him get in range. We transfer the disruptor to the decoy, and we activate it when the boat is not in Igor's line of sight yet. He will freak out and have no choice but to get closer to investigate. Even if he suspects it's a trap, he won't turn around and abandon the pursuit. He's too invested by now. And even if he does, we can still get him with the helicopter."

Turner shook his head. "Again, we can't risk the helicopter like that. Without a proper distraction, Igor will see it coming and shoot at it."

"What if the decoy just stops?" Kian asked. "It can pretend a malfunction. After all, it's an old clunker. It can even signal an SOS, claiming loss of power. Losing the signals from the trackers at the same time the ship breaks down may prove odd enough for him to want to get closer to investigate."

"I love it," Onegus said. "He'll probably think that his people tried to overpower their captors, and we killed them all, and that's why the trackers stopped transmitting."

"No, he won't." Turner let out a sigh. "Don't forget that we are also transferring some of the human-made trackers on board the decoy, and they would have continued transmitting even after their hosts were dead. I believe Kian's prior assumption that Igor will get closer on his own accord is correct. His aim will be to compel everyone on board."

Kian felt smug for a brief moment, but the truth was that he hadn't suggested anything that hadn't been discussed before in one way or another.

In fact, all the different scenarios and possibilities were scrambled in his head, and he needed a few quiet moments alone to sort it all out. But perhaps Turner's analytical brain had already done that.

Leaning back, Kian looked at the strategist. "So, what's our next step, Victor?"

"I need to make a few phone calls. Can we continue in half an hour?"

It seemed that Turner also needed time to organize his thoughts.

"No problem." Kian pushed to his feet. "I could use a walk in the fresh air and a cup of good coffee." He looked at Onegus. "Do you want to join me at the café?"

The Chief shook his head. "I have a few things I need to go over as well."

Kian nodded. "I'll see you both in half an hour."

SOFIA

*a*s Sofia walked out of the elevator with her mother, she was surprised to find Toven standing outside Valstar's cabin.

"I hope you don't mind me butting in." He pushed away from the wall. "After you asked me for permission to see Valstar, it occurred to me that you might need my help to get truthful answers from him. He can't lie to me. "

Joanna snorted. "He can still manipulate you. My father is very smart."

"Your English is very good." Toven regarded her briefly. "Your daughter must have inherited her talent for languages from you." He smiled. "She definitely didn't inherit it from Jarmo."

If Toven hoped to get some response from Joanna by bringing up Jarmo's name, he would be disappointed. Joanna had never cared for him, and she hadn't expected to get pregnant. Then again, she had engaged with him while in her fertile cycle, so maybe she had?

But why? What had she tried to prove?

"We both got the talent from Valstar," her mother said. "Can we go in now? I want to be done with this."

"What do you want to achieve by speaking with your father?"

Joanna closed her eyes and let out a sigh. "I want to make my peace with him before he dies. He might not want me there, though. He has a better relationship with Sofia than he has with me, which is ironic given that our falling out was because of her."

Sofia's ire ignited as if Joanna had thrown a match into a vat of gasoline. "It's not my fault that you wanted to piss off your father by taking a human to your bed. I'm the result of your actions. And even if you didn't have me, what kind of a relationship did you expect to have with the pureblood who fathered you? In his eyes, you are an inferior. Not only because you're a hybrid but because you are a female. Back on the home planet, where females ruled, that would have been an advantage, but not in Igor's camp."

She'd wanted to say that for so long to get back at her mother for all the years of neglect, but up until now Joanna had never admitted the reason for her indifference.

The truth was that the purebloods didn't interact much with the children they produced with human females, so Valstar's and Joanna's lack of a relationship wasn't unusual. But the hybrids were more accepting of their children.

Many of the hybrid males didn't want to produce human offspring, using protection to ensure that they didn't procreate with the humans they took to their beds, and there had been very few children born to them. Aside from Sofia, all the others were males, and they had some sort of relationship with their fathers. The hybrid males who had sons couldn't get too close to them without undermining their position in the Kra-ell society, but none pretended that their children didn't exist, like Joanna had done.

"I can't argue with that," her mother said. "I hope things will be different under Jade's rule, and the purebloods will treat the hybrids better. As Sofia pointed out, we didn't choose to be born. The choice belongs to our parents, and they should take responsibility for the results of their actions." She looked at Toven. "Can we please go in?"

That was as close to an apology as Sofia could expect. It wasn't enough to douse the fire burning inside her, but it sufficed to smother it to a mere smolder.

"Yes, of course." Toven rang the bell.

A Guardian opened the door and motioned for them to come in. "He's ready for you."

"Good afternoon." Valstar smiled at them. "What a special treat it is to get a visit from my daughter and granddaughter. Please, sit down."

He looked no worse for wear, but his attitude was unrecognizable. It was disconcerting to hear Valstar talk like a human grandfather.

Had Toven compelled him before their arrival?

"How are they treating you?" Joanna asked in Russian.

"As well as can be expected for a prisoner awaiting his execution."

Toven pulled out a chair from the dining table and brought it over. "I spoke with Jade and asked her to consider allowing you to stand trial."

Valstar's eyes flickered green with hope. "Who will be the judge?"

"It remains to be decided, and Jade hasn't given me her answer yet."

Valstar dipped his head. "Thank you for doing this for me."

"You're welcome. Now I want you to answer Joanna's and

Sofia's questions truthfully. Don't lie to them, and don't try to manipulate them."

Sofia could feel the compulsion even though it hadn't been directed at her, and given Joanna's shiver, she'd felt it too.

Looking like a new male, Valstar cast them a bright smile. "What do you want to know?"

"Did you ever care for me?" Joanna asked.

"Of course, I care. You are my daughter. But it's not the Kra-ell way to show emotions. You're half human, so your need for coddling is greater than that of a pureblooded child, and your mother supplied that in excess. You were always rebellious and did not show proper respect to your elders like the other hybrid children did. Then you took a human lover, which you did for the sole purpose of getting a rise out of me. When you got pregnant, and none of the pureblooded or hybrid males claimed your child, making it obvious that the child was fathered by a human, I had to beg Igor not to punish you. He wanted to whip you in front of the entire community to scare the other females from taking humans to their beds."

Joanna's eyes widened. "He wanted to whip me while I was carrying a child?"

"You disobeyed the rules, and you should have been punished. You escaped punishment thanks to my intervention. I told Igor that you were mentally unstable and incapable of proper Kra-ell behavior."

Her mother's shoulders stiffened. "That could have cost me my life. If Igor thought I was defective, he could have executed me."

Valstar shook his head. "I knew that he would never execute a female. You were too valuable, and your womb could still produce other children regardless of your mental instability."

"That was smart," Sofia said. "You found a way to manipulate Igor."

"Regrettably, to a minimal extent." Valstar sighed. "I did what I could."

"What about me?" Sofia asked. "Did you care for me?"

"Naturally. How do you think you got to spend nearly eight years in the university? I convinced Igor that we needed a linguist and suggested you. I told him that as my granddaughter, you had an exceptional talent for languages."

"Thank you. I loved the university. But when you trained me for the mission, you didn't act as if you even liked me, and when I told you that I had a heart problem, you were dismissive."

Valstar nodded. "As I said before, the Kra-ell don't show emotions, but that wasn't the only reason I didn't express my concern when you told me about your fake heart problem. Igor had all the phones tapped, and he often listened to my conversations. I suspected that you were lying, but I couldn't confront you about it without undermining us both."

KIAN

*W*hen Kian returned from his coffee break, Onegus nodded in greeting, and Turner swiveled his chair around and looked at him. "Did William get back to you about the gerbils?"

Kian had forgotten about that. Since nothing major had been happening the day before and they had just been waiting for Turner to find a decoy vessel, he'd used the time to catch up on work and spend time with his family.

"He did." Kian pulled out a chair and sat down. "The trackers work even when implanted in gerbils."

"Good." Turner swiveled his chair back to face the table and tapped his pen on his yellow pad. "I've already spoken with Captain Olsson and told him about the refueling stop in Copenhagen. I've also spoken with Merlin, and he said that all the purebloods he's scanned so far had the alien trackers. I asked him to scan several of the hybrids to check what kind of trackers they had, and all those he tested had human-made ones that don't require a living host to operate. After doing some math, though, I figured that Igor must have more of those alien trackers than the number of purebloods, so Merlin might find more of them among the hybrids he hasn't checked yet. It's also possible that Igor is keeping the alien trackers for the pureblooded children to be implanted when they reach maturity and for those yet to be born."

Kian lifted his hand to stop Turner from continuing. "I'm very interested in hearing that math."

Turner flipped to the previous page on his yellow pad. "I asked Yamanu to sit down with Jade and go over the number of purebloods in her community and who came from where. There were eighty-seven adult purebloods in the compound, of which seventy-eight are on board the *Aurora*. Fifty of them are females, but only twelve were born in the compound. The other forty came from other tribes. Out of the forty, four came from Igor's pod, and twenty-five came from other pods. The remaining eleven were born in the other tribes. If we assume that most pods contained four females and sixteen males, then to obtain the twenty-five females, Igor had killed ninety-six original settler males and extracted their trackers. Since only fifty-three purebloods were born in his compound, and eleven Earth-born females came from other tribes, Igor still had about thirty-two alien trackers to spare. The question is what he did with them. We know that he put one in Sofia, but the two hybrids that were assigned to her had simple trackers in them. My bet is that he saved the rest for the pureblooded children and special missions like the one he sent Sofia on."

"Makes sense," Onegus said. "So, given that fascinating math exercise, how many gerbils do we need?"

"Merlin said that he can extract trackers from about sixty of the purebloods, so sixty gerbils, or maybe a little more just in case some don't make it. I don't know how resilient gerbils are."

"What about the kids?" Onegus asked. "He might have implanted them already. Would there have been a reason for him to wait until they were fully grown?"

"It's irrelevant whether they do or don't. Merlin can extract about sixty trackers by the time the ship docks in Copenhagen and no more. It doesn't matter who he extracts them from."

"Right." Onegus nodded. "We need to get the gerbils to Merlin by tomorrow afternoon." He cast an amused sidelong glance at Kian. "You should be happy that we don't need to get sixty cats. The gerbils don't take a lot of space and can be kept in a cage."

"Cages," Turner corrected. "They can't be all clustered in the same spot. The Guardians will have to distribute them around the ship."

"Can you take care of that as well?" Onegus asked. "Or should I do that?"

Kian wondered how one went about getting sixty gerbils in Copenhagen, but he was confident in Turner's ability to do so.

"I'll have my secretary arrange that." Turner flipped to the most recent page on his yellow pad. "It might be a good idea to get Mey and Jin off the *Aurora* while she's docking in Copenhagen. I wish we could have gotten the humans and the children off as well, but we can't. The adults still have trackers in them, and we won't have time to remove them. We also don't have time to prepare fake passports, even for the children. Copenhagen's international airport is modern and sophisticated, and we won't be able to smuggle people out through it on a commercial flight or even on a chartered plane. There are too many security cameras and fail-safes."

"Mey and Jin will refuse to leave." Onegus turned to Kian. "Not unless you order them to disembark. Since it's a security issue, you can use it as an excuse."

"Not really. If I don't order Mia to leave, then I can't order them. And in any case, I wouldn't do that. I'm not risking getting in trouble with Jin."

Onegus chuckled, thinking it had been a joke, but Kian was

serious. That girl's talent was scary, and with her contrary character, the Fates knew what she was capable of when feeling slighted.

"Mia can also disembark," Turner said. "And even Toven. His compulsion over the Kra-ell will hold until the *Aurora* arrives at Greenland. He and Mia can fly there and wait for the ship to arrive, and if they do that, Mey and Jin might choose to accompany them."

"I'll talk with him." Kian swiveled his chair to face Turner. "The next thing we need to figure out is what to do once we get Igor and his men, either dead or alive. Even if the decoy remains intact after the confrontation, it can't catch up to the *Aurora*, so we have to fly our men out of Norway, either to meet up with the others in Greenland or back home."

"By the way, the decoy's name is the *Seafarer*." Turner flipped through his yellow pad until he found what he was looking for. "The helicopter is capable of transporting twelve fully armed soldiers. Assuming that it is still operational and didn't get hit, it can fly them to a nearby airfield in two trips. I can arrange a chartered plane to pick them up from there, but it will be much easier to arrange a flight to Greenland than to fly them all the way back to Los Angeles. We've already made arrangements to pick everyone up from Greenland, but I still need to supply them with a final destination." He looked at Kian. "Did you decide where we are taking the Kra-ell and their humans?"

"It depends on whether we catch Igor. If we do, I'll put the Kra-ell inclusion in the village up for a vote. But since I need the big assembly's unanimous approval, it will have to wait until the Guardians are back."

"We need to put them somewhere in the meantime," Onegus said. "We don't have enough space in the keep, and we rented out all the apartments in the building across from it. Any ideas?"

Kian shook his head. "Not yet, but I will come up with something."

"What about our fake campsite?" Turner asked. "It's already fenced off and equipped with William's security system. We already have twenty-seven mobile homes parked there, but there is enough room to double the number. It will not be comfortable, and they will be cramped for a few days, but it will give us some breathing room until we find a different solution."

The campsite had been built close to the tunnel entrance leading to the village to explain the extra traffic on the road. Housing over three hundred people in there would attract too much attention, but it could work as a temporary solution.

PHINAS

*W*hen Onegus and Kian finished explaining their newest plan, Yamanu looked at Phinas. "I don't have enough Guardians I can assign to the decoy. I will need some of your men, but I will lead the mission. I can leave Arwel in charge."

Phinas shook his head. "I'm going to the decoy with my men. Your Guardians are much better at babysitting the Kra-ell than my men and I are, so they need to stay on the *Aurora*."

Phinas had thirty men with him, and Yamanu had only sixteen Guardians, including Arwel, who was technically on vacation. Together with the two of them, their force was forty-eight warriors strong—too small to secure the Kra-ell on board the *Aurora* and to go after Igor, but it would have to do. He would capture the bastard for Jade and bring him hogtied to her so she could chop off his head while he was immobilized.

There was no greater gift he could give her.

Yamanu flashed him a toothy smile. "Thank you for the offer, but I insist on having Guardians on board the *Seafarer*. You can contribute half of yours, and I'll contribute half of mine."

That was reasonable, except for the fact that it would be difficult for him to choose who would go and who would stay, and those that stayed would have to assist the remaining Guardians babysitting the Kra-ell.

"Fine, but I lead the mission. I'll transfer command of my remaining men to you."

Nodding, Yamanu turned to the tablet to get the Chief's approval.

"That's fine with me," Onegus said. "In fact, that was what I wanted to suggest." He looked at Phinas. "You seem confident in your ability to face Igor and capture or eliminate him, and so far, you've done exceptionally well on this mission. That being said, it has been many years since you've led men into battle. Are you sure that you can handle the task?"

"I'm sure. For better or worse, the training I received was hardwired into me. My instincts and response times are still excellent."

Phinas was also a fast thinker and a decent strategist, but he didn't want to toot his own horn. Actions spoke louder than words, and he would prove his worth by delivering Igor to Jade.

Onegus nodded. "Agreed. You lead the mission with half of your force and half of Yamanu's. Max will lead the Guardians, but he will answer to you."

Phinas nodded.

"Let's move to the next item." Onegus shifted his focus to Toven. "Since we are docking at Copenhagen, you and Mia can get off and either fly home or to Greenland to meet up with the *Aurora* when she arrives."

"Why would we want to do that?"

Kian leaned forward. "Because you have a Russian cruiser on your ass. Don't you want to get your mate out of harm's way?"

"She won't go unless I do, and I don't feel comfortable abandoning these people. My compulsion will hold until they get to Greenland, but I prefer to stay on the *Aurora* in case the unexpected happens. Especially since half of the force is transferring to the decoy."

"He has a point," Turner said.

Kian let out a breath. "Then I guess I shouldn't suggest the same to Jin and Mey."

"Probably not," Yamanu said. "But I'll give it a try. Arwel can go back with them as well. He's not on official duty on the *Aurora*, and if I'm not leaving to lead the force on the *Seafarer*, he doesn't need to stay."

"I'm putting him back on official duty," Onegus said. "You need him."

Yamanu nodded. "That I do."

"Next." Onegus glanced at his notes. "As soon as the Aurora docks in Copenhagen, you will receive a crate that will be marked as live lobsters. But instead of lobsters, it will be packed with sixty-five gerbils for Merlin to implant the alien trackers in. Get it to him as soon as possible. I've already spoken to him about arranging an assembly line for that purpose. Once all the gerbils are implanted, they will be put back in the same crate and transferred to the *Seafarer* along with other provisions for the voyage. We will do the same with the other supply crates, except the other ones will be empty when they leave for the *Seafarer*. We want Igor to think that we smuggled his people out in them, so they will be making the rounds for most of the day. Any questions about that?"

"What about food for the gerbils?" Yamanu asked.

"There will be food for them in the crate," Turner said. "They will be delivered in individual small cages, and the food will be inside. When you take them out of the crate on the decoy, spread them throughout the ship in a way that you would've spread out people."

Yamanu still looked worried about the critters. "Won't they be making a racket, chirping and scratching, or whatever other noises gerbils make?"

Turner returned to typing on his laptop when he gave Yamanu the answer. "They will still be sedated after the operation when they are put back in their cages and transferred in the crate to the *Seafarer*. Any other questions?"

Phinas lifted his hand. "What do I tell Jade?"

"You can tell her our plan," Kian said.

"She'll want to be aboard the decoy and help capture Igor."

Kian nodded. "I bet she will, but she's needed on the *Aurora*. Her people cannot lose their leader, and given her vendetta, I don't think she should be on the decoy. She might be more of a liability than an asset."

Marcel raised his hand. "Do I need to be on the decoy to activate the scrambler?"

"You can show someone else how to do it," Kian said. "I prefer for you to stay on the *Aurora*."

Marcel looked relieved. "I can show Max how to do it."

"Or you can show my tech guy," Phinas offered.

"Show both of them." Onegus solved the problem.

"We are going to arrive a day late to Greenland." Toven leaned toward the tablet. "Did you change the charter plane's schedule?"

"There's no need," Onegus said. "Since the *Aurora* is refueling at Copenhagen, it no longer needs to conserve fuel, and she can go faster and still arrive on time."

"Awesome." Yamanu grinned. "I just hope we don't get hit. I would hate to miss that flight."

58

JADE

*W*hen Phinas finished explaining the plan, Jade pushed to her feet and started pacing the length of the cabin. "I want to go with you. I can leave Kagra in charge."

How could they deny her the satisfaction of catching Igor and ending him on the spot? She wasn't one of their soft females who they coddled and protected. She was a capable warrior, stronger, faster, and better trained than the Guardians and Phinas's men.

He looked at her helplessly. "I know that, and I told Kian that you would want to be there when we catch Igor, but he said that you are too important to lose. Your people need you."

She stopped and glared at him. "Does that imply that you are dispensable?"

"Yeah, I am."

The conviction and acceptance in his tone made her angry, but then wasn't she also guilty of regarding males as dispensable?

It was the Kra-ell way for males to fight and die honorably in battle. Reaching old age was considered a failure for a warrior. When she was younger, Jade had accepted the Mother's doctrines without question. But it had been a very long time since she'd attended a sermon, and without the high priestesses drumming it into her head, she'd pondered the validity of those teachings over the years.

Perhaps the priestesses were not the mouthpieces of the Mother, and maybe tradition should not be followed blindly.

After her sons were murdered, her doubts had doubled. It wasn't only her anger about the way they had died, it was about the way she still missed them. She would have missed them just as much if they had fallen in battle while performing heroic acts of bravery, but perhaps she wouldn't have been as bitter and consumed by the need for vengeance.

Jade was a Kra-ell warrior herself, and dying in battle was how she'd always expected her corporeal life to end and her afterlife to begin in the idyllic fields of the brave.

She would never have tried to shield her sons from battle and rob them of the opportunity to earn their place as well. But it wouldn't have been easy, and pride in their bravery would have never compensated for their loss. She wasn't like the soft human females who dreamt of attending their sons' weddings and holding their grandchildren in their arms, but after spending most of her life on Earth, she could understand them better.

"You are not dispensable, Phinas."

He smiled. "Are you going to miss me?"

Of course, she was, but she wasn't going to admit it. "Don't flatter yourself."

He kept on smiling. "Admit it. You'll miss me when I'm gone."

"Fine. I admit it." She plopped on the couch next to him. "But don't you dare breathe a word of it to anyone. I have a reputation to uphold."

"I know. The Kra-ell way." He wrapped his arm around her shoulders and pulled her toward him. "We had all kinds of traditions where I grew up, and none of them were worth preserving. Perhaps you should rethink yours as well. I don't think that the Kra-ell's tribe-style family is natural. I think it was a solution to a problem and that the Kra-ell are not so different from the gods and the humans in that regard."

"You're projecting your values onto us."

He rubbed his hand up and down her arm. "And yet, here you are, cozying up to an immortal and totally uninterested in the pureblooded males of your species."

"It's the novelty." She put her head on his shoulder. "And it's the fact that you are an outsider, and I don't need to keep up the leader persona with you. I can relax and be myself. Being with you is like a sanctuary, but it doesn't mean that I'm in love with you. I'm not capable of that. But I admit that I like you a lot."

Was it true, though?

Could she still think that when the thought of not having him sleeping next to her depressed her?

How would she go back to sleeping alone? And why did it bother her so much that he wouldn't always be there?

Perhaps she should establish a new tradition of the extended Kra-ell family all sleeping together in one huge bed, with those who wanted to engage in sexual activities using a different room and returning once they were done.

Dipping his head, he kissed the top of her head. "I like you a lot too, and I promise to bring Igor to you, hopefully still alive. I'll drop him at your feet, so you can finally get your revenge and chop off his head."

She lifted her head and smiled at him. "You say the sweetest things."

59

TOVEN

"I need to get to the clinic." Mia wheeled her chair to the door. "They should be getting the shipment of gerbils any minute now."

Toven put a hand on her shoulder. "Are you sure that you can handle the little critters? What if they bite you?"

She smiled. "I'm an immortal now, so I will heal fast. I have a way with animals and a gentle touch. I can make it easier for them. Besides, it will be fun to work with people for a change."

Toven crouched next to her wheelchair. "I thought I was the only company you needed."

When he wasn't busy planning the mission, they were working together in silent harmony. Mia worked on illustrations for her next children's book, and when she needed a break, she sketched environments for Perfect Match adventures.

He worked on a science fiction dystopian romance that was very loosely based on their shared virtual adventure.

Toven found that he enjoyed writing science fiction and exploring the different possibilities of where humanity could be in five hundred years or more. With his perspective on history, his predictions were probably more accurate than most, but probably not as good as the ones produced by artificial intelligence. The computer could process nearly endless pieces of information and base its predictions on all of the history stored in its database, which was infinitely more than Toven could store in his head.

Mia cupped his cheek. "I love working side by side with you. I wouldn't trade it for anything in the world, but from time to time, I crave the company of other people." She leaned to kiss him on the lips. "I also love animals."

"I would like you to reconsider getting off and taking a flight to Greenland."

She shook her head. "We talked about it. If you are staying, I'm staying with you. There are children and pregnant women on board. Leaving while they have to stay would be cowardly on my part."

"You are one of the bravest people I know, but you have restricted mobility, and they don't. That's why I'm worried about you."

She smiled indulgently. "I'm still an immortal who will not get hypothermia if the ship sinks and we can't get into the lifeboats for some reason. That can't be said about the humans and the children. I'm in less danger than they are."

There was one more thing he could try. "If you agree to fly to Greenland, Mey and Jin might consider that as well. If you don't, they won't either."

"They are not going to consider it even if I do." She patted her stumps. "As you've pointed out, I'm the one with mobility issues. They are not. My departure will not influence their decision to stay."

Letting out a sigh, he pushed to his feet. "I'll take you to the clinic." He opened the door and wheeled her chair out into the corridor.

She turned to look at him over her shoulder. "What are your plans for today?"

"I'll be supervising the Kra-ell and making sure that none try to leave the ship. We locked up those who are still loyal to Igor, and we keep an eye on the others."

She was quiet on the way to the elevator and then turned her head to look at him again. "How come you are not joining the team on the decoy? Not that I want you to, but I assumed that we were needed to compel Igor. I understand why I can't be included, but what about you?"

When the elevator door opened, he wheeled her inside and pressed the button for the level the clinic was on. "Everyone on the decoy will have earpieces. If they capture Igor, they will tranquilize him and keep him that way until they get him to Greenland for me to interrogate, so there is no reason for me to be there. Though frankly, I don't think Igor will be captured alive. They will most likely have to kill him."

"What makes you think that?"

"It's just a hunch. If Igor can't escape, he'll choose death over captivity. He will fight to the death."

60

JADE

Jade stood at the entrance to the ship's loading dock and waited for Phinas to come back to her.

Everything was ready. The gerbils had been implanted with the gods-made trackers, each member of the decoy team was carrying two human-made trackers in his pocket, the crates were being loaded on forklifts, and it was time to say goodbye to Phinas.

Neither the *Anatolov* nor the *Helena* had followed the *Aurora* into the port, and both were keeping their distance from the harbor, which was good news for the team leaving for the decoy.

Nevertheless, they were maintaining a low profile and keeping up the charade. Large crates had been loaded onto the *Aurora* and were now being offloaded to be driven across the harbor to the decoy. The Guardians and Phinas's men would follow on foot. If Igor had informers in the port, they would report the transfer of the crates, and he would assume that his people had been transported inside them.

Watching Phinas with his men, she felt tears prickling the

256

back of her eyes, which made her angry, and the anger burned through the moisture.

She wasn't some weak human female, watching her lover leave for war and anxious for him to return to her unharmed.

Except, that was precisely what she felt.

Would she let him kiss her in front of everyone like the humans did in the movies?

Yes, she would.

None of her people were there, so only the Guardians and Phinas's men would see them kissing, and they wouldn't make a big deal out of it.

She couldn't let him go without showing him how much she cared about him.

What if he didn't come back?

She would never forgive herself for sending him off, thinking that he was only a temporary distraction and that she would forget him in no time. She couldn't say the words, but she could show him by kissing the living daylights out of him as the humans liked to say. She wasn't sure what the phrase meant and what was the significance of daylights, living or dead, but it was supposed to indicate a particularly passionate kiss.

He would get what she was trying to communicate.

As he turned around and strode toward her, she forced a smile. "Ready to go?"

He tilted his head. "You look worried. Don't be. This is not my first rodeo, and I know what I'm doing."

"I know." She closed the distance between them and wound her arms around his neck. "Don't get killed. It would really piss me off."

Getting over the initial shock of her initiating a public display of affection, Phinas grinned and wrapped his arms around her. "Don't worry. I'll come back as promised, with Igor bound in chains with a pretty bow on top."

She wanted to kill Igor, but more than that, she wanted Phinas to come back in one piece. "Don't take unnecessary risks to take him alive. Just blow him out of the water if you can."

As he looked into her eyes, his grin turned into a frown. "You really mean it."

"I do."

"You'll give up the satisfaction of chopping off Igor's head just to get me back."

"Yes. I owe you a life debt. I'm not allowed to accompany you to protect you, but I can sacrifice killing Igor myself to keep you safe. Knowing that he's dead will have to satisfy my need for revenge."

With a smile tugging on his lips, he pulled her closer against his chest. "I know it's not about the life debt. Admit it, you love me."

"The Kra-ell don't feel love, but you have my respect and friendship in addition to the life debt."

"Right." He smirked. "I'll play along for now, and I won't take unnecessary risks to get the bastard alive. The safety of my men and the Guardians comes first. But if I can get him for you, I will."

"Thank you." She pulled his head toward hers and kissed him hard.

When his hand closed on her bottom, she felt her cheeks warming, but she didn't do anything to stop him and kept on ravishing his mouth.

"Save it for later," Yamanu said behind Phinas. "You need to get going."

Phinas didn't let go of her right away, and she didn't let go of him until they were both out of air.

"Get back to me," she whispered.

"I will. I promise."

61

PHINAS

*S*aying goodbye to Jade had been oddly difficult. They were not parting ways for an extended time, not unless something went terribly wrong.

Phinas was heading out to a potential battle on board the decoy, and Jade was on the *Aurora*, which had been shadowed for days by a Russian navy cruiser that they surmised would attempt to sink them at some point. They were both heading into danger, but that was only partially responsible for making the separation so hard.

Somewhere along the way, during the several short days they had shared, he'd gotten accustomed to spending his nights with Jade and waking by her side in the morning. They had both been busy during the days, but he could find her whenever he pleased, and he'd done it several times each day, and so had she.

It was as if they couldn't stay apart for too long without an invisible cord getting pulled too taut and forcing them to seek each other.

Not having her near was a lack he was constantly aware of, and Phinas felt like something was missing even while attending the command meetings to which he'd been invited as of late.

He hadn't admitted the extent of his feelings to her, and she hadn't either, but his guess was that she felt the same way.

The parting kiss she'd given him was proof of that. For Jade to do that in public was a sign of a significant change in the way she viewed herself and their relationship.

What was at play was not entirely clear to him yet, but when he came back, hopefully with Igor in chains, he intended to explore it together with Jade. They both needed to get over their reluctance to open up and share their feelings with each other.

It had been almost two days since the *Seafarer* and the *Aurora* cleared the Baltic and sailed along the coast of Norway toward Bergen, and a couple of hours since the *Aurora* changed its heading, sailing toward the Shetland Islands on its way to the North Atlantic.

Phinas was still staring in the direction the *Aurora* sailed, but she was long gone from sight. Max walked over to him. "We are on in five."

"Captain's quarters?" He fell in step with the Guardian.

Max nodded. "If you can call them that. Berg is on the bridge, and he let us use his quarters for the call. Don't get excited. They are just as bad as the rest of this ship."

Compared to the *Aurora*, the *Seafarer* was a rusty old bucket that seemed to cut through the waves with effort. It was manned by volunteers from Captain Olsson's crew, and led by Second Officer Mateo Berg, who was its acting captain.

When they entered the captain's quarters, Phinas saw what Max had meant. The place needed a major remodel, and if not that, at least a good scrubbing and a coat of paint.

They sat at the small table, and Max put the tablet in front of them and made the call.

"Good evening." Max lifted the tablet and turned it in a circle to show the room to the other team members. "Phinas and Max reporting from the lovely *Seafarer*."

"Good morning, gentlemen," Kian said.

The screen was split, showing Kian, Kalugal, Turner, and Onegus on the left side and Toven, Yamanu, and Marcel on the right side.

"I am pleased to share that our assumption was proven correct. The *Helena* has maintained its course and is now following you, while the *Anatolov* changed course and is now shadowing the *Aurora*. If both vessels maintain current speeds and heading, the *Helena*, which we assume has Igor on board, will get in position to fire at the *Seafarer* within ten hours, but that doesn't mean it will do so right away. He might keep following you up the coast until he's comfortable to launch the attack, which could take a day or two."

On board the *Aurora*, Toven leaned forward. "What about the Russians?"

Kian shared his screen so they could all see what he was looking at. "As you can see, the Russian cruiser, represented by this red dot, is mirroring the *Aurora*'s heading and did not pick up speed to close the distance between the ships as of yet."

Phinas calculated the timeline. "It's almost noon here. It will be dark by the time Igor catches up to us. I don't think he will attack at night."

Turner leaned in. "I agree. Igor will prefer daylight for better aim and assessment of the damage when he hits the *Seafarer*. He will also prefer it because it will be a little warmer, giving the Kra-ell, who are not good swimmers, more time to float before hypothermia gets the better of them. They can't regulate their body heat indefinitely. He will also have an easier time fishing them out of the water. "

"I assume that someone is monitoring the tracking feed

twenty-four-seven," Yamanu said. "We need to know right away if there is any change in the Russians' cruiser speed or heading."

"Of course," Kian said. "We arranged for the war room to be manned around the clock until this crisis is over. Have someone on your side available to respond to a call at all times as well. Once the *Anatolov* or the *Helena* pick up speed, we will have very little time to coordinate our moves."

Kalugal lifted his hand to get their attention. "Also, please make sure to have life vests distributed and handed to all hands onboard and double-check on the lifeboats, first-aid kits, and emergency rations. If events go south and we end up with people in the water, remember that at these temps, the humans will only last for minutes, the children possibly less. Go over the emergency plan with your men and with the passengers and make sure to communicate calm and confidence. I'm sure there are a lot of frayed nerves on the *Aurora*."

Phinas was surprised by Kalugal's concern. The guy was typically myopic when it came to humans. It seemed that Jacki was rubbing off on him.

Perhaps her influence was also responsible for the new energy between Kian and Kalugal. Syssi definitely had something to do with Kian's change of attitude and his proposal to offer Kalugal two seats on the council.

However, it still remained to be seen if the council would approve the move.

"How far is the helicopter?" Toven asked. "And how fast can it respond in case Igor surprises us and attacks at night?"

"The helicopter is fully equipped for night missions, so that won't be a problem," Turner reassured the god. "It's currently at a small airstrip to the north of the *Seafarer*'s current position, about twenty-two miles east. A flight plan for the next leg was already filed, and they will soon take off to keep up with the boats' northbound progress. The plan is to land close to the shoreline by early morning. This will make the flight to intercept a quick affair. Depending on how late in the morning Igor decides to make his move, the helicopter will be about fifteen to twenty minutes away. We will have enough warning before Igor gets within weapons range."

Phinas was disappointed that Kian had abandoned his quest to attack first, for the simple reason that they couldn't determine beyond a shadow of a doubt that the *Helena* had Igor on board and intended to fire on them. In case they had all been mistaken about the yacht and its crew's intentions, Kian didn't want to be the aggressor.

It was probably a mistake that would cost them, but he could understand Kian's reluctance.

"Let's make sure everyone has their earpieces fully charged and within reach," Turner said. "I want everyone to wear them starting at dawn. From now until this is over, you should all carry your sidearms at all times as well."

Phinas wondered if these instructions had been meant for his team's ears. He doubted Turner would have repeated such basic instructions to the Guardians.

Onegus took over from Turner. "As soon as we are done here, have a couple of guys that have experience with shoulder-fired rockets on deck with the missiles ready. Launching a missile at the *Helena* will further focus Igor's attention on you, helping the pilot sneak in, and will keep Igor in a defensive mode, which might give us just the time we need in case the helicopter is not yet on the scene."

The Guardians, as an active and heavily trained force, practiced with shoulder-fired missiles as part of their weapons training, while the last time Kalugal's men used that type of weapon it was called a bazooka and probably looked nothing like its contemporary grandchild.

Turner had been able to get four shoulder-launched missiles delivered onboard the *Seafarer* before they'd left the port, but Phinas hadn't seen them yet. They had been delivered in unmarked crates.

"Any questions?" Kian asked.

When there were none, he saluted them with two fingers. "Be safe and good hunting to all!"

62

KIAN

*K*ian rubbed the sleep out of his eyes.

It had been less than two hours since he'd gotten in bed to get some shuteye, but anxiety had made it impossible to rest, urging him to check his phone every so often for updates about new developments.

Telling himself that he would have received a call if anything had happened didn't help.

With a sigh he got out of bed, got dressed, and headed to his home office.

After a few minutes of rapid texting exchanges with the two teams in the North Sea and his war room, he was reassured that there were no new developments.

So far, the morning and afternoon out in the North Sea had passed without incident. Igor's yacht maintained a ten-kilo-meter distance from the *Seafarer*, and the Russians maintained their heading and speed as well.

Evidently, Turner's assessment that Igor would wait to attack until the decoy was further up north was correct, and so was his assumption that the Russian was waiting for the *Aurora* to get further away from land before making his move.

Kian suspected that very few had gotten a good night's sleep on board either the *Aurora* or the *Seafarer*, and that was probably true for many in the village as well.

Everyone seemed to be collectively holding their breath, part in anticipation and part in worry.

Regrettably, his people were well acquainted with danger and crisis. So much of their time and resources were spent to avoid detection by Navuh and humans. Kian had lost count of how many times he had to shepherd the clan through one crisis or another throughout the many centuries he'd been leading it. At first, it had been a simple matter of protecting his family, but as the clan grew and his mother's mission to continue the gods' work of enlightening humanity had caught momentum, Navuh had realized that Annani had survived and was meddling in what he considered his affairs, and the real battle had begun.

There had been so many close calls that Kian suspected the Fates had a hand in protecting the clan, but this crisis felt different.

They were dealing with a large group of people from a different species who had fought the gods and had persevered despite the gods' technological and genetic advantage. If he allowed them to join the village or even settle nearby, and they became adversarial for some reason, they would pose a serious threat.

The Kra-ell negated most of the advantages immortals relied upon for their survival. They were faster and stronger than the Guardians, and they were immune to mind tricks. And now, Jade and Kagra knew about the clan's existence and had a measure of its capabilities.

They had no real reason to go against the clan, but they harbored old resentments against the gods, which the Kra-ell could easily project onto the gods' immortal descendants.

The flip side of the problem was that they could be a huge asset as allies—a secret weapon he could deploy against the superior military power of the Brotherhood. Not that a couple of hundred Kra-ell would make much of a difference if Navuh attacked full force, but Navuh wouldn't dare do that on American soil, and the force he would be comfortable deploying against the clan on its home turf wouldn't be more than two or three hundred strong.

The Kra-ell would be indispensable against a force that size.

Except, the two hundred or so Kra-ell came with the complication of excess baggage that couldn't be discarded. The large group of humans who had lived with them in the compound was completely dependent on the aliens. Most of the humans, if not all, had been born in the compound, and they would be lost out in the world. Surprisingly, those who Arwel and Yamanu had talked to didn't mind staying with the Kra-ell as long as they were fairly compensated for their services and not coerced into breeding hybrids for them.

Perhaps it was just fear of the unknown, and with the clan's help they could sever their ties to the Kra-ell. But the problem was that their knowledge of the aliens couldn't be erased by thralling, and compelling them to keep quiet about it was not a permanent solution. Compulsion faded over time and had to be periodically reinforced.

In a way, the humans were more of a problem than the Kra-ell, and Kian didn't know what to do with them yet, but their issue had to be addressed as well.

And there was Igor, an adversary who was not only a terrifyingly powerful compeller but also ruthless, cunning, and resourceful. Now that he could potentially learn of the clan's existence, the neutralization or elimination of this threat was critical.

63

JADE

*J*ade pressed the ringer button for Yamanu's cabin and took a step back as she waited for the door to open. She knew he wasn't there, but she hadn't come for him.

She was there to borrow his mate's phone.

After all, Mey was part Kra-ell. They might not be friends, but they were on friendly terms.

As Mey opened the door, her eyes widened momentarily. "Good evening, Jade. Yamanu is not here."

"I know. I didn't come to see him." Damn, she hated asking for favors. "I came to ask to borrow your phone. I want to talk to Phinas, and I know you have a secure connection that Igor can't track. If you need to ask Yamanu's permission to let me make the call, that's okay. I will wait out here for your answer."

A smile lifted Mey's full lips, and she opened the door wider. "Please, come in."

"Thank you." Jade followed her inside.

"Take a seat." Mey waved her hand at the couch. "Do you have Phinas's number?"

"I hoped you had it."

"I don't, but I can get it from Yamanu. Anyway, I need to check with him whether you can call Phinas, but not because it is you who is requesting to make the call. I need to ask him if anyone is allowed to call the people on the decoy. I'll text him."

Evidently, Mey had no military training.

They were in the middle of a crisis, about to face a dangerous enemy, and Jade was an unconfirmed ally at this point. If the roles were reversed, she wouldn't have allowed Mey to make the call unsupervised, or maybe not at all.

Mey sent the text and shifted her eyes to Jade. "Can I offer you something to drink while we wait?"

"No, thank you." Jade could use some water, but she didn't want to inconvenience the female.

"A glass of water, maybe?" Mey asked.

Jade tilted her head. "How did you know that I was thinking about water?"

Had the female read her mind? If Mey could hear echoes of past conversations that had been embedded in the walls, she might be able to also read minds.

Mey chuckled. "I didn't read your mind. I can't, and not just because you are a pureblooded Kra-ell."

"So, how did you know?"

"You licked your lips. Besides, I also get thirsty when I'm anxious."

"I'm not anxious." Jade squared her shoulders.

Mey arched a brow. "So, what's the urgency to speak to Phinas?"

Lifting her chin, Jade briefly closed her eyes. "I don't know what's going on with me. I've never felt like this before."

"Let me guess." Mey sat down next to her on the couch. "The longer you are away from Phinas, the worse the pain here gets." She patted her chest. "You are going crazy, and you figured that talking with him is the only thing that would help."

The female claimed to not be able to read minds, and yet she'd nailed it, describing precisely what Jade was feeling.

"How are you doing that?"

Mey smiled. "I know what you feel because it's the same for me. It gets easier after a while, and the longer you are with your mate, the longer you can tolerate being away from him. I can be away from Yamanu for two to three days now, but at the beginning, a separation of even a few hours was too difficult."

"What are you talking about? Love? I'm Kra-ell. I don't do love."

The woman cast her an indulgent look. "I'm talking about the bond, which is stronger than love. For some, it forms before the couple realizes that they are in love."

"The Kra-ell don't bond. We don't work the same as the gods, and we are physically incapable of forming bonds. It would have been disastrous to our society. Phinas might be experiencing what you're describing, but I shouldn't."

"And yet you are." Mey lifted her phone and looked at the screen. "Yamanu says that you can talk to Phinas, but I should make the call and hand you the phone." She lifted her eyes to Jade. "I'm sorry. I didn't expect him to ask that."

"It is exactly what I would have done if the roles were reversed. You just don't have the military training and experience that Yamanu has."

Mey smirked. "You'd be surprised, but that's not something I can talk about."

Her curiosity was piqued, but as Mey made the call, the cryptic comment was forgotten, and all Jade cared about was hearing Phinas's voice.

PHINAS

*O*ver forty hours had passed since the decoy had left the harbor, and as night had fallen, the anxious energy on the *Seafarer* had subsided.

Igor wasn't likely to attack at night because of the visibility. Shoulder-fired rockets were not a precise weapon, and the yacht most likely didn't carry the kind that was self-guiding. Those were premier weapons, and the oligarch who owned the yacht had no reason to have one of those on board.

But the problem with should haves and could haves was that they were just educated guesses, and those were not always correct.

Phinas groaned. "I could kill for a bottle of Snake Venom."

"No booze allowed on missions." Dandor pulled a pack of cigarettes out of his pocket. "But smoking is okay." He tapped the bottom of the pack to push one cigarette out and offered it to Phinas.

"No, thanks, but you can go ahead. It doesn't bother me."

They were on the decoy's top deck, sitting on loungers while huddled in their puffer jackets and keeping their gloved hands inside their pockets for warmth. If it weren't so damn cold, Phinas might have indulged, but it wasn't worth taking his gloves off for a smoke.

Neither of them was a regular smoker, not since their days in the Brotherhood. Back then, they'd used to smoke while on missions, and Dandor remembered the tradition.

It evoked memories of camaraderie, and for a brief moment, Phinas was tempted to light up, but smoking before a battle was one of those traditions that were better abandoned.

Jade had a bunch of them that she should shed, but he understood why she was clinging to them. It was because Igor had pissed on the Kra-ell customs, turning them on their heads.

Perhaps once she had her revenge, she could reexamine her beliefs. She was a smart female, rational and pragmatic, and adhering to religious doctrines did not suit an independent thinker like her.

In Phinas's humble opinion, religion was propaganda, a way to control the population and give people a false sense of control over the chaos of life.

Fates, he missed that stubborn, magnificent female.

Phinas chuckled at his own hypocrisy. Why was he invoking the Fates? He had grown up with Mortdh's teachings shoved down his throat, and he'd detested that even as a teenager. He'd never been a devout follower of Mortdh, and when he had joined the clan, he hadn't adopted their belief system either. But invoking the Fates felt better than invoking Mortdh, so there was that.

When his phone rang, he fumbled to pull it out of his pocket and frowned at the name on the screen.

Why was Mey calling him?

Touching the screen with his gloved hand produced no result, so he pulled it off with his teeth and was finally able to accept the call.

"Good evening, Mey. How are things on the *Aurora*?"

"As well as can be expected from a bunch of people stressed out of their minds, but thank you for asking. How are the gerbils?"

"The gerbils?" He chuckled. "That's who you want to check on?"

"I know the men are all right."

"The gerbils are fine. They are enjoying a cruise in shitty little cabins, but since they are just small critters, they think that they are in a huge palace."

Mey laughed. "Is it that bad?"

"After spending time on the *Aurora*, yeah. It is. Not where I would choose to spend my honeymoon, not even if I was given a ride for free."

"Speaking of honeymoons, someone is waiting impatiently to talk to you."

Phinas's heartbeat accelerated. He'd wanted to call one of his guys and tell them to find Jade and give her the phone, but he'd thought she would be angry if he did that. Public displays of affection and all that. But here she was, doing it herself.

"Hi," she said. "How are you doing?"

"Missing you. Do you miss me?"

She hesitated for a moment. "Yes."

"Is Mey standing right next to you?"

"Yes. I'm still not trusted enough to make outside calls without supervision."

He needed to have a talk with Yamanu about that. If they wanted Jade as an ally, they needed to start treating her as one.

"I'm sorry. I'll have a word with the boss about it."

"It's okay. I would have done the same if I were in Yamanu's position. You and your people are heading into a dangerous confrontation, and keeping security tight is of the utmost importance."

274

He smiled. "Did I tell you already how much I enjoy chatting with a female warrior?"

She chuckled. "How many females do you usually chat with?"

"Not many," he admitted. "I'm not the chatty sort."

"You could have fooled me."

"I'm like that only with you, gorgeous."

This time the silence lasted even longer. "How are you holding up?"

Phinas stifled a snort.

Evidently, Jade had reached her limit of mushy, personal talk.

"Everyone is antsy. Igor is keeping a steady distance from us, and it's nerve-wracking to wait for him to make his move. I liked Kian's plan much better, but he changed his mind about luring Igor to get closer and attacking the yacht first."

"I'm with you on that. You and your friends are basically sitting ducks, waiting for Igor to launch a rocket at your ship. What if people get hurt?"

"They'll heal. We are immortals, and we've all gotten injured at one time or another. It's not a big deal."

"It is if he can blow up the bridge or hit an area where your people are. There is only so much that our bodies can heal. If the injuries are too massive, we die."

"Don't worry. I promised to come back to you in one piece, and I always deliver on my promises."

65

KIAN

Syssi's light footsteps pulled Kian out of his reverie.

"Good morning, love." He pushed to his feet. "Did I wake you?" He gathered her in a hug, savoring her warmth.

"You didn't." She lifted her face for a kiss. "Or maybe you did. My subconscious mind must have sensed your absence from our bed and woken me up to check in on you."

He kissed the tip of her nose. "I'm fine. You can go back to sleep."

Syssi shook her head. "I want to keep you company, but first, I need some coffee. I'll make us cappuccinos." She pulled out of his arms.

"Let me make us some tea. It's four in the morning, and I want you to go back to sleep."

Yawning, she nodded.

Kian took Syssi's hand, led her to the kitchen, and sat her down on a barstool.

"Any updates?" she asked.

"Not really. Everyone is waiting for Igor to make his move."

While waiting for the water to boil, Kian pulled out the box of assorted teas and a bag of cookies from the pantry and put them on the counter next to Syssi.

She took a cookie and nibbled on it for a brief moment. "You need to decide how you are going to deal with Igor once you catch him. Toven promised his life to Jade, and she wants to execute him on the spot. But since you want to interrogate him, you'll have to persuade her to wait." She adjusted her night robe over her knees. "I'm curious whether he had anything to do with the Kra-ell interstellar ship's sabotage."

"I doubt it." Kian pulled out two cups from the top cabinet and put them on the table. "I don't think anyone would have wanted to delay the ship's arrival for thousands of years and then make it explode." He poured hot water into the cups.

"On the contrary." Syssi dunked a teabag in the water. "If he was a fugitive, he might have wanted to arrive on Earth long after whoever was looking for him was dead, and to prevent anyone on board from discovering who he really was, he did something to make it explode, but only after the escape pods were safely deployed."

That was a very plausible scenario that Kian hadn't considered before.

Smiling, he leaned to take her lips in a quick kiss. "Did I already tell you how brilliant you are?"

"Many times. It's just something that occurred to me during the night when I couldn't fall asleep because you weren't in bed with me."

More than sleep had been sacrificed on the altar of this crisis. Intimacy with his wife had been sacrificed as well.

"I'm sorry." He sat on the stool next to hers and swiveled it toward her. "Soon, things will go back to normal, and we will spend a lot of time in bed together." He leaned to kiss the spot on her neck he liked to bite.

She shivered. "Don't tease me. It's not fair."

"It's not a tease. It's a promise." He leaned away and dunked a teabag in the fast-cooling water. "We still have two potentially major battles on our hands, but I believe they will both go down soon."

Holding the warm cup in her palms and breathing in the aroma of the tea, Syssi closed her eyes and sighed. "That's why you need to decide now what to do with him once you catch him."

"It's not a foregone conclusion that we will catch him. We might kill him, or he might escape."

"You'll catch him."

The small hairs on the back of Kian's neck tingled. "Are you simply thinking ahead, or do you have a feeling?"

When Syssi 'had a feeling,' Kian knew better than to second-guess her.

"I didn't have a vision if that is what you are asking, and it's not a feeling or a premonition either. It's a logical assumption and calculated probability. I know you, and I know how competent our Guardians are. Igor will be caught alive, and you'd better decide now what to do with him and what bribe you can offer Jade to agree to give him a stay of execution."

If it wasn't a premonition, all possibilities were still open, and he didn't need to deal with that until it became relevant.

"I don't have the bandwidth to deal with that now. I'll decide on that when and if we catch him."

ONEGUS

"About damn time." Onegus rubbed his hands.

It was just his luck that it was his turn to sit in the war room when things were finally starting to progress toward resolution.

Nearly forty-eight hours had passed since the decoy had left the Copenhagen harbor and about forty hours since it had started up the Norwegian coast while the *Aurora* continued to the North Atlantic. Everyone had been getting antsier in anticipation of the confrontation.

Kian, Turner, and Kalugal had left about two hours ago to shower and change clothes, but they would have to drop everything and rush back.

Imagining Kalugal walking in with a towel wrapped around him made Onegus's lips twitch, but this was not the time to amuse himself. He needed to act fast.

The first order of business was to call the pilot. "This is McLean. The *Helena* has increased its speed and is heading toward the *Seafarer* at thirty-seven knots. It will be in weapons range in under an hour." He gave the pilot the estimated coordinates.

"Got it. I'm taking off and will be there in under twenty minutes. I'll find a spot to land and wait for your signal."

"Roger that." Onegus terminated the call.

The next went to Phinas. He would have preferred to talk to Max, but Phinas was in charge of the mission, and he was the one Onegus needed to call.

Phinas answered immediately. "Are we on?"

Onegus repeated the information.

"Finally." The guy let out a breath. "I'll get everyone in position."

"Don't forget to double-check that everyone's earpieces are secure in place and well fitting."

"I've already done that, but I'll do it again. From now on, the earpieces stay in."

"Excellent. I'll keep you posted."

The last call was to Kian.

"Talk to me." The boss's gruff voice was laced with urgency.

"The *Helena* started increasing its speed about seven minutes ago, and if it maintains current speed, it will reach the *Seafarer* in a little under an hour. I've already notified the helicopter pilot, and he'll be in position in about twenty minutes. I also spoke with Phinas, and our guys are getting in position and checking their earpieces."

"Very well. Did you notify Turner and Kalugal?"

"Not yet."

"I'll do it. Call Yamanu to let him know and keep monitoring the situation."

"Yes, boss."

"I'm on my way. I'll be there in ten minutes."

Unless Kian had one of the golf carts parked in front of his house, he would have to run to get to the underground war room in such a short time.

Taking a quick look at Roni's laptop and the two flashing

red dots following the two blue ones, Onegus placed a call to Yamanu.

"Good morning, chief. What's up?"

The *Aurora* command team was using one of the cabins as their war room, but with Phinas gone, only Yamanu and Toven remained.

"Is Toven with you?" Onegus asked.

"He's right here. Do you want to talk to him?"

"I need you both. Just activate the speakerphone."

"Done."

"Igor is making his move," Onegus said without much preamble. "The *Helena* picked up speed a few minutes ago and is heading toward the decoy. The ETA is a little under an hour, and the helicopter will be there with plenty of time to spare. There is no indication that the Russians changed their speed or heading as of this time."

His update was received with a silent pause as the gravity of the news sank in. For better or worse, it was finally happening, and the confrontation they had all been waiting for was about to unfold in less than an hour, or rather one part of the confrontation. It still remained to be seen if the Russian captain would engage.

If he did, Nils would take care of that problem.

"Thank you for letting us know," Toven said. "We will keep everyone here on high alert from now on. I'll get Mia up here in case you need our help with Igor, his men, or both."

Onegus doubted that Toven would be able to do that remotely, even with Mia's help, but he kept his opinion to himself. After all, Toven probably suspected the same.

"Thank you. I will keep you updated."

As Onegus ended the call, Kian arrived, and less than a minute later, Turner and Kalugal walked in, neither wearing a towel nor a bathrobe.

Roni was the last one to arrive. "I'm taking over monitoring the ships."

"Be my guest." Onegus turned the kid's laptop toward him. "This application is your baby, your brilliant invention."

Roni sighed. "It is brilliant. I just wish it had more market potential."

Kalugal moved to the chair next to Roni and looked at the screen. "Your invention has plenty of market potential. I bet we can sell it to navies around the world."

"We?" Roni arched a brow. "Are we partners now?"

"If you want to make money from this application, then we are."

KIAN

*W*hen the *Helena* started to slow down to match the *Seafarer*'s speed, Kian signaled Onegus and Turner. "Let's put the main players on."

Regrettably, the live broadcast would be audio only because they hadn't thought to send the surveillance drones with the decoy team.

Turner put the pilot on speaker for a live update from the helicopter, and Onegus put Phinas and Max on speaker as well.

Later, they would switch communications to the earpieces, but for now they could still use their phones.

"The captain is aware of the *Helena*'s approach," Phinas said. "He's maintaining steady heading and speed, pretending that he didn't notice the fast-approaching yacht. He is also aware of the helicopter's ETA. We put two guys on the observation deck with strong binoculars that transmit information straight to Max's phone. We can see what's happening on the yacht's front decks, and the moment we see activity that indicates they are preparing to launch an attack, we will shoot first. Other than Max and me, the rest of the team is out of sight and hidden from anyone on the *Helena* trying to see what we are up to."

Max took it from there. "I have four Guardians with shoulder-fired rockets in position and ready to engage, but they won't be visible from the yacht because they are behind the waterslide and hiding under a tarp. As soon as the yacht is within range, and provided that our guys on the observation deck report signs of aggression from the *Helena*, we will fire two missiles simultaneously at her."

Max followed the finalized battle plan that was a compromise between all the various iterations they had come up with before. The *Seafarer* team would not attack until they were certain that Igor intended to shoot at them, but as soon as his intentions to launch a rocket at them became clear, they would give him hell first.

Hopefully, Igor didn't have superior rockets like self-guided missiles on board the yacht, and having two incoming missiles would get his full attention and give the helicopter pilot a chance to shoot its missile and get away before Igor could shoot back.

Kian's objective was to avoid, or at least minimize, casualties on all sides. The only death that was acceptable to him and wouldn't weigh on his conscience was Igor's.

"The *Helena* is now five minutes from weapons range," Roni said from his station in front of the laptop.

"Time to switch to the earpieces," Onegus said.

Kian ended the call and activated his earpiece.

The others did the same.

"We are in the air," the pilot reported. "ETA is seven minutes."

"The *Helena* will be in weapons range in one minute," Roni updated.

"The *Helena* is now in weapons range." Roni was starting to lose his calm, and his announcement had come out a squawk.

"No sign of activity on the Helena yet," Phinas said. "We are holding fire for now."

"We are one minute out," came the pilot's garbled voice.

"Hold on," Max said. "There is activity on board the *Helena*. It looks like they are wheeling in something. Now they are removing the cover. Fuck! It's a damn missile battery. Fire!" Max gave the command.

PHINAS

*a*s soon as Max issued the fire command, the whoosh of the missiles exiting the launching tubes sounded.

The sound was filtered through the specialty earpieces and was a little off, but it was still the most satisfying sound Phinas had heard in a long time.

The *Helena* was still a far-off blob to the naked eye, even for an immortal, but the Guardians had telescopic scopes, and their aim was true.

"The *Helena* is changing its heading," Max said. "It is trying to avoid getting hit."

Clearly, someone on board the yacht had noticed the approaching missiles and was attempting evasive maneuvers while those in charge of the missile battery were still fumbling with it. Those kinds of missiles were self-guided, and once fired they would hit their target even if those operating them had a shitty aim.

The *Seafarer*'s first missile missed the target. The second didn't.

"We have a hit," Max said. "Damage is minimal. The missile only grazed the side of the boat."

Max cursed under his breath. "It's up to the helicopter now."

Phinas held his breath as a race against time ensued. Who would manage the first shot? The *Helena* or the helicopter?

If the missiles launched at the same time, they were all fucked. Both vessels would start taking in water. The *Seafarer* had life rafts, and probably the *Helena* had them as well, but it would be a major shit show if the crews of both fought their way to the ladder that the helicopter would drop to collect their team.

"We are in range," the helicopter pilot announced. "Locking target. Missile fired."

Phinas didn't dare take a breath, clutching his binoculars as if his life depended on it.

Why hadn't the *Helena* deployed its missiles yet? A battery could fire them all at once and do so much damage to the *Seafarer* that they might not survive.

Was the battery defective? Its operators inexperienced? Or were the Fates looking out for them?

"Why aren't they firing?" Max asked.

"They must have a malfunction." Phinas kept his binoculars trained on the *Helena*. "Someone just rushed in with a handheld rocket launcher. He's getting ready to fire. Missile away."

As a clear white plume rose from the front deck of the *Helena*, a flash of light was seen a split second before a loud boom sounded.

"Yes!" Max pumped his fist in the air. "We have a hit."

"Hit confirmed," the helicopter pilot announced.

Phinas let out half a breath as his eyes locked on the incoming missile.

The captain had initiated evasive maneuvers as soon as the *Helena* had deployed the missile, but the *Seafarer* was large and slow to turn.

Phinas braced for impact…that never came.

As the missile missed the *Seafarer* by mere meters and splashed into the water without detonating, a cheer arose from all team members on board.

Max pulled him into a brief bro hug. "Thank the merciful Fates."

Another loud explosion drew all eyes to the *Helena*.

The helicopter's guided missile must have caused serious structural damage, and the yacht caught fire. When it reached the fuel tank, or maybe the munitions onboard, it caused a major explosion.

The *Helena* was sinking fast.

"There was a big explosion on the yacht," Max updated the war rooms in the village and on board the *Aurora*. "The *Helena* is sinking, and people are jumping overboard."

"What do you want me to do?" the captain asked on the com.

"Please bring the *Seafarer* about to collect the survivors," Kian said. "But stay on the bridge and do not assist our men. The same goes for your crew. Everyone stays at their stations."

The crew was equipped with specialty earpieces like the rest of them, but they were human, and they needed to stay out of the fray.

"We are circling above to provide coverage and assistance as needed," the pilot announced.

As their team came out of hiding and assembled to get instructions, Max pulled out his tranquilizer gun. "Switch your weapons from firearms to tranquilizer guns and check your earpieces."

Phinas could barely contain the grin that threatened to split his face.

After the many days of cat and mouse with the guy, he had grown larger than life in all of their minds, but they had defeated him, and if he was still alive, he was in the water and at their mercy.

It wasn't over yet, and Igor might still pull the proverbial rabbit out of his hat, but Phinas doubted that. He was moments away from bagging the guy, and he couldn't wait to deliver Igor to Jade with a red bow tied around his neck.

JADE

*J*ade alternated between pacing in front of the cabin designated as the *Aurora*'s war room and sitting on the floor right next to the door. It was pathetic, and it made her feel like a beggar, but she was beyond caring.

She hadn't stooped so low as eavesdropping with her ear to the door, mostly because the ship's doors were so thick and the fit so precise that even with her Kra-ell hearing, it was impossible to discern what was being said inside. But if Toven or Yamanu stepped out for even a moment, she would badger them for information about the battle until they gave her something.

They had been in there for hours, and even though no one had told her a thing, she knew in her gut that the battle had begun.

Closing her eyes, she prayed to the Mother not for Phinas to emerge victorious or perform exceptional acts of bravery, and definitely not to die as a hero and forever find peace in the fields of the brave.

She prayed for him to come back to her alive and well.

To pray for his life bordered on blasphemy, but she no longer blindly believed in the sermons she'd heard as a young female, and she could not suffer another loss.

The Mother forgive her, but she couldn't lose anyone else she cared about.

When the door opened, and Toven stepped out, she jumped to her feet. "Tell me what's going on."

He smiled. "Everyone on the *Seafarer* is okay. No one got hurt."

Her hand landed on her chest. "Thank the Mother. Did Igor fire on them?"

"He tried. They had a missile battery on board the *Helena*, but the Fates must have smiled upon our men, and the battery malfunctioned. They managed to fire one handheld rocket, but it missed."

"What about the other side?"

Phinas had told her the plan, but she didn't know which parts of it had been implemented and which had been discarded. It had gone through so many changes and back and forth that she'd lost track of the final plan.

"The helicopter got a good shot, causing a fire that must have ignited the fuel tank or the munitions on board, the yacht exploded and sank. People were seen jumping into the water right after the explosion, but we don't know yet who the survivors are and if Igor is among them."

"Do we even have proof that he was on board?"

Toven shook his head. "We don't."

At this point she would be satisfied with a confirmation of his demise, but until she saw him or his dead body, she wouldn't have a moment's rest. Even if the other survivors claimed that he'd been there, she wouldn't believe them.

"You need to keep looking. If he's not among the dead or the living, we are back to square one, and all of this insane effort was for nothing. He could have compelled those on board the *Helena* to follow his commands and to claim that he was there when it exploded. I wouldn't put it past him to plant explosives on the yacht just in case it was overpowered and detonate them to throw us off his tail."

Toven smiled. "It's a bit of a stretch, but at this point, I would believe anything when it comes to Igor. He's a cunning bastard."

"When will we know?"

"They are fishing the survivors out of the water as we speak. Let's pray that he's one of them just so we can end him ourselves and know for sure that he's no longer a threat."

Jade bared her fangs. "We are not going to kill him. I am. He's my kill, not yours."

"If we catch him alive, he's yours. But perhaps you could wait a few days to have your revenge, so we can get some information out of him first."

The fire in her gut ignited. "Unless you are a stronger compeller than he is, he's not going to tell you anything unless you promise to spare his life, but it's not yours to spare. It's mine, and I'm not going to spare it in exchange for information or anything else."

PHINAS

"*N*ine people in the water," the helicopter pilot reported. "They are clinging to debris, but they are not going to last long in the freezing water. Do you want me to drop the ladder?"

"Do not engage," Phinas replied. "And don't get any closer. We will get there in a few minutes."

"They might not have those minutes," the pilot argued.

The guy's good intentions might cost him and his crew their lives if they got within earshot of Igor.

"I repeat. Do not engage and keep your current altitude. Don't get any closer to the survivors. They are all extremely dangerous criminals, and some of them are highly-trained commandos."

"Roger that."

They were about to shoot tranquilizer darts at the survivors, and although he didn't owe the hired pilot an explanation, it was always good to have people cooperate willingly and not grudgingly.

Max lifted the binoculars to his eyes. "Is it possible that's the entire crew, including Igor and his three compadres? How many people are needed to operate a yacht this size?"

Max's words were delivered by the machine voice, sounding exactly the same as everyone else's on board, but even though Phinas was used to that by now and despite the excellent quality of the computerized voice, it was still jarring.

"I don't know," he admitted. He had never gone on a naval mission, let alone had been part of a crew. "I've been on very few sea voyages and only as a passenger."

"There couldn't have been just nine people operating a vessel this size. Even if the others were killed, where are their bodies?" Max lowered his binoculars. "Aren't bodies supposed to float?"

It was a rhetorical question, but Phinas answered anyway. "They are."

"You said that the Kra-ell bodies are dense. So Igor and his guys could have sunk all the way to the bottom of the ocean."

"Their bodies are denser than ours, but they will still float when dead. Besides, they are not that easily killed."

Or so he hoped.

According to Jade, the Kra-ell didn't enter stasis when severely injured like the immortals did. They'd had to be put into stasis artificially and placed in life-sustaining pods to traverse the universe in a spaceship.

If Igor had been killed in the explosion, but his body wasn't found, they would have no proof of his demise, and Phinas would have no trophy to bring to Jade.

That would be very disappointing.

Lifting the binoculars again, he scanned the ocean where the *Helena* had been. All that remained of her was a field of scattered smoldering debris. The rest had sunk. It was possible that Igor's body, or whatever was left of it, was trapped in the parts that were on their way to the bottom.

It was also possible that he hadn't been on board at all and had been puppeteering the crew from afar.

When the *Seafarer* neared the field of debris, the survivors became clearer through the binoculars, and Phinas released a relieved breath. The four Kra-ell were easy to identify thanks to their long black hair, and when the ship got even closer, he could even see their alert, glowing red eyes.

The humans were in much worse shape, and if they didn't get to them soon, they would lose their hold on the debris and drown.

The helicopter was still circling at a low altitude overhead, but Phinas couldn't allow it to go lower before the Kra-ell were apprehended and muzzled. Besides, the humans were in a bad state and wouldn't be able to climb the rope ladder. It was a difficult feat even for trained combat soldiers who were not suffering from hypothermia.

Hopefully, the noise of its engines and rotor would be enough to disperse the sound waves of Igor's compulsion.

Phinas lowered the binoculars, put them aside, and tapped his earpiece. "Three minutes until we are in range. Lower the lifeboats at the back. The rest come to me, but stay away from the railing."

After the Kra-ell were hit with the tranquilizer darts, the men in the lifeboats would have mere seconds to fish them out of the water. If they didn't get to them in time, the males would drown, and that was unacceptable.

Four lifeboats with two men each should be enough to get the Kra-ell and the humans.

As the rest of his men and Guardians rushed over, he turned to Max. "You and I take out two?"

Grinning, Max nodded.

"Boleck and Dandor will take the other two."

They were the best snipers on board, probably better than him and Max.

"It's time to go hunting." Phinas motioned for Boleck and Dandor to come forward. "The Kra-ell do not succumb to hypothermia as quickly as the humans, and they are still in full command of their bodies. Expect them to be armed and open fire the moment they have a shot. Take cover and shoot only the Kra-ell. By now, the humans are too numb to pose a threat."

When the men nodded, Max took over. "The humans will be pulled out first. I need five of you to get a human each and treat them for hypothermia. You know what to do. The rest of you will help us deal with the Kra-ell."

Phinas didn't know what the treatment for hypothermia was, and neither did his men, but evidently the Guardians had gone through medic training.

"Don't shoot more than two darts if both hit target," he reminded Max and the two snipers.

From experience, they knew that one dart might not be enough to knock out a Kra-ell, and sometimes a second one was needed, but four could be deadly. They wanted to catch Igor alive, although for different reasons.

Kian wanted to interrogate him, but all Phinas wanted was to deliver him to Jade.

He didn't know why Kian thought that Igor would have more information about the gods than the other original settlers on board the *Aurora*, who were more than happy to answer Toven's questions, even without him having to resort to compulsion.

But Phinas didn't care about that.

All he cared about was delivering Igor to Jade. Other females might be thrilled with expensive jewelry or luxury vacations, but there was no gift his female would appreciate more than Igor's head on the proverbial platter.

He and Max and the two snipers took positions behind the lifesavers attached to the railing at even intervals and took aim, each at the Kra-ell closest to them.

When the captain slowed the *Seafarer*, and it started turning sideways as planned, Phinas tapped his earpiece. "Fire at will."

All four darts hit their targets almost simultaneously, but three of the Kra-ell had to be shot with another dose before going limp in the water and starting to sink.

The rafts arrived in the nick of time, and only one Guardian had to dive into the water to fish out the Kra-ell who'd been hard to get to with the raft because of the debris. Somehow, the humans were still conscious and clinging to the flotsam when the men got to them, and they were pulled into the rafts and wrapped in blankets right away.

Phinas allowed himself a brief moment to exchange high-fives with Max before they gave Yamanu an update while walking over to where the winch operators were pulling up the first human.

He was wrapped in several blankets and held by a harness, but he was awake, and the hard look in his eyes reinforced Phinas's assumption that the five humans were employees of the oligarch, a weapons dealer with ties to the Bratva.

"I got him." A Guardian released the man from the harness and threw him over his shoulder before running with him to where they'd prepared a treatment area.

The static noise in Phinas's earpiece preceded the helicopter pilot's machine-translated voice. "Do you need me to evacuate anyone to the hospital?"

Given that the humans were still conscious, Phinas didn't think that they needed more medical attention than they were getting from the Guardians.

Besides, these weren't innocent civilians. They were most likely members of the Bratva and dangerous as hell.

"That's a negative, captain. How are you doing on the fuel?"

"I have enough for another round, and then I need to head back to refuel."

"Then do it now and come back with a full tank. You know the plan."

The helicopter was to shuttle them and the Kra-ell to a nearby airfield where a plane would wait for them to take them to Greenland.

"Roger that."

He and Max waited impatiently until the last human was pulled up and rushed away, and the Kra-ell's turn finally arrived.

They were still unconscious and bound in titanium chains, and as they were hoisted up one by one, they were laid out on the deck and covered in blankets.

"How long before they wake up?" Max asked, although his guess was as good as Phinas's.

"Not long. Minutes probably for the one who was shot with one dart, and longer for the others."

"That's the hybrid." Max pointed at the one who looked more human. "He's been shot with only one dart."

"Then maybe they will all wake up at the same time."

They hadn't gagged them on purpose. Igor would reveal himself readily enough as soon as he tried to compel them to release him and his men.

Phinas couldn't wait to find out which one it was. He hadn't asked Jade for a description because he didn't want her to think about the bastard even more than she already did, and Sofia's description could have described nearly all of the adult Kra-ell males.

Tall, slim, with long black hair. The one feature that distinguished Igor from the others was the look in his eyes that had given Sofia the creeps. She'd told Phinas that he would know it when he saw it.

The first one to stir was a pureblood, and as soon as he opened his eyes and they became focused, Phinas knew who he was.

"Release my men and me immediately," he said in heavily accented English.

Phinas grinned. "Hello, Igor. It's my distinct pleasure to finally make your acquaintance. Jade is looking forward to seeing you again."

Those probably were not the words Kian would have chosen or would have wanted Phinas to say, but they achieved the desired effect, dimming some of the bravado in Igor's eyes.

Even paralyzed and in captivity, he still didn't appear beaten or subdued by any stretch, but maybe he was starting to realize that he'd underestimated what and who he'd gone up against.

Phinas put his hand on Max's arm, stopping him from tapping his earpiece. "Allow me."

The Guardian nodded.

The moment they had all been waiting for had finally arrived, and once Phinas said the words, everyone on board the *Aurora* and in the village could take a collective breath, at least for now. They still had the Russian destroyer to deal with.

Phinas tapped his earpiece. "We got him."

To read the first 3 chapters JOIN the VIP club at
ITLUCAS.COM —To find out what's included in your free
membership, flip to the last page.

After two decades in captivity Jade is finally free, her quest for revenge within grasp, but danger still looms large. A storm is brewing on the horizon and threatening to obliterate Jade's tenuous hold on hope for a better future.

Dear reader,

Thank you for reading the Children of the Gods.

As an independent author, I rely on your support to spread the word. So if you enjoyed the story, please share your experience with others, and if it isn't too much trouble, I would greatly appreciate a brief review on Amazon.

Love + happy reading,

Isabell

Also by I. T. Lucas

68: Dark Alliance Kindred Souls
69: Dark Alliance Turbulent Waters
70: Dark Alliance Perfect Storm

PERFECT MATCH
Vampire's Consort
King's Chosen
Captain's Conquest

The Children of the Gods Series Sets

Books 1-3: Dark Stranger trilogy—Includes a bonus short story: **The Fates take a Vacation**

Books 4-6: Dark Enemy Trilogy —Includes a bonus short story—**The Fates' Post-Wedding Celebration**

Books 7-10: Dark Warrior Tetralogy

Books 11-13: Dark Guardian Trilogy

Books 14-16: Dark Angel Trilogy

Books 17-19: Dark Operative Trilogy

Books 20-22: Dark Survivor Trilogy

Books 23-25: Dark Widow Trilogy

Books 26-28: Dark Dream Trilogy

Books 29-31: Dark Prince Trilogy

Books 32-34: Dark Queen Trilogy

Books 35-37: Dark Spy Trilogy

Books 38-40: Dark Overlord Trilogy

Books 41-43: Dark Choices Trilogy

Books 44-46: Dark Secrets Trilogy

Books 47-49: Dark Haven Trilogy

Books 50-52: Dark Power Trilogy
Books 53-55: Dark Memories Trilogy
Books 56-58: Dark Hunter Trilogy
Books 59-61: Dark God Trilogy
Books 62-64: Dark Whispers Trilogy
Books 65-67: Dark Gambit Trilogy

MEGA SETS

INCLUDE CHARACTER LISTS

The Children of the Gods: Books 1-6
The Children of the Gods: Books 6.5-10

TRY THE CHILDREN OF THE GODS SERIES ON AUDIBLE

2 FREE audiobooks with your new Audible subscription!

FOR EXCLUSIVE PEEKS AT UPCOMING RELEASES & A FREE COMPANION BOOK

Join my *VIP Club* and gain access to the **VIP** portal at
ITLUCAS.COM
(http://eepurl.com/blMTpD)

Included in your free membership:

- **FREE** Children of the Gods companion book 1 (includes part 1 of Goddess's Choice)
- **FREE** narration of Goddess's Choice—Book 1 in The Children of the Gods Origins series.
- Preview chapters of upcoming releases.
- And other exclusive content offered only to my VIPs.

If you're already a subscriber, you'll receive a download link for my next book's preview chapters in the new release announcement email. If you are not getting my emails, your provider is sending them to your junk folder, and you are missing out on **important updates, side characters' portraits, additional content, and other goodies.** To fix that, add isabell@itlucas.com to your email contacts or your email VIP list.

Made in the USA
Middletown, DE
28 March 2023